Laurence W. M. Lockhart

Mine is Thine

A novel. Part 2

Laurence W. M. Lockhart

Mine is Thine
A novel. Part 2

ISBN/EAN: 9783337051549

Printed in Europe, USA, Canada, Australia, Japan

Cover: Foto ©Andreas Hilbeck / pixelio.de

More available books at **www.hansebooks.com**

MINE IS THINE

A NOVEL

BY

LAURENCE W. M. LOCKHART

AUTHOR OF 'FAIR TO SEE,' ETC.

IN THREE VOLUMES

VOL. II.

WILLIAM BLACKWOOD AND SONS
EDINBURGH AND LONDON
MDCCCLXXVIII

MINE IS THINE.

CHAPTER XVII.

WE must now borrow the wings of Cosmo Glencairn's fancy, and fly back to the Lake of Como, where the golden summer days passed pleasantly and peacefully for the occupants of the Villa Bianca; so pleasantly, indeed, for Lord Germistoune—who was hard to please—that, as the period of his tenancy drew to a close, he began to turn scowling glances on the mountains of the Engadine, and to use language of bitter scepticism about Gull and the rest of the faculty, *apropos* of his approaching sojourn in the Alpine paradise. "Empirics and blunderers—all of them!" he would grumble. "Because it is the right thing for Sir Peter Rabbits to go to that detestable place" (Sir Peter was a civic dignitary whose "case" had been mentioned as having points of similarity to his own), "why should it be the right thing for me? Monstrously improbable that my organs could ever have resembled those of an alderman, even before he had bedevilled them with gross living and Guildhall banquets! Name of Rabbits, too! Preposterous!" But, after all, this constituted a grievance without which his life would scarcely have been in order.

Pleasantly, too, the days passed for Esmè—all unconscious of the influence she was exercising over the lives and destinies of others—happy in fancy-free meditations and in pursuits congenial to a graceful and cultured mind. The weather continued to be faultless; the sun shone every day in a cloudless sky, but the mountains lent themselves to nature's pleasant conspiracy, and sent down light airs, that came tempered from the abodes of snow, to fan the favoured district. As for the Ravenhall party and Tom Wyedale, the delights of the place were not so patent to them. Poor Mrs Ravenhall! long, long ago had the bloom of young enthusiasm for anything in this weary world been brushed from her *blasé* spirit; the voices and the aspects of external nature had no message and no meaning for her. But her walk and conversation were so artificial, that it came like a second nature to her to simulate whatever for the time being seemed to pay; and thus to all her little circle she was untiring in her raptures over the lake and its environs, which, from morn to night, never ceased to be " quite too divinely lovely and enchanting," to say the least of it.

The few people whom she knew at Cadenabbia were impressed with this. It showed, they said, such freshness, simplicity, and soul; for here was a lady, ordinarily involved in the turmoil of the great world of fashion, retiring without regret from its seductions, at the call of duty, and finding more than consolation in the sweet teachings of the beautiful and the sublime. All this factitious enthusiasm was focussed upon Esmè, into whose confidence and affections it was her design to penetrate; and since it appeared that freshness, simplicity, and soul would be the proper " wear " under the circumstances, she thus masqueraded accordingly.

Esmè was rather perplexed by it all, and even, at times, a little bored, when she would say to herself, with unconscious truth and humour, " I wonder why Mrs Ravenhall seems to think that *I* must take it as a personal compliment when she says anything pretty about the scenery?"

Of course, the whole thing inexpressibly bored Mrs Ravenhall herself. Her heart was far away in the crush and scramble of the London season. She was missing everything; she was not being seen at the right places; she was losing ground, perhaps—even, perhaps, being forgotten. The Honourable Nora Hackbut, who contributed Anglo-Continental gossip to one of those weekly papers which are so frank and so exhaustive in describing the private lives and doings of even trivial people, did, indeed, let the world know what Mrs Ravenhall was about, and what a high opinion she had of the beauties of nature; but this could not compensate for a dreary blank in the 'Morning Post,' where Mrs Ravenhall's place knew her no more.

Nor did these vexatious circumstances by any means exhaust the list of Mrs Ravenhall's trials. She was somewhat in the position of a manager of amateur theatricals, who, besides composing the piece and playing a part in it himself, has to fulfil the combined duties of stage-manager and prompter—now hustling a sluggish member of the *corps* on to the stage, now suggesting a "cue" to the forgetful, and at times even dashing "on" in person to supply the place of an absentee. Her *corps*, it will be observed, was divided into conscious and unconscious *dramatis personæ;* and the former—her husband and brother—had to be constantly instructed, cajoled, and stimulated in private,—so that, with the additional necessity of keeping the whole company in good-humour with each other, her trials were heavy and incessant. If one of them, even, would have heartily co-operated, it would have been different; but not even Tom, for whose benefit the whole thing was devised, could be got to do so—he was sluggish and procrastinating, and, indeed, played his part in a way that left much to be desired.

As to Mr Ravenhall, whose *rôle* was almost a negative one, he gave her continual trouble. He very soon grew tired of the place, and, being indifferent to Tom's interests, could not see why his convenience should be sacrificed to them. Hence he became very restive, and anxious to move on, which involved yet other calls on his wife's powers of stratagem. His wish to escape was, perhaps, not to be wondered at; for, inde-

pendently of everything else, his relations with Lord Germistoune soon made his position somewhat irksome. The bluff member for —— had, in truth, been utterly cowed by the noble lord. At first, things had gone very smoothly between them, for Ravenhall, laying his wife's precepts to heart, carried himself deferentially in the presence of the autocrat, who, mindful of his gallant promise to Mrs Ravenhall, and moved also by propagandist considerations, was studiously temperate in sentiment and courteous in tone to Mr Ravenhall. His wife had spoken of the "struggle" going on in his mind—implying that the contest lay between Reason and Radicalism; and the keen old partisan felt that a little tact and diplomacy might be well bestowed in settling the "struggle" in favour of Toryism and Truth. Lord Germistoune, by the by, occasionally rather mystified Mr Ravenhall by subtle allusions to the "struggle" in question, for Mrs Ravenhall had not revealed to her husband the existence of that phase of his own consciousness; but his stupidity guarded him from untoward discoveries, and things went on serenely for a time.

The characters of the two men, however, made it impossible that they could long do so.

Mr Ravenhall was one of those people who must either trample, or be trampled, upon; and being misled by Lord Germistoune's unexpected complaisance and moderation, he presently began to recover his self-assurance, to lose his deferential tone, and even to develop very decided symptoms of bluffness. Lord Germistoune, with a hawk's eye for all ·this sort of thing, noted the change resentfully; but, in consideration of the "struggle," was able to subdue the feelings of the man to those of the partisan for a little. There are limits, however, to all human endurance; and it is equally certain that, in this country, the majority of men will much more readily endure a strongly-expressed dissent from their views, as to principles merely, than as to the personal qualities of this or that party leader whom they follow or oppose.

The principle and the measure may be amicably discussed by the week; but when the Man is introduced, the hour of explosions has arrived. Lord Germistoune's politics were strongly flavoured with the personal element; so were Mr Ravenhall's.

And thus it one day befell that the latter, finding himself in a mixed company, and stimulated by the presence of an admiring constitu-

ent, ventured to speak reckless words in eulogy
of a great leader, as to whose character—whether purely diabolical or altogether saintly—a
keen controversy then raged; whereupon Lord
Germistoune forgot all about his gallantry, and
the propaganda, and the "struggle," and made
short work of the eminent man and his rash
disciple. Mr Ravenhall, alluding to a recent
speech of his hero's, had affirmed that "there
was no disputing *that*, at all events;" and
added some bluff remarks about "malignant
stupidity," as distinctive of all those who might
think otherwise, not only on this point, but
upon the general question of the great man's
perfection. The words were not addressed to
Lord Germistoune, but they reached his ear, and
he at once came into action.

"Let me beg you, then, Mr Ravenhall," he
said, "to write me down 'malignant and
stupid.'"

"No, no, Lord Germistoune! no, no!"
laughed Ravenhall; "we all know *you* are too
clear-headed a man to differ with what I have
just said."

"I protest, sir, your test of clear-headedness
astounds me—it really does. As to the—the
individual of whom you speak, I differ with you

to this extent, that I think if he were expelled from the British realms — and with every circumstance of ignominy—it—it would be a fortunate circumstance for the realms, sir.   What?"

"It would be a black day for England when that took place ; and in the depths of your heart, I am convinced you agree with me."

"Now, isn't this a great deal too monstrous? What the dev—, how, may I ask, do you venture to assert that my words and my real sentiments are at variance?"

"Pooh! pooh! pooh! my lord, you take the matter too strongly.   I merely mean that I am sure there is room in your mind for admiration of a man's intellect and uprightness, apart from political considerations.   That man gives a tone to public life——"

"Yes, he does—a tone of political recklessness and effrontery; and, let me tell you, there is no room in my mind for anything but abhorrence of a traitor."

"Oh! ho! ho!"

"Ah! but it isn't 'oh! ho! ho!'"

"'Traitor,' Lord Germistoune? you'll scarcely make that out, I take it."

"Yes, sir, I *said* 'traitor'—and I'll swear to the word, if you please—a traitor whose intellect is perverted, whose uprightness robs us piecemeal of the constitution, tampers with the coronation oath, filches and perverts the Prerogative, sacrifices every conviction to self-interest, and—and—oh! by the Lord Harry, sir! your boldness in speaking of this man as *not* a traitor, passes my comprehension."

Ravenhall was white, partly from anger, partly from consternation; but he was not going to cave in, before a constituent, without another struggle.

"Come, Lord Germistoune," he said, rallying his courage, "let us speak as common-sense, patriotic men of the world, and——"

"I should be glad to hear you in that vein, Mr Ravenhall—monstrously glad."

"And make allowance for differences of judgment, temperament, and so forth."

"No; I will make no allowance for iniquity, however it may be begotten."

"These are hard words, but hard to prove, I fancy. If I chose, I might say some hard words about a certain great man on your side who——"

"Now, Mr Ravenhall, if you think I am going to bandy *tu quoques* with you, you are mistaken. Legitimate argument, conducted in a temperate tone, I always court; puerilities of this sort I am in the habit of resenting as a personal affront. I simply repeat that the man you speak of is a traitor and—and a disgrace; and there is no kind of sophistry that can disturb the facts which support my definition. There! enough of him."

"There is one thing about him——"

"I distinctly decline to discuss him any farther; and, for the future, you will greatly oblige me by avoiding the subject. It disgusts me."

Lord Germistoune looked so awful, and so aquiline, and rapped his words out with such forcible intonation, and with such an air of uttering axioms, that Ravenhall fell before him mute, prostrate, and permanently cowed—shunning intercourse with him for the future as much as possible, and, when in his company, observing, as a rule, a rather sullen silence.

And all this gave grievously superfluous trouble to his wife, who, in her ignorance of the passage of arms which had taken place, went on wasting a world of diplomatic *finesse* and vigilance in hope of promoting more intimate relations between Lord Germistoune and her husband, and thereby of lightening her task of diverting the attention of the former from her serious manœuvres.

It was, of course, Mrs Ravenhall's grand object to bring Esmè and Tom into contact. To "do things together" was therefore her constant aim. But there is not much to be done at Cadenabbia beyond its delightful *spécialité* of floating about on the lake, and indulging in the poetry of idleness; and this did not favour her schemes, which pointed to a good deal of *tête-à-tête* intercourse between the young people. She liked to do things which involved loitering in quiet places, where the party might, insensibly as it were, separate, and Tom and Esmè, without perceiving how it came about, might drift away in company together. Her ingenuity in devising pretexts for such excursions was really wonderful. One day it was "such a dear little road-side shrine" she had heard of as really remarkable if you looked into it, which they had not yet done; another, it was a picturesque old woman, of whom dear Lord Germistoune *must* make a drawing for *her;* or a church deserving of a similiar distinction, or a tree, or a cow—no matter what the object, or how commonplace, for she always contrived to invest it with some imaginary interest, which caused the pilgrimage to be made, and gave point to it. Then she would set Lord Germistoune to his task, and remain beside him, full of interest, query, and suggestion; while Tom and Esmè naturally moved about, or went away together to search, at her suggestion, for some mythical point of view affording scope for Esmè's sketching powers. The two young people soon got on terms of friendly intimacy; for Tom was extremely frank, cheery, and amusing, and Esmè's unconsciousness of the plot which circled round her was not disturbed by any aggressive action on his part. In fact, he was much more at ease with her in a *tête-à-tête* than when with the rest of the party, which, considering he was a suitor, was exactly what he ought not to have been; but, in truth, it was his sister's presence which mainly reminded him of the part he had undertaken to play. His state of mind about the whole matter was very ambiguous. He did not quite know *what* he wanted. He was perfectly certain, of course, that he would like Miss Douglas's fortune, and that the state of his affairs made such an acquisition desirable. Moreover, when his mind turned upon his financial troubles, it did, in some mysterious way, take comfort from feeling that there was, in *possible* reserve, this *possible* something—this off-chance—upon which he might *possibly* fall back, and perhaps successfully. But his heart was untouched; he had no turn for matrimony; he was sadly deficient in those arts which his sister believed him to be practising; and he shrank from the disturbance and opposition which he knew must arise, even were he successful with the lady herself. So he drifted on, procrastinating and temporising, forced to deceive his sister as to his real relations with Esmè, since a knowledge of them might probably have led her to throw up the game which he was not helping her to play, but which he could not bear to abandon — as a last resource, which might come in usefully some day or other.

Now and then, indeed, when the post had brought him some desperate menace from a creditor, and when his sister had improved the occasion with urgent rhetoric, he would make some quaint, spasmodic approaches to the subject with Esmè; but they were so clumsily made, and so adroitly withdrawn, that they passed altogether unobserved and unsuspected.

Mrs Ravenhall, of course, catechised him often and searchingly; and since, to a certain extent, she regulated her tactics towards Esmè from the impressions she received from him, she was often in a state of mystification which gave rise to cross-purposes.

"Another day gone, Tom," she would say, "and what progress?"

"Well, it is difficult to say, Lucy."

"But *some?*"

"Oh yes, I think so."

"You are getting to like her very much?"

"Very much."

"Now, be frank with me; do you observe any change in her manner?"

"Ye-es, a decided change, I should say."

"Is it at all fluttery when you are left alone together, or when you meet?"

"Rather fluttery."

"And you adapt your manner, I hope?"

"Oh yes; I flutter too."

"Be serious. I sometimes think your manner is a little too familiar and easy. Avoid that. If you loved the dear girl as she ought to be loved, there would be no familiarity."

"Well, you know, we *are* getting pretty intimate; we couldn't well help it—thanks to your management."

"Ah! but you mustn't be intimate. Check that sort of thing at once. It kills sentiment. And there ought not to be too much conversation. It is, of course, unnecessary to say how fatal your ordinary style of rattle would be. If

his facings, would occasionally go over to the other camp, and while she played a *coup* or two for her brother, endeavour, from the other point of view, to discover how the land lay. To Esmè she was in some respects incomprehensible — without the key to her plot it could hardly be otherwise, act she never so adroitly; but her unfailing geniality and kindliness of manner were sufficiently attractive, and she was sure of a sincere welcome, on her frequent visits.

"Here is the tiresome, gossipy old woman coming again to worry and interrupt you, dear Miss Douglas," she cried, as she entered Esmè's room, on one of these occasions, towards the close of the Cadenabbia campaign, and when Mrs Ravenhall began to think that she must intervene more actively herself. "But I hope you are not too busy — I hope I am not too dreadfully in the way?"

Esmè reassured her on these heads, and she went on to propose the inevitable expedition; "but," she added, "it is not for a common reason I propose it to-day; and since Lord Germistoune is not busy — for he is walking on the pier — and since you are always so sweet and good, I am sure you will oblige me, if you can."

"Oblige, Mrs Ravenhall! of course I shall be

delighted to go with you—I always am. Where do you think of going to ?"

"Ah ! I *have* got a little gem for Lord Germistoune, about five miles down, on the Chiavenna side. But, to be quite frank with you, I have a selfish object—yes, quite a selfish object —in proposing an excursion to-day. To tell you the truth, I am miserable about my brother Tom. He is so depressed and low. He will admit nothing ; but I can't bear to see the dear fellow suffer. So I wish to distract him, if I can —to take him out of himself; and I think, if we can get him to go with us, we cheerful people ought to be able to do him some good among us."

None of Love's ensigns displayed themselves in Esmè's face, but she expressed all due sympathy for Tom, and asked simply what was wrong. That, Mrs Ravenhall said, was what she could not make out ; but his depression had existed for some time, and was increasing ; and probably Miss Douglas had noticed it ? But Esmè could not say she had, by any manner of means. "He has given you no hint," said Mrs Ravenhall, "that there is something preying on his mind, you are certain ?"

"Most certain ; and surely it is most unlikely he should have spoken to me about it."

"I don't know about that. I *do* know that he has a strong feeling of sympathy and *rapport* with you; so I thought he *might* have made you his confidant, though he admits nothing to me. But he has said nothing?"

"Nothing. By the by, he sometimes speaks with a good deal of anxiety about a horse which he is interested in, for some race; perhaps he has had some bad news about it."

Mrs Ravenhall's face fell, and she replied, "Oh dear, no; he makes no secret to *me* of any trouble of *that sort*. This is something far, far deeper." Furtively scanning Esmè's face as she spoke, and seeing no desired change in it, she said to herself, "If this is dissembling, she dissembles skilfully; and dissembling it must be, unless Tom is deceiving himself, which, in his calm state of mind, is not likely." Then she went on to say, confidentially, that they must extract Tom's secret from him, if possible. "You will help me, will you not, my dear Miss Douglas?"

"I? Oh, Mrs Ravenhall, I don't see how I can possibly do that. I think it would be——"

Here Esmè paused, and Mrs Ravenhall thought her manner and expression more satisfactory.

"At all events," she said, "you will help me to try and cheer him, I know."

The idea of that rattling talker and *farceur* requiring to be cheered made Esmè smile ; but as he *might* be depressed in private—must be, indeed, or his sister could not be so concerned about him—she laughingly said that she would heartily co-operate. "I daresay," she added, "he is only bored. It must be dreadfully dull for any one of his tastes, down here, with none of his usual pursuits, and no congenial companions. Probably the best advice we can give him is to go away."

"Probably," thought Mrs Ravenhall, "this is a feeler."

But here she was rather in a logical difficulty; for, having just stated that Tom was excessively unhappy, it was hard to affirm (which she would have liked to imply) that all his happiness centred in Cadenabbia. She could not do this, or even throw out any broad innuendo as to the attractions which the place had for him, without showing her hand, which, sorely hampered as she was by her ignorance of the exact relations existing between Tom and Esmè, she could not venture to do. So she merely said, with some *intention*, that she felt certain "*that* would not meet the difficulty, but rather aggravate it *materially*."

And then she went on in a side-strain, *apropos*

of Esmè's allusions to Tom's tastes and pursuits, to suggest that, in reality, his soul soared above the vulgar pastimes of his coevals, to which he merely addicted himself from the disgust incidental to a *carrière manquée;* moreover, that the underlying vein of thoughtfulness and earnest feeling which he undoubtedly possessed, was concealed by the *mauvaise honte* and artificial cynicism so constantly to be observed in the Anglo-Saxon when disappointed in his loftier aspirations. In fact, she gave quite a romantic colour to Tom's pigeon-shooting, polo-playing, and race-frequenting propensities—winding up with a firmly-expressed conviction that from them he might be satisfactorily retrieved by the *right influence,* if only it could be brought to bear upon him; for, "Ah, dear me," she concluded, with a deep sigh, "it doesn't bear thinking of! It is the sorrow of my life; and I *had* such hopes of him! We all had. Yet I can't bring myself to despair. No. I constantly say to myself, 'Under tender and noble influences, what might not that gifted creature do, even yet!' for he is full of heart and sympathy. Well, well; forgive me for boring you. Dear Tom is so very much to me, I forget myself when I begin to speak of him."

Mrs Ravenhall did this passage excessively well, and Esmè's kind heart was touched for the "sorrow of her life." It was impossible, indeed, that Esmè should not feel a little perplexed about this strangely unobtruded side of Tom's nature, but it could not be altogether imaginary; and, in any case, Mrs Ravenhall's anguish was obviously sincere, and to be respected.

On the morning of this expedition the sorrowing sister had discovered her "gifted" brother gazing in some consternation at a sheaf of newly-arrived duns, and had, then and there, well battered him with counsel, suggestion, and reproof as to the progress of his suit; and after the start, while the party were still together, she was so observant and manœuvring, and so plied Tom with secret telegraphy, that for once he really became conscious, constrained, and silent, thus favouring the recently-coined theory of his depression. Then, when Mrs Ravenhall's tactics had ripened for the separation of the party, she contrived to whisper Tom, before he and Esmè sauntered away, "Just continue as you are doing; be low, be depressed, but, at the right moment, *empressé* and earnest. I have paved the way for you, I think." These words of wisdom Tom did not long bear in mind, but presently fell into such wild spirits, and rattled away so continuously, that Esmè, thinking partly of Mrs Ravenhall's revelation, partly of Tom's recent eclipse, and having no reason for constraint with him, laughingly congratulated him on the recovery of his spirits. "Recovery of my spirits!" he cried, and then (remembering his sister's words, and suspecting some move of hers to which he ought to play up), "ah!—ahem! did you think I was out of spirits?"

"Oh yes; your gloom was quite tragical, and visible to every eye."

"Ah! perhaps; I didn't think it would be observed. I'm sorry it was. A man ought to conceal these things—to—to wear a mask, and that kind of thing."

"I think it is very hard, when one is really bored, to conceal the fact."

"Well, it is; but I ought to have concealed it."

"I was right then; I knew I was. You *are* bored with this place, and I think it is very natural."

"Bored?" cried Tom, aghast at his clumsy *lapsus,* "of course I didn't mean that. I meant low, depressed."

"Which you are?"

"Yes, now — now you press me; I must admit that I am — horribly so."

"But yet not bored with this place?"

"No; I never was happier than I am here."

Esmè laughed. "What a very curious state of mind to be in!" she said.

"Isn't it?" said Tom.

"Horribly low and depressed, yet never happier—all at the same time?"

Tom was not so logical as his sister: besides, he had a dim notion that this was the normal phase of a lover's mind; so he stuck to his paradox, trying to look lugubrious, with fun threatening to break out in his eyes and all over his face.

"It is impossible, then, for your friends to know whether they ought to congratulate or condole," said Esmè, demurely, humouring his whim, and expecting a *dénouement* in connection with Tom's ever-execrated banker and some turn of fortune on the turf.

"Ah!" said Tom, "I wish I knew which they ought to do. No one could tell them except yourself."

Here he was, up at the very point, long before he meant it; whereupon, immediately, great consternation fell upon him, so that he swerved, and adroitly added, "Of course I don't mean *you* specially, but you or some other tremendously clever person, who understands metaphysics and that kind of thing."

"Really, Mr Wyedale, I wonder what you will credit me with next? Metaphysics! I don't think I even quite know what the word means."

"Oh, neither do I, for that matter; but it's a good big word, and means something wise."

Esmè laughed, and said, "Well, I don't think I need go very deep into metaphysics to discover what would be a remedy for that part of your state of mind which is not 'exquisitely happy.'"

"A remedy? What is it?"

"Some pigeons to shoot, for one thing."

"Well, the place would be more endur—— would be the better for something of the sort."

"Or a polo-ground."

"Ah! *if* we had some polo."

"Or a race-meeting, within reach, now and then."

"Don't tantalise me, Miss Douglas."

"And a few sympathetic men under sixty, to talk to and play tennis with."

"Oh yes; the men here *are* maddeningly old

and stupid. They can do nothing. They break one's heart."

"Exactly; in other words, you are severely bored."

"No, no, no."

"Oh yes, you are; and, strange to say, I can suggest an alleviation to you, which I don't think you have discovered for yourself. Giuseppe, our chief boatman, tells me there is splendid sport to be got here in spearing trout at night in the lake—what they call 'burning the water' in Scotland."

"You don't say so!"

"Giuseppe does."

"And—and large trout?"

"Gigantic, according to Giuseppe."

"And how do they work it?"

"Ah! I must refer you to Giuseppe for the particulars."

"I can't tell you, Miss Douglas, how much obliged I am for the hint. I'll get at Giuseppe this very afternoon. I'll try conclusions with the trout before I'm a day older. There's really no sport much better. That *will* be something to do at last." And so, forgetting his sister, matrimony, depression, and all the real business of the hour, he rattled away upon the intoxicating subject, till, coming abruptly upon the rest of the party, he stopped short and pulled so long a face — remembering how hopelessly he had broken down in his duty, how far he had wandered from the prescribed path—that his sister almost feared she read in his guilty features the announcement of his rejection.

From all this it will be seen how little Esmè's unconsciousness was to be wondered at; what a waste of power was involved in poor Mrs Ravenhall's sleepless exertions; with what poetic justice nature, working through Tom's natural instincts, buried her intrigues, for the present at least, in bathos; and how little cause, for the present at least, Cosmo Glencairn had to torture himself, as he often did, about the rival who had communicated his designs with such offensive *nonchalance.*

CHAPTER XVIII.

THE month drew to a close at last, and Mrs
Ravenhall had the mortification of feeling that
the campaign in which she had displayed so
much strategy was perhaps, at best, only a
drawn one. Misrepresent as he might, Tom
could not point to a single position of advantage which had been gained. He could
only keep on reporting, like the telegrams from
despairing armies, "the *morale* of the troops is
excellent," "the situation is easier," "the de-
finitive blow is postponed for strategic reasons,"
and so forth. All was cruelly vague and unsatisfactory; and from the opposite side no
cheering symptoms came to the anxious eye of
her who conducted the siege operations. It
was hard to draw off now—with nothing to
look forward to but a renewal of the campaign
in a new field, under circumstances that could

scarcely be so favourable, and when her own supervision might not be available.

She was at her wits' end about Tom. She wished him to go on to the Engadine, and at least preserve the *status quo*; but Tom was obstinate. He wanted a rest, a change from this *toujours perdrix* of ladies' society, polite small-talk, boredom, dissimulation, and physical inactivity. But he put it otherwise to his sister, asserting (and this reasonably) that in her absence the field would not be conveniently open to him; also, that a little absence often did good—making the heart (as he was instructed) grow fonder; and lastly, that he had a presentiment that the thing would be done at Dunerlacht, and nowhere else. It was hard, he added, to fight against a presentiment—which Mrs Ravenhall felt to be true, when, as in this case, it merely signifies an obstinate resolve; so she was reluctantly obliged to give way before it. And what was Tom going to do now? Tom's heart was already beating high with the thought of Homburg. The siren-song of " faites le jeu," the " innumerous " crisping of *billets de banque*, the diapason of shovelled gold, was sounding in the ear of his fancy; but it was part of the matrimonial scheme that he was to appear *rangé*—so he said he required bracing, and would go to bathe at Biarritz or Ostend for a month. In this melancholy way matters stood, when, two days before the break-up of the party, Mr Ravenhall, who had been detrimental all along, at last came in useful; for his wife, on returning from a long excursion that afternoon, found him in a high state of fuss— his portmanteaus packed and in the hall, and he himself fuming at the non-arrival of the steamer which was to convey him on the first stage of his journey to London. Mr Ravenhall, be it known, had come away from Parliament without "a pair," and on that very forenoon he had received telegram after telegram from Hustler the Whip, imploring him, in agitated terms, to return on the instant; for, two nights thereafter, the Opposition—"strong, united, and jubilant" —were going to "try a fall" with the Ministry, which was shaky and despondent, and required every vote which could be scraped together, if it were to be saved at all.

"So I am off, of course," said Ravenhall, "to save Ministers."

"And what am I to do?" asked his wife.

Mr R. had not given her a thought; but, as he rushed to the steamer which now came up,

he said that she might do what she liked—that
was to say, come home at her leisure, securing
the escort of Tom; and so went on his way.

What, then, was she to do?   It was grievous
to miss a season; but to go back to London
when two - thirds of it was over, to set the
machinery of season-life agoing when the rest
of the world were beginning to think of the
wind-up, was by no means remunerative—and,
in this case, there was a special reason against
it.   Her resolution was taken at once.   She
would "go home by the Engadine," with Tom
as escort, and linger as long upon the way as
seemed advisable.   Had not Ravenhall given
her *carte blanche?*   Without a word, therefore,
to Tom, she went straight to the Villa Bianca;
and relating how her husband had been suddenly called home on "urgent business," she
explained her new plan, which she thought
would be *quite* delightful, were she only convinced that the prospect of her continued
society would not be irksome to the Germistounes.   Nothing could be more flattering than
their response to this: and what, they asked, of
Tom?   Tom, his sister said, would accompany
her; it would be a *delight* to him; the *poor
fellow* had been *quite dismally low* about the

break-up of their *charming little coterie!* And when Tom's accession had been also hailed with kindly acclamations, she went into the plans for the journey; and, in a few minutes, it was arranged that they should travel together, and, "to prolong the enjoyment, and make quite a picnic of it," start for Chiavenna on the following afternoon, sleep there, and make their way over the Maloja Pass next day. With all details cut and dried, Mrs Ravenhall then sought her brother, to communicate what she called this "rare stroke of fortune." Strange to say, the "poor fellow" heard of Fortune's bounty in a spirit of utter thanklessness; for he fell into a violent passion, and protested, in most unloverlike language, against being "swindled" into further association with the *objet aimé* for the present.

"But," urged his sister, "they are so pleased you are coming—*quite* in ecstasies."

"Gammon!" cried Tom, whose faith in "ecstasies" the events of the month had crushed—"ecstasies be hanged! They are thrown away, at all events, for I'm *not* going. There!"

"Now, Tom, do be reasonable."

"No, I won't. I've been in the mill long enough. I'm off to Ho—— to Biarritz. I require bracing. Health before every consideration."

"But what am I to say to them?"

"Exactly what you please."

"But I've pledged you."

"That is your affair."

"And who is to take care of me?"

"Again your affair."

"And all our schemes?"

"All *your* schemes may slide. I'm dead tired of them."

Here was ingratitude, base and brutal; but Mrs Ravenhall knew that Tom's wrath was ever evanescent, and his nature kindly—so she turned away very silently to the window, applied her pocket-handkerchief *very* furtively to her eyes, and gave a *very* little sob. There was pathos in the silence, and dramatic power in the suppression of the tear and the sob. Few men —not brutal—can resist this sort of thing: Tom was beat at once. "Come, Lucy," he said, "I didn't mean to be so harsh; but it *is* hard on a fellow, admit that."

"A great deal harder upon me," replied Mrs Ravenhall, with her back still turned and a *tremolo* in her voice. "See what I've been doing and sacrificing for you, and this unkindness the only return ! "

" Well, I *am* a brute, but I'm sorry for it."

" And you'll go ? "

Tom had felt from the first that this was a foregone conclusion ; but he replied, " If there *is* no help for it,"—adding, with a sudden flash of the predatory instinct, " if I can *get*, that is to say ; for unless you pay my hotel bill, I'm afraid the manager may be rather pressing in his invitation to remain."

His sister reassured him on this head, and pointed out that, when such a stake was at issue, a little money was of no consideration. This healthy financial sentiment opened up to Tom a new field of auriferous possibilities, which helped to console him, though 'he continued all day sufficiently " low " and " depressed " to have covered himself with distinction in the most protracted " love " scene with Esmè.

The next afternoon saw them on board the steamer for Colico. Lord Germistoune and his daughter were very sorry to go ; and the retainers of the Villa seemed very sorry to part with them, thronging to the pier with bouquets and benedictions, and breaking out into a choric song of love, admiration, and regret as the vessel moved away. This, as the words of their little hymn implied, was a tribute to the sweet English girl whose gracious ways and fair Madonna face had captivated the simple folk. His lordship, however, took it all as for himself, stiffly raised his hat, and observed to a bystander that he was gratified; also, that these were a goodish kind of poor devils, who lied and thieved like fury, but had an eye for a gentleman when they saw him, and knew how to treat him. Mrs Ravenhall was only too thankful to turn her back upon the lake; but she was still "before the footlights:" so when they left it and drove away to Chiavenna, she kissed her hand sentimentally to the last of it, and murmured, "Lago, mio! mio bel lago, addio! Ci bisogna partire! ma i nostri cuori staranno sempre con te!"

And Lord Germistoune, gallantly affecting to catch her enthusiasm, waved his hat in the same direction, and cried in the same melodious tongue, "Addio, bel lago! La signora se ne vada, e con lei tu perdi la tua più cara bellezza!"

And Esmè laughed and said—

"Al rivederti, bel lago!"

And so they all said "good-bye" to the lake,

in its native language—all except Tom, by the by, who was still "low," and who said nothing, but looked as if he never wished to see its waters again; and so the curtain fell upon beautiful Como.

Pleasant is the route through the Val Bregaglia, by which Italy speeds her parting guests, and sends them upwards from her summery plains to the solemn haunts of winter. Upon the massive crags that overhang the way, the South still spreads her mantle of deepest foliage, whose exquisite verdure is blended from the green of the chestnut, the walnut, and the oak. Thickets of shrubbery clothe the levels in dark luxuriance, relieved with flashes from the rhododendron's bloom; there are glimpses of sward still enamelled with souvenirs of the Land of Flowers; even the boulders which have tumbled to the river-side have brought their gala covering of wondrous mosses, purple, amber—a wealth of indefinable colour—which tells no tale of winter. The Maira, fresh from some glacier up above, meets the tender grasses and the flowers upon her margin, and checks her haste. It is still the Land of Summer, and the Val Bregaglia will summer it with every art, as long as may be.

But we go on and up. Here is Castegna, and

we are across the frontier. Farewell to Italy! On we go and up, through gradual transformations. We begin to miss the walnut-leaf; we lose the chestnut; we pass through galleries of unclothed rock. Over the dark crests of pine and alpine cedar, flashes from sunlit snow-peaks begin to reach us. The Maira is a torrent now, sometimes a waterfall. The alpen-rose and heather nestle on her rough banks; the mountain-ash trembles over her angry tumult. On we go and up, with a sudden steepness of ascent. Suddenly a mist falls around us—a cloud. We hear the jingling of the horses' bells and the roar of a waterfall; we feel by the angle of the carriage that the gradient increases; and though we can see nothing, we know that we are breasting the western face of the MALOJA. The mist lifts, and, behind, we have a dream-like glimpse of far-away plains sleeping in the sun—Elysian —beautiful exceedingly; and below us, in the foreground, a deep, dark, piney gorge, whence, in a ghostly column, the spray of a cascade rises up, quivering with the voice of its hidden waters. Down comes the mist again; nor does it rise till, the horses springing forward in their supreme effort, we suddenly find ourselves upon the level, and everything is clear again. We are in the

Engadine. We stand on the edge of an upper mountain-world—on a plateau 6000 feet in height, where the great mountain-peaks separate themselves at last from the family chain, and, rising up to heaven in sublime loneliness, assert their magnificent individuality.

By this route, and with some such experiences, the combined party made their way from Chiavenna to Maloja, much favoured by the weather. Then, after a brief halt, they continued their journey to St Moritz, through the unexpected green pastures and by the blue waters of the Upper Engadine, where everything *is* so unexpected and strange—where the air is so still and the woods so songless, and everything wears such an impress of solemn pensiveness, it would seem as though some awe from the near presence of the mighty hills saddened the valley, or the weight of their pine-clad feet oppressed it with too sore a burden. The day was waning when they started from Maloja, and when they left the Silser-see the sun's last rays died on its quiet surface. Up in mid-heaven the rose light still bloomed on the peaks of the Julier and Bernina; but twilight deepened apace as they drove swiftly down the valley, so that when they reached Campfer the last of the after-glow was fading from Piz Languard, and they entered St Moritz in the dark. Up to a certain point things had gone most satisfactorily *en route*. Tom had rather a bad time of it, to be sure ; for whenever Esmè remarked on anything in the shape of a plant or a flower by the wayside, his sister, finding telegraphic measures vain, frankly ordered him to descend and secure the specimen—and as Esmè's botanical sympathies were quick and wide, his exits and entrances, notwithstanding her protests, were incessant. Nor when he had half filled the carriage, and escaped to the *banquette*, under plea of smoke, did he find sanctuary there, being perpetually harassed by his sister's parasol arousing him to some bit of scenery which Esmè admired, and which he was consequently assured was " quite in his style." There is a good deal of labour and sorrow in the conduct of a courtship at best, when all the *petits-soins* are inspired by the heart of the suitor, and Tom often felt that this " machine-made" wooing was becoming perfectly intolerable ; and over and over again, on this day, he bitterly compared himself to a barrel - organ, whereof the grinder was Lucy, who, with no fear of the police before her eyes, was grinding his works to destruction. Lord Germistoune had begun the morning "gouty," by which euphemism (strongly recommended for use in families) he described a general fractiousness of temper and desire to put every one else in the wrong ; so that the prospect of the journey was not lively. But suddenly remembering that he had unlawfully partaken of Chiavenna beer the night before, and deciding that Stefano, the courier, was in some mysterious way responsible for this infraction of medical ordinance and his master's *malaise*, he packed his " gout " neatly up in half-a-dozen sentences of malediction, flung them on his scapegoat's back, consigned him to the arch-brewer of all mischief, and, thus relieved, became as pleasant and ungouty as need be. Nothing could be neater than his gallant little speeches to Mrs Ravenhall, or more graceful than his patronage of the scenery, or apter than his remarks, botanical and geological—nothing, at least according to Mrs Ravenhall, and even Tom (when not engaged in rooting up something tough and bulbous by the roadside), for Tom was still the faithful *claqueur* of the proprietor of the " best mixed shooting in Scotland." And then, his lordship's anecdotes ! so racy ! so full of sarcasm ! so interesting ! If they were old they were " historically instructive;" if their satire clung, like yew's roots, round dead men's bones—well, it served the bones right; for Lord Germistoune was great, and wise, and infallible—when Mrs Ravenhall was his prophet. So things went cheerily and well, till they were more than two-thirds up the Pass. But neither the temper of a gouty noble nor the weather of an Alpine pass can be depended upon. A little thing will disturb the equilibrium of either. It became suddenly rather chilly, and there was a check in the flow of Lord Germistoune's converse. A haze came over the sun; it became chillier. Lord Germistoune began to look a little dangerous — to put his ears back, as it were. Symptoms of an impending mist showed themselves; Lord Germistoune shivered angrily, and was pulling his plaid tighter round him, when his arms dropped, and glaring with all his eyes at the second carriage which followed close behind, he almost screamed—

"By heavens! the HOUND is actually *drinking* before me—*me!*—in my very face!"

And there, sure enough, was Stefano, seated in the *banquette*, positively refreshing his inner man from a flask, in the august presence of his employer! "A d—d low Neapolitan lazzarone" drinking (with gusto too !) " in the whites of the eyes " of the Right Hon. Archibald, Viscount Germistoune, Baron Dunerlacht, K.T., and a Baronet ! If ever there were a provocative to " gout," here surely it was. His lordship succumbed to it instantly. The *cortège* was halted on the edge of the precipice with some difficulty, and even peril, and the courier, being extracted from his perch, was "brought up," and received such a *warming* about "roistering ruffianism," and " brutal, mutinous insolence," as would have closed the mouth of a timid courier against *schnaps* for the remainder of his days. Then the flask was confiscated, and its contents poured as a libation to the infernal gods, whom Lord Germistoune had continuously invoked during the " incident." But this time the ebullition brought no relief; the scapegoat went in vain to the wilderness, and Mrs Ravenhall's blandishments fell flat, — for the mist swooped down and wrapped them in its cold wet blanket, so that the thin blood of the old man had need of all the fire of his anger to keep it on the move at all. There was, fortunately, no lack of this stimulant. If Sir William Gull had, with devilish art, concocted " this accursed cloud," and conveyed it through the air, and caused it drop on the Maloja Pass, so as to meet his noble patient there, he could not have been held more personally responsible for its existence. Awful superlatives were tacked to the doctor's name, and even Alderman Rabbits came in—as a sort of accessory—for the tail of the storm, the most ungenerous strictures being passed upon his interior. Nor did matters greatly improve when they emerged from the cloud and found themselves upon the plateau of the Engadine. The whole thing was pronounced to be a mistake, if not a swindle; the air would give a seal bronchitis; the levels about the river and lakes looked malarious enough to kill herds of the strongest elephants. Scenery? there *was* no scenery; it was an infernal desert invented by the doctors as a sort of theatre for empirical practice. "Let them," he cried, "make their experiments on aldermen if they please; they may vivisect Sir Peter Rabbits if they choose—probably they couldn't do better; but it's monstrous that a really valuable life should be tampered with by the scoundrels." He was in the state of mind which prompts the "Tax-payer" to write to the 'Times;' and perhaps he might have done so had it *not* been the habit of the "tax-payer," and if he had not regarded " *l'organe de la cité*" as the root of all national evil.

Few places in Europe are more loved by its visitors than the Engadine, many of whom regard it with a kind of bigoted enthusiasm which will scarcely allow that there can be any qualification of the praises due to it ; but even these will, *perhaps*, admit that, at first (*only* at first), there is a certain dishevelledness — a general happy-go-luckiness—about the hotels, to which one requires to get accustomed. At all events, they will be quite able to conceive that a man arriving in the dark, and in Lord Germistoune's frame of mind, might very probably not be soothed by his first impressions even of the Hotel " Zur frohen Aussicht " at St Moritz.

CHAPTER XIX.

It was dark when the party arrived. All the
guest-world were at " evening-meal," and all
(the few) waiters were feeding them—the porter
even assisting. Thus, when the Germistoune equi-
page clattered up, there was none of that rush
and *élan* of welcome which, at smaller altitudes,
greet parties less illustrious. All the shouting,
and jingling, and cracking of whips was met
with a bathos of darkness and silence. Only after
a very prolonged ringing did a leisurely form,
with a shaggy head, and its hands very deep in
its pockets, lounge to the door. This was the
landlord himself, at that time a worthy Switzer,
with the fear of God, perhaps, but certainly not
that of man, before his eyes; and who—being
a republican, or rather because his hotel was
always full, and because a contract price is
equally valuable, be it paid by peer or prole-
tarian—had no sort of leaning to a lord, but

rather contrariwise,—the servants of the noble being often troublesome. This individual, then, remained at the top of the steps, leaning against the door-post, and making no sign whatever.

"What does it mean? what the d—l does it all mean?" shouted Lord Germistoune; "where are the people? the servants? the landlord? the —speak to that man, Stefano! speak to him— if he *is* a man!" Stefano reascended the steps, and a low, sleepy, growling sound ensued, on the part of the man, which was presently interpreted to his master by Stefano, to the effect that the growler *was* a man, that he was also the landlord, and that he too wished very much to know "what it all meant."

"Tell him," cried Lord Germistoune—"tell the idiot that we want rooms, and our luggage taken down, and—and what people usually want at hotels."

"Tell him," replied the growler, "that he can't have rooms here."

"Then I'll go straight to the mayor!" shouted his lordship, springing to his feet. Whereupon the growler announced that *he* was the mayor, and ready for him and all comers. "Then, by the Lord Harry, I'll go to the president of the district, wherever he is!" But there was no checkmating the monster—he was also president of the district! Great heavens! here was a pretty pass! Lord Germistoune had got beyond the law, or rather he found all its machinery concentrated in the hands of a brutal pluralist, who would certainly not use it against himself. What was to be done? All kinds of vituperation and menace fell upon the growler as spray upon an iron-bound coast. Eventually, in some of his capacities, he might probably lock his lordship up for inciting to a breach of the peace; in the meantime, he rather seemed to enjoy the fun of the thing in a dim, ruminating way.

Things were in this state of dead-lock when a smart and intelligent young woman, who proved to be the landlord's daughter, appeared on the scene, and who, receiving nothing from her father but an unintelligible grunt in answer to her inquiries, tripped impatiently down to the carriage, and asked the pleasure of the party, and their names — on hearing which she gave a cry of astonishment, assured them their rooms were reserved and ready, rushed upstairs, tolled the bell, dashed into the house, cried shrilly for the attendants, and, when she had put everything in train, turned upon her father sharply, and asked him, as Lord G. had done, "What it all meant?" To which, in the same grim monotone, he simply replied, "They didn't tell me their names. They only said they wanted rooms. Am I a prophet?"

And this is the kind of thing that did, and may perhaps still, occur in the Engadine; but, after all, it is only the people's way—only their way—which, of course, makes it as right and pleasant as possible. The poor old lord was really quite crushed by this last scene. The terrible immobility of the landlord had been too much for him, after the trials and fatigues of the day; and he went to bed entirely subdued, and without a word of bitterness, save the remark that an egg, which he had encountered at supper, was sufficient to "account for everything—*almost* everything;" the exceptions being, perhaps, the mysterious clemency of Providence, which could permit the continued existence of the growler, and the savagery of a political system which could place him in a double-seated curule chair.

The Engadine, as has been said, enjoys an affection on the part of its visitors which is quite enthusiastic. Some give all their love to Pontresina, others to St Moritz, others to Campfer, others (the sybarites) to Samaden; and, among the partisans of each, there is often hot contention and dispute. Yet, as against an outsider, all true Engadiners will sink minor differences, and "go for" the Engadine, the whole Engadine, and—it would *almost* sometimes seem—for nothing but the Engadine. Well, it cannot be said that their enthusiasm is much misapplied, for it is a goodly and a glorious region — Lord Germistoune's first impressions notwithstanding. The air alone makes the region unique. Is there anything like it anywhere else? so dry, elastic, and champagney? The *genius loci may* be solemn and pensive, but we laugh at him; we defy his contagion, breathing this brave atmosphere in the brave summer time. You seek delight in the glories of nature? in vast expanses of mountain panorama, in the splendours that dwell about the world of snowfield and glacier? Elsewhere you may purchase fleeting glimpses of these, with toil and weariness of the flesh. But here, at ease, on a high green oasis, in the midst of the glittering ice - world, you can watch, like a lotus-eater, the restless phenomena of light and colour, which dream over it in tender ripples, or surge across it in gorgeous floods, incessantly, from the first streak of dawn till the after-glow has faded from the tallest summits. And here, without effort to distress the feeblest, you can reach points where all the Alpine world lies before you—all the giants of near and far, from the Tyrol to the Oberland, from Palü to Monte Rosa and the Matterhorn. And if you are muscular and ambitious, and wish to enjoy, with vast ranges of vision, the "swagger" of braving crevasse and avalanche, *circumspice!* many of the highest and severest mountains in Europe are beside you ; you are half-way up them all, and thus can achieve your objects and earn glory at, so to speak, half-price. Here then, living in neighbourly intimacy with mountains and glaciers, young, old, lusty, feeble, athlete, and sybarite, can all taste the best delights of the high mountain life, each in his own way and degree. Yes, it is a goodly place. The splendid air, the noble scenery, the sound sleep, the conscious bound into a new vitality, after the languor of the plains—all these things are good ; but, behind these positive delights, a negative advantage gives them exquisite point —there are no tourists here. The tidal wave of noisy vulgarity and brutal selfishness which swamps Europe, "affronts" the desert, and "puts a girdle round the earth," does not rise to these altitudes. We are beyond the zone of Cook and Gaze. Let us not pause to consider how it is so. Let us be simply thankful for the mystery, that in these pleasant places they are not.

It might have been expected that Lord Germistoune would not remain to appreciate the delights of the locality, and that earliest dawn would see him and his suite flying in the direction of monarchical institutions. But, strange to say, when he came down in the morning, whether it was the magic of the air already, or of a wonderfully sound sleep, or what not, his tone was temperate in the extreme. "We must try the place for a day or two, at all events," he said. He did not even allude to the landlord. Indeed, the relations between these two remarkable men were very singular from first to last. Manœuvres were of course resorted to, to keep them apart. Still, Lord Germistoune could not be kept from going occasionally for his letters to the bureau, in a corner of which the landlord was habitually ambushed; thus they would meet from time to time. Could it be that the imperviousness of this republican pachyderm to Lord Germistoune's wrath and general augustness paralysed the latter by its utter novelty, and so quelled him? Certain it is that no further "scenes" occurred between them.

As soon as his lordship's eye fell upon the landlord, his back would stiffen, his nostrils dilate, and he would breathe short. As soon as the landlord beheld his lordship, he would rise slowly from his chair, with *his* back very much in the air, and his hands very deep in his pockets, and his eyes very much fixed upon the noble lord, and thus remain — alert, and, as it were, ready to spring—until the latter marched warily out of the room, with the cautious dignity of a large dog retiring from the presence of another large dog who looks as if he "meant business."

But the existence of the landlord did no particular harm. The place *was* tried for a few days, and it suited. The air and the waters were all that could be desired ; the hotel was comfortable ; the food was respectable ; my lord's appetite immense. There was no talk of moving. Gull was rehabilitated, and the name of Rabbits was not heard any more.

As yet there were few English in the place ; but the foreign visitors were plentiful, pleasant, and *comme il faut.* There was a charming contingent of high-bred Italians at the hotel, and some official Prussians—all padding and bureau-cratic *morgue*, but of much distinction; and several Russian princes and princesses of the most charming description; and, among all these, there were several persons of real emi-nence in the world of statecraft, diplomacy, and fashion. At once Mrs Ravenhall let loose all her tentacles into this shoal of eligibles, and had captured at least half-a-dozen distinguished "friendships" in a week. Poor woman! after all her vicarious love-making, she had certainly earned some relaxation. Who could grudge it to her? And here it was for her, as she best loved to take it. Lord Germistoune, too, was pleased with the society, particularly with its diplomatic and political elements; and the society received him with distinguished consideration.

He was always fond of political talk, and it was his foible to believe that he understood the foreign policies of all nations—even of England. So he posed as a statesman here, and harangued at large, occasionally being kind enough to ex-plain the drift of treaties and memorandums to the men who had devised them. "I have been a Minister myself," he said, and they all called him "Excellency." One observes that people with far fewer advantages—with less voice, less presence, less money—will always find a gallery for their prose and their platitudes if they only assert themselves; and Lord Germistoune was quite the centre of a little peripatetic *salon* down at the Kurhaus, of mornings. There he walked about, dropping words of wisdom, in the intervals between the prescribed tumblers. The air about him was foggy with turgid sentences, of which one continually caught such fragments as —"I told Beust very distinctly that I could not sanction——" "Cavour, who was a charlatan, implored me——" "Buol knew what my distinct opinion of *his* policy was ——" "Louis Napoleon frequented my society at that time, and took my advice; if he had continued to do so——" &c., &c. People listened to all this respectfully; how much they swallowed, is another question. "Que diable!" said Prince Latschki to an American friend, "I have turn that old man inside out in five minute. It is a shell! Void! Pah!"

It is probable that Latschki expressed a pretty general sentiment, but it was certainly not the sentiment which met his lordship's ears and eyes; and he was delighted with every one, especially with himself.

Mrs Ravenhall's "weather eye" was, notwith-

standing other allurements, by no means neglect-
ful of the young people. The Engadine seemed
full of promise for her projects, at first. Here,
there was no call to rack the brain in devising
expeditions, and excuses for them. There was
something of the sort to be done every day in
the week, without apology, and, indeed, almost
de rigueur. These excursions are usually made
in large parties, involving many vehicles, so
that a very little generalship enabled her to
make such travelling combinations as suited
all her purposes. To one carriage she would
invariably "detail" herself and Lord Germistoune, with some gentleman who would amuse
and flatter him; and, for fourth, the lady of distinction whose "friendship" she happened to be
stalking at the time.   In another conveyance
Esmè and Tom would find themselves *vis-à-vis*
with a neutral matron and some strangely unattractive old man, — generally Schnoll, the
German publicist, a dungeon of learning per-
fumed with garlic — or Angus Slorach, the
Edinburgh metaphysician, who had one eye,
reckless ways of snuffing, and an intolerable
fund of anecdote about the late Dr Chalmers.
Tom sometimes grew restive about these old
men, inquiring bitterly *who* on earth the late

Dr Chalmers was, and *why* on earth he should be disinterred for his benefit.

Things, however, seemed to go along pretty satisfactorily. Tom's occasional bulletins were as rosy as need be; and being, from various reasons, less searchingly verified than hitherto, they passed muster, and Mrs Ravenhall was tolerably content for a time. But matters changed. For it chanced that there was in the hotel a certain young Count Roderigo Fori, of monstrous fascinations, with large, lustrous, and tender brown eyes, and a tenor voice that had simply no right to be off the stage,—a youth, indeed, "framed in the very prodigality of nature," and dressed by Poole; and this splendid creature, who had no doubt desolated many female hearts before, introduced grievous care and agitation into the soul of Mrs Ravenhall. And it also chanced that there was sojourning there a certain young American damsel —not beautiful, as it is the delightful habit of her young *compatriotes* to be, but endowed with that kind of wit and *espiéglerie* which is calculated to fascinate *that* kind of young bachelor who, as a rule, sharpens his face against female allurements. And this Miss Krupper—in full, Eudoxia G. Krupper—to whom Mrs Ravenhall had never done any harm—beyond never looking at her—yet cast upon that lady the curse of the sleepless eye. For, if the alluring Count had only had the sense to fall in love with Miss Krupper, all might have been well; or if Miss Krupper had followed her national instinct in favour of a coronet (even when it only exists in the imagination of the nobleman or on his cigar-case and pocket-handkerchiefs), and cast her glamour over Count Roderigo, things might still have been supportable. But this regrettable Count fell desperately in love, or seemed—for these Italians are nice, but—well, fell in love with Esmè; and "that impossible" Miss Krupper fell in love with, or at least did her best to throw glamour over, Tom Wyedale. And these two tragical threads of circumstance interweaving, presented themselves almost simultaneously to the observation of Mrs Ravenhall, and wrought her woe. The party in the hotel spent their evenings together in the common drawing-room—for they were, on the whole, of the same *monde* (except, perhaps, Miss K. and her mamma); and, since there were many Italians among them, much music was made. Roderigo was the musical star; for his playing on guitar and piano were worthy of his performances as a tenor, and he had such a dramatic method of singing and playing—such a way, as he sang, of fixing his beautiful eyes, with passionate intensity, on some inanimate object, and then gradually shifting his gaze to the face of some pretty woman, on whom it would rest in pathetic dreaminess during his tenderest phrases—that he was justly the object of admiration, and in perpetual requisition, particularly among the pretty women, of whom there was abundance. Esmè's singing was also justly admired; but since her playing was unequal to it, what more natural than that so apt an accompanier as the Count, should be ever ready to assist her? And thus they were brought together, and Roderigo very soon began to favour Esmè with a monopoly of the dreamy gazings above recorded.

About the same time, the charming young man developed a strong partiality for Tom's society, frequenting it so assiduously, that where Tom was, there, too, generally was the Count, or thereabouts. Thus Mrs Ravenhall's scheming in favour of her brother had a reflex action in favour of his new friend, who was almost as much in Esmè's society as was Tom—except, indeed, when the latter shared the happiness with Herr Schnoll or Dr Slorach. But let us be

just.   The Count's affection for his English
friend must have been, in part at least, inde-
pendent of the *arrière pensée* of access to Miss
Douglas.   Otherwise why should he have invited him, night after night, to his rooms, when
all the world slept?   He certainly did so, and
Tom as certainly went; and, since it would have
been but dull work for two young fellows to
sit doing nothing, could anything be more
natural than that they should trifle with a
pack of cards?   And although the count was
(he said) a perfect noodle at *écarté*, could anything be more in keeping with a chivalrous
nature than that he should hospitably engage
his guest. in a game to which he was partial,
being, indeed, favourably known in connection
with it at "The Turf" and similar literary
institutions?   And if he won?   Well, chivalrous conduct *sometimes* has its reward, and the
battle is not *always* to the strong; so that Mrs
Ravenhall need not have been so very bitter
against Roderigo, *apropos* of his little *soirées*—
all about a trumpery three hundred sovereigns
too! which paltry sum she had to pay for Tom
in a fortnight—Tom having "no effects," and
debts of honour being "the very devil."   Mrs
Ravenhall *was* perfectly blind to the romantic

element in the incident, and thought, and said, quite dreadful things about the amiable young nobleman.

This, however, was comparatively a trifle. The Count's daylight conduct became markedly aggressive. Fellows of this sort are no laggards. At all the excursions, he was at Esmè's side from the moment of debarkation, fetching and carrying, bounding up steep rocks for flowers and what not; anticipating every want; prostrating, worshipping, wriggling like a spaniel, with the eternal look of a spaniel's devotion in his beautiful brown eyes. Every night, at music, the *intention* of his singing and his dreamy gaze became more pronounced. One night the wretch even ventured on a serenade with his guitar : but here justice overtook him ; for, mistaking Lord Germistoune's chamber for Esmè's " bower," he had not achieved the second verse of " Com' e gentil " before the window was thrown up, and he was ordered, in the most unfeeling terms, to stop " that infernal caterwauling, and be off about his business." Another day, Esmè having remarked at dinner that she did not possess a specimen of the *edelweiss*, at breakfast-time next morning she found a bouquet of the same upon her plate, with the legend attached to it, in Italian, " AN OFFERING FROM THE DAWN ! CULLED THIS MORNING AT 11,000 FEET ABOVE THE SEA BY FORI." Dr Slorach swore to several people who had observed the tender incident, that he had seen the "whupper-snapper" buy it in the market-place ten minutes before, and was in a mind to expose the imposture; but he didn't: so that the imaginative count scored the feat to his credit.

All these extravagances of worship were lost upon their object. Esmè admired the young man's singing, and thought him very good-natured but supremely ridiculous, and treated his arts of devotion as the mere stock-in-trade of an Italian youth of artistic proclivities. Don't let the profane thought that she flirted with him enter any one's mind. Any repudiation of the sort on her behalf is indeed unnecessary; for it is obvious that the smallest sign from her would have brought the Count to a prompt declaration. Between the tender thought and the earnest glance and the burning word, there are but short intervals with combustible gentry of the Fori type.

The ordinary " Mees Anglaise " might—probably must—have succumbed at once to his wiles and graces; but Esmè was not an ordinary "Mees Anglaise"—which, of course, Mrs Ravenhall knew; still she could not know how completely the Count, so to speak, missed fire. Great, therefore, was her dismay. That wretch Tom could not be roused by her to a sense of the peril. "Do you wish me," he asked, "to shoot the fellow, before he has given me my revenge and you have got back your money?" and instead of being alarmed, went and straightway fell into the toils of E. G. Krupper, and flirted with her—for he *could* flirt with a certain kind of females who amused him and took all the trouble off his hands—and was seen lurking with her in the verandah at the back of the hotel, and on the terrace, in the suggestive gloaming; where Mrs Ravenhall, with her own ears, overheard "the artful minx" confide to Tom that she had 8000 a-year!—"what they *always* say," Mrs Ravenhall afterwards assured Tom, "and which *always* turns out to mean, in green-backed dollars, worth about sixpence apiece or so. So don't you go and add madness to folly." Tom, too, addicted himself yet the more to the society of his friend the Count; and, instead of manœuvring against him, seemed to be for ever playing his game. The thing could not go on long. Mrs Ravenhall was getting quite thin, and had no heart for her own little pursuits. But the crisis came. A party was organised for the Morteratsch glacier. Tom and Esmè were, as usual, to share a carriage with the metaphysician and the old Baroness Blinkenschwag. But, by the fiendish arts of Miss Krupper and Roderigo working upon, and through, Tom, the plan was upset. The doctor and the Baroness were beguiled and diverted to alien vehicles, and Esmè found herself driven rapidly off with the three conspirators, unchaperoned, before there was time for inquiry or remonstrance. They were ahead of the rest of the party : and when Mrs Ravenhall arrived at the scene of the picnic, the spectacle which met her eye was, Tom and Eudoxia huddled together, like a pair of love-birds, and sharing one plaid (for your glacier gives a chill to the air); and, at a little distance, the Count, posed as William Tell, on the edge of the ice-cataract, and singing divinely to a group of maidens below, in the centre of whom was Esmè, focussed, of course, by the dreamy gaze of the songster. This was altogether too much. The cup ran over. Mrs Ravenhall resolved now to make short work of William Tell, and to be

quit of Eudoxia. For the return journey, she
very demonstratively took Esmè into her own
carriage, and manœuvred her off the ground,
almost before Roderigo was aware of the change
of programme. When he *did* make the discovery, his face was a sight to see. Tom roared
out laughing. Eudoxia openly made game of
the poor wretch, and tendered him bantering
advice, which he rashly took *au sérieux*; for
he ran after the carriage and hurled a little
farewell bouquet of thyme into it, but, missing
his mark, smote Viscount Germistoune, K.T.,
on the nose withal—and *that* was pretty nearly
the last of the Count. The throwing of the
bouquet at all was a liberty—the accident that
it impinged upon his lordship's nose was an
outrage. Lord Germistoune and Mrs Ravenhall
both felt this,—especially Mrs Ravenhall, who
took the incident as the text for a discourse,
commenced then, and afterwards finished in
private with Lord Germistoune.

This bore on the innate depravity of Italian
counts in general, who were often impostors,
wearing aces in their sleeves, as necessary acces-
sories of raiment; who were usually connected
with the " CAMORRA," and *always* heiress-hunt-
ers. The application of all this to the luckless

Roderigo took place on their return home. "I never liked the man, dear Lord Germistoune. His eyes are quite enough for me, and I *do not* like his companionship for my brother. He has begun to get money out of poor Tom, who is *so* trusting; and I can't stand *that*." The recollection of the Count's little *soirées* and their financial aspects, as affecting herself, gave great intensity to this passage. "In short, I really must get Tom away from his influence." Then, with exquisite tact, and speaking as an old and fondly-devoted family friend, she gradually insinuated that there *was* danger for "that sweet unconscious child." She had seen, she said, things—attentions—which had made her *reflect*. Her eyes, sharpened by womanly tenderness, had noted the wolfish ways of Roderigo. Speaking *as* a woman, she felt that the Count might gain a *deplorable* influence over *any* woman. He was horribly magnetic and glamorous; and, being in *absolute want*, there was little doubt that he meant to bring his magnetism and his glamour, and all his other diabolical properties, to market here, and was, in fact, doing so now. No doubt Esmè was so superior, so very superior, she—still, as a matter of parental principle—— But there was no need to argue the point. Lord

Germistoune's soul was in arms at once. The
bare idea of such a monstrosity as that this—
this hound should lift his eyes to *his* daughter,
had never occurred to him. He towered, in his
arrogance, above such a suspicion. The giant
walks with his nose in the air, and trips over the
mole-hill. But—once suggested! *Donnerwet-
ter!!* Well, he did exactly what Mrs Ravenhall
intended. He had his bill and ordered a chaise
for Pontresina, as did Mrs Ravenhall and Tom ;
and, with bag and baggage, the combined party
thither shifted camp. "There is too much sharp-
ness in the air of St Moritz" was his lordship's
explanation of the move to Esmè. The last
object they beheld at the hotel was Roderigo's
green and chapfallen face. His sympathetic
southern nature told him exactly how matters
stood. He saw them go, without an *œillade* for
Esmè, or a bouquet for her father's nose. With
a solemn sweep of his Tyrolese hat, he bade
adieu to Love and *écarté* and a thousand golden
dreams.

CHAPTER XX.

Cosmo Glencairn did not remain very long at
Edlisfort, after his memorable interview with his
father; he returned to town, and, while all the
world made holiday, lived a hermit's life in his
chambers. Now fully resolved on a parliament-
ary career, he plunged into certain ponderous
lines of reading which bore on the political
science, or manfully explored the dreary literature of blue-books for instruction upon special
subjects. Everything about his political life
was to be honest, solid, complete. On no half-
knowledge were his opinions to rest—from no
vague opinions were his political actions to flow;
and, since he proposed to himself not the stationary see-saw of a hobby-rider, but keen partici-
pation in everything, it will be seen that his
earnestness promised to be a hard taskmaster.
All measures for the restoration of Phil Denwick
to a well-ordered life were put in train; there

was no difficulty about the money, which was
to be forthcoming in the beginning of autumn;
and at that time Phil himself was, according to
agreement, to commence his period of probation
and practical instruction in Mr Hopper's office.
In doing what he was undertaking to do for
Phil, Cosmo wished really to benefit his friend
—not merely to extricate him from his present
penury, but to make his life stable; so that his
bounty carried with it the benevolent condition
of work. Phil's gratitude was unbounded, and
it would have been a hard condition to which
he would not have subscribed to show it, and to
please Cosmo. But, indeed, the idea of work—
suggesting, as it did, everything that was the
converse of his late miserable experiences—was
welcome for its own sake; and he, like Cosmo,
sprang forward to anticipate it in preparations.
Hopper was most affable to the prospective
shareholder, let him know what to study in the
meantime, and how to set about it; and Cosmo
sent him out of town to a quiet place by the sea,
where he devoted himself to mastering the theo-
retical mysteries of commerce and the *arcana* of
the iron-trade. So Phil, living cleanly with the
parson of the parish, who was an old Cambridge
chum, was a reclaimed prodigal, for whom the

swine of Leicester Square and their husks and other abominations were only an evil memory or occasional nightmare. Mr Glencairn, indeed, shook his head rather violently over that part of the plan which involved Phil's future admission to the hierarchy of the Company ; but, on Hopper assuring him that the probation was to be stringent, and that the prospect of Phil's qualifying was almost *nil*, he said he " was glad to sanction an arrangement which might benefit his dead friend's son,"—which Mr Hopper assured him was most magnanimous, and exactly like himself—in fact, " quite." And everything for the present was comfortably settled, as far as Phil's affairs went. Cosmo had returned to town in the early days of June, and, in seven weeks thereafter, Parliament was prorogued : for as yet there were no " Obstructionists " to paralyse the Legislature and befriend the grouse ; and the noodles who addressed the House and wasted its time, could then only be counted by the dozen, instead of, as now, by the hundred. So that her Majesty was able to dismiss her faithful Commons for the recess, on the 20th July—which is not like to occur again, unless some one can invent a gag for Jawkins, M.P. And during these weeks, and now, Cosmo was on the *qui vive;* for the incumbent nurse of the "healthy local interest" of the borough of —— was expected to resign. And Cosmo had prepared an address for the electors, and written speeches, and studied the local maggots of the borough, and, in short, armed himself at all points for the electoral campaign. Phil Denwick, who came up to see him now and then, used to assist at private rehearsals, when, after listening to the flowing periods of his friend's speeches, he would take up the *rôle* of a "heckler"—which is the Scotch name for the political excrescence who puts questions to the candidate at political meetings, and who, although always the shallowest dunderhead in the assembly, yet, by dint of not knowing what he is talking about, and of not being able to display even his ignorance in any sort of grammar at all, can undoubtedly trouble and mystify and exasperate a candidate, and is therefore dangerous, and to be considered beforehand. Phil could imitate the ways of this monster, and heckled to perfection; but, on such occasions, Cosmo always passed with flying colours, and was, *nem. con.*, declared to be a fit and proper person, &c. &c.

Alas! it was all premature. The member for the borough changed his mind. " Circumstances," he wrote to Mr Glencairn, "had occurred which made it his bounden duty to remain stanch to his post;" and so, though Mr Glencairn was resolved that his "post" should not continue stanch to the honourable gentleman any longer than *he* could help, there was nothing for it at present but to await the general election, which could not be distant.

This was very trying to Cosmo, under all his circumstances. In the first place, he was feverishly anxious to begin. Dim, in the far distance, but overtopping every other motive, there was a light to be reached, and not even to have started in its direction was distressing. Then the near prospect of the contest had naturally brought its preoccupations, besides specially stimulating his studious energy in fields which are sometimes of no great interest in the abstract. And now, in the reaction from this, he lost, for the time, that vantage-ground from which he had been able to discipline his love, and once more, at times, became a sport for "the tempest of the heart," with its ecstatic contemplations, its agonies of longing, and those cruel lulls of blank despondency which are the cruellest of all to bear. At such times it was in vain that he invoked Ambition, Duty, Manhood—in vain that he nerved his resolution, and tried desperately to immerse himself in the dry routine of study. Sentences read and re-read, conveyed no impression. Subtle spirits of the air filched the thoughts from the words, or interwove them with strange fantasies, or flashed the image of a haunting face, over the meaningless page, or overwrote it with a haunting name in the splendour of prismatic colours. These spirits come in a note of music, in a sunbeam, in a breath of meadow-fragrance. There is no exorcism that can prevail against them. In truth, the burthen of his love was over-great for him, now that he had lost the assistance of that spring of a present excitement which derived its virtue from the hopes with which it was connected. This being gone, spirit and flesh alike began to cry out for relief. And a desire to see Esmè again, to hear her voice — but even only to see her, to be near her, though she should be unconscious of his proximity, to breathe the same air, to look at the same mountains, to establish between him and her *some* chain of association, however faint and visionary, — this pathetic desire became more and more clamorous, and grew daily to be less resisted. And a longing for a freer air than this of the town fell upon him. Here he began to feel stifled, cramped, and jaded. He would have the quickening breezes of the north; he longed for the hills and the heather, and the clear streams, and space, and freshness, and movement.

"I require a change," he said to himself. "I am overworked; but my preparations are well advanced; and, let an election come when it may, I am ready: so that I can afford a change; it will not do to be overtrained when the time arrives. I must go away for a change; the question is, whither?" In such prosaic words of feeblest self-deception did he put the case to himself. Yes, he required a change — a change from this twilight life of separation; and the question, "Whither should he go?" was answered by his yearning for the Highland hills, where he knew that she now must be.

But how? whither *exactly?* under what pretext?

It had got to this approach to the concrete, when, one fine morning in the beginning of August, the eminent Mr Snowie of Inverness, whose wintry name has sunny associations for all northern sportsmen, waited upon Cosmo at his chambers.

" Just to see, Captain, before I leave town, if we can't even yet come to an arrangement about Finmore. It's still open; full of birds; never was a finer season; pity to lose the chance; cheap, too." Thus Snowie,—and exit in ten minutes, with a look on his face which told that Cosmo's questions, " How ? whither *exactly?* under what pretext?" had found an answer which was entirely satisfactory to the worthy agent at least.

No one would for an instant venture to stigmatise Mr Snowie as a poetical character; but on this occasion it appeared to Cosmo that

> " A Voice
> Went with him, Follow, follow ! thou shalt win !"

Let all true-hearted readers hope that the voice *did* say so, and may not prove an impostor.

CHAPTER XXI.

"It will pe somepody that iss koing to Feen-maur."

"What wye to Finmore mair nur ony ither gate?"

"Pecause there iss a crayt few ither dogs will pe koing to there twa days syne; which I haf saw on to the rod."

"But this isna a dug, Alistair; it's a man."

"You are a pretty smert fel-lo, Tchon Tcheemyson, and so iss your mither; and she leeves in Glasco toon, where aal the shops iss; and you haf a hat on the Saabuth dess, which iss like the mecnister's hat; but you are ferry much into the wrong, for aal. This iss not a man."

"You'll no be sayin' it's a wummin, ony wye?"

"That iss pretty truc, too. She iss not a wummin, and she iss not a dog; but she iss not a man naythers. She iss a tchentelmans."

"Haw! haw! haw! haw!"

"Goot life! Tchon Tcheemyson, do not mek that tammd noise with your ucklee mouth. Stop it haystilee, or you will fricht aal the sheeps that iss on to the hullside. She iss a tchentelmans; and ferry certainly, she will pe the tchentelmans that iss com to Feenmaur; and her dogs will pe koing to there twa days syne, and I haf saw them on to the rod mysel; and her horses and her consarn and her sarvint lasses, and ither things."

"And wha *is* the gentleman? What do they ca' him?"

"She will pe a captin frae apoot England some gate. Look to her. She is takkin' the rod for Feenmaur."

.   .   .   .   .   .

An interval of intense observation and silence, tempered with the sound of riotous snuffing.

.   .   .   .   .   .

"Goot life! whaat will the craytur pe standin' glowerin' at the castel for, aal this time?"

It is a godsend to a Highlander in a lonely district, when any living thing above the rank of a sheep or a grouse comes within the range of his vision, for it affords him a valid excuse for abandoning his lawful occupation, and devoting himself to the phenomenon as long as it remains in sight. The questions who, whence, whither, why, and how, with many minor problems, are grappled with according to the most exhaustive methods; and where there are two philosophers to compare their hypotheses, and squabble over them, the excitement and the idleness may be quite indefinitely prolonged. The dialogue, of which the brilliant fragment above recorded formed a part, took place a few days after the events which occupied our last chapter.

The scene was a hillside overhanging a beautiful glen in the mid-Highlands of Scotland, and the speakers, as their dialects may have suggested, were a Highlander and a Lowlander— the former an ancient shepherd supposed to be " tenting " his sheep, the latter a keeper supposed to be " giein' a bit look ower the hill," in anticipation of " The Twelfth." The subject of their remarks was a gentleman who was making his way along the highroad which ran below their post of observation; but since he was merely a pedestrian, and therefore scarcely worthy of the mystery enshrouding the " two figures "— invariably on horseback—which used to pioneer our boyhood into the delights of James's novels, we may frankly admit, at once, that he was no other than Cosmo Glencairn. Mr Snowie had dangled the bait of Finmore before his eyes at the right moment. Cosmo had risen to it with an impulse which only gave special expression to a fixed, though half-unconscious, purpose; and here he was, on the 11th of August, in the heart of the Highlands, and *en route* for the shootings in question. His dogs, by a covenant with his father, were quartered, during the off season, at Edlisfort, with training and exercising privileges on that domain ; and these had arrived, two days before, in charge of his own keeper, or rather *shikari*. Nor was old Alastair at fault in any of his other surmises ; for Cosmo's horses, and a small establishment hastily got together by his trusty *factotum*, had also preceded him, so that everything might be in readiness within the lodge, as well as without on the moor, against his arrival. At the conclusion of his railway journey, of some fifteen hours, from London, he felt rather cramped and fagged ; so he dismissed what Alastair called "the consarn," which awaited him at the station, and started on foot, meaning to take to the heather and strike across the hills when he reached the borders of his own territory. A stretch on the hill would, he assured himself, be a beneficial and even necessary preparation for the work of the morrow. It is barely possible, however, that he had some other motive in addition.

The glen which Cosmo entered, shortly after leaving the railway, was almost wide enough, at its entrance, to be called a strath, but narrowed in rapidly, and at its farther extremity was little more than a gorge. The inner sides of the hills which formed it, were marked by strange and picturesque irregularities—now projecting bastion-like bluffs and salients of displaced strata, now falling back in ravines and corries and dells. Over all, deep stretches of pine-wood drew their dark covering, smoothing harsh outlines into mellow curves, and melting abrupt discords into flowing transformations ; while the lights and shadows, in following the ever-changing contour of the ground, relieved the monotony of the all-pervading and sombre green with a variety more dignified than mere contrast of colour can afford. The river, which found a channel in the centre of the glen, rested here, in a level reach, from its struggles with rock and precipice far above, and murmured melodiously along between fair slopes of heather, which came down from the foot of the hills on either side, interspersed with bright bosquets of young larch and hazel, and birch and oak, and all that aromatic shrubbery which makes the Highland wilderness a garden of delight. The majestic silence of the summer noon was marked, rather than broken, by the voice of the water, the song of birds, and the minor sounds of Nature, which rippled, as it were, on the surface of its profound depths. At the top of the glen, high spurs from the opposing hills met and closed it in with a sheer precipice, over which the river passed from its upper to its lower channel in a noble fall. The ruins of an ancient keep hung over the caldron on a dizzy ledge, showing dimly through a haze of spray which rose from the abyss below; and on a spacious plateau farther down the right bank of the stream, a baronial edifice, in the ancient Scottish style, stood out from its background of precipice and wood, and scaur and falling foam. The season had been backward, and the first freshness of vegetation still lingered here. The young larches by the river still met the sunbeams with their tenderest green; the splendid purple of the bell-heather had not yielded to its graver substitute; the golden broom fringed the wayside; and all the riparian bells and plumes and tassels of early summer, still swung joyously in the breath of the passing stream. Some slight showers had fallen on the previous day, but they had cleared the sky of every cloud, and left a legacy of thymy fragrance to the valley, which greeted Cosmo, as he entered it, with a sweet Highland welcome.

The aspect of the glen was familiar to him. He knew all its beauties by heart. Before now, as he turned into its solitudes, tired with the whirling din of London's high-pressure life, he had felt its stillness fall round him like the benison of some spirit of rest and peace ; and, before now, the first inspirations of its unpolluted air had reawakened in him childhood's ecstatic sense of the goodliness of life. Here, to-day, was the same infinite repose and the same virgin air; there was nothing changed in the bravery of wood and hill ; the river warbled its hymn of content in the same music as of yore, and the song which rang in the thickets was old as the glen itself. But for Cosmo, all to-day was changed and transfigured. The glen of other times was remembered as a faint and colourless sketch. Light, colour, fragrance, sound, the sweep of outlines, the harmonious whole, all now seemed instinct with an intense and beautiful vitality. Life had come into them — a soul, and a voice, borrowed from every harmony of nature, which cried to him that the world was fair, but here for him the climax of all its charms. This was Glenerlacht; and, as he turned a curve of the road, and caught the distant thunder of the waterfall, Esmè's home—the real shrine of his pilgrimage—burst upon his view.

About half a mile from the house, the river, whose banks had by this time become high and precipitous, was crossed by a bridge; and this being the formal commencement of the avenue, it was shut from the highroad by lofty iron gates, flanked by a Gothic lodge, with a warder's tower. The arch, which formed the gateway, bore on its keystone the Germistoune escutcheon, assuring the wayfarer, by its innumerable quarterings, of the noble alliances of the family, though the ominous motto which surmounted it—

"Nicht and Micht mak Richt"

— suggested that the origin of their possessions was perhaps not altogether so respectable. About this point the highroad turned sharply to the right, as if respecting the privacy of the demesne, and wound up the hillside, till, at a discreet distance from the avenue, it resumed its direction parallel to the river. Exactly opposite the house another road branched inland to the right. This was the road to Finmore; and it was here that the hawk's eyes of the gossips in the heather above had first detected the lingering form of Cosmo.

Herrick says that—

> "Love is a circle which doth endless move
> In the same sweet eternity of love;"

and this being so, we are confident that readers will gladly be excused, now and then, from following the lover in his spiritual circumambulations under our pilotage, and will kindly fill in for themselves—some, perhaps, with the freshness of recent personal experience—the various phases of exaltation and so forth with which Love's pilgrim drew near the shrine of his divinity. To their imaginations, therefore, we commit the interval which separated Cosmo's first emotions on entering the sacred glen, from the moment when Alastair (as though resenting the misuse of time) remarked, "Goot life! whaat will the craytur pe standin' glowerin' at the castel for, *aal* this time?"

We may well believe that Cosmo had got through a good deal of this sort of contemplation, as he came slowly up the valley; in fact, that from the moment the castle became visible, his eye had rested upon no other object, and all the more intensely when a Union-jack, proclaiming the presence of the family, was seen to float from the central tower. Yet, when he got to the cross-road, he had by no means looked his last, for he sat down, and pulling out a powerful deer-stalker's glass, proceeded to sweep therewith the castle and its grounds. Cosmo strained his eyes across the glen; but he could descry no living thing about the place; the esplanade, the terraces, the walks on the wooded hill beyond, the very windows of the house—all were scanned over and over again, but vainly. A glimpse of any one, however remotely connected with Esmè, would have been a relief; even Lord Germistoune, if he would only have condescended to show himself, would have been quite a godsend. But no one came. An hour passed. Where were all the people? Would no one ever come? What did the flag mean? He got quite peevish about the flag. If the family were not at home, why didn't some one have the common honesty to come and haul it down? It was a swindle. He grew bitter; he felt aggrieved; the petulance of a lover rose in him; and after an hour and a half of fruitless vigil, he took the road for Fin-more. But—oh blessed backward glance, which no true lover e'er denied his lady or his lady's bower!—just before the road dipped, and cut him off from hope, he turned and looked once more, and this time not in vain. Figures—one, two, three—a host of figures were streaming from the castle doors; and it is needless to say that Cosmo sped back to his post of observation, and again, with trembling hands, brought his glass into position.

By this time there were at least a dozen people on the esplanade—male and female forms; but though the glass was a good one, it failed to reach the *minutiæ* of human features, polish and readjust it as Cosmo might. Figures, gestures, colours of dress—all could be distinguished; but the faces were blanks: and even about the in-dividuality of the figures it was at first diffi-cult to speculate, as the party remained massed together.

Presently there appeared in relief on the steps in front of the house, a figure which there was no difficulty in identifying. Tall, erect, and stiff, it extended its arms towards the group, as if directing them to some particular point; and in the blended characteristics of the lamp-post

and the lion rampant, Lord Germistoune shone
revealed. Apparently his instructions were not
at first comprehended ; for the lion's paws shot
out, and sawed the air impatiently, and at angles
which defied heraldic canons. And now from
the group below, an airy form detached itself,
and ascended the lion's pedestal, and seemed to
lay playful and soothing hands upon the agitated
arms. Some one asking for an explanation, of
course. Some one ? Ah! here, at least for
Cosmo, there was no vagueness, no uncertainty.
Cruel distance might veil the divine features ;
but the contour, the attitudes, the undulating
graces of movement—these, at twice the distance, would have proclaimed the adorable per-
sonality to the eyes and the instincts of love.
Esmè! The glass shook in Cosmo's hand; his
colour went and came, and his voice quivered
as he murmured aloud the name which, for him,
was the epitome of all music. But the rapture
of steady contemplation was denied him. Esmè
immediately left her father, and ran back to the
group, which now broke up and streamed down
to a terrace by the river, and a good deal nearer
to Cosmo. And now he could see Esmè's face.
Ah !

A good deal of conference and arrangement seemed to take place; a couple of footmen brought down from the house a large oblong box; and at last, mystery and chaos solved and evolved themselves in the disorderly order of lawn-tennis. Two sets engaged in the game, which was played with much spirit by all concerned, the firm and nimble rushings and boundings of the male performers being not more full of *élan* than the wondrous swoopings and gyrations of the ladies. They played with only too much spirit to suit Cosmo's purpose; for, though a lover's eyes are quicker than other eyes, his telescope is as fractious and unmanageable as every other telescope is. And thus, when he essayed to track Esmò through the mazes of the game, this perverse instrument was never up to time. Now she would be in repose, and, the focus having been brought warily across the lawn, he would just have begun to drink in the rays of an aureole, when, lo !—a flash ! a jerk !— and Cosmo's amorous gaze was lost in a bank of senseless turf. Or now, with the energy of desperation, the telescope would give chase, and participate in all the acrobatics of the game—up, down, right, left, scouring, rushing, scurrying— but doomed to eternal disappointments, for ever

settling on the blue flannel body of a corpulent
male, or painfully travelling up a skirt to reach
a female waist of the most revolting dimensions.
The sorrows of Tantalus, or of a man attempting
to shoot rabbits with an Enfield rifle, sink into
insignificance when compared with Cosmo's present ordeal. Exasperating, truly; so exasperating that he was just pronouncing lawn-tennis a
game only worthy of Mænads and Satyrs, in
which, if a Sylph permitted herself to take part,
she was—— when ah! thank goodness! it was
over at last. Esmè retired to the bench of
spectators, and a new game began. Everything
looked promising. Now, telescope, now! Vain
hopes! When the focus struggled into the proper
position, it collided with a pair of male legs, and
ascending, was hopelessly stopped by a broad
back in a jersey striped with all the colours of
the rainbow. The body thus arrayed was actually
standing right in front of Esmè, and by its gestures appeared to be very gay and conversational.
But surely the — the *brute* was not going to dare
to stand there for ever, intercepting *her* view of
the game? He might; Cosmo said to himself
that he very possibly might, seeing that a fellow
with stripes of that description must be capable
of any enormity. But no; another figure came

to the rescue—a female figure of dignified movements—who had been standing, hitherto somewhat apart, looking up, as if in conversation, to
the terrace above, from the edge of which Lord
Germistoune appeared to watch the game. When
Esmè retired from the contest, this lady, who
was veiled and unrecognisable, at once got under
way; and presently the hyperbolical jersey was
replaced on the disc of the telescope by a curtain
of blue serge of equal opaqueness. This woman
was as bad as the man ! Right in front again !
What on earth was she about ? She seemed to
be engaged in a little amicable struggle with the
invisible princess, and in which a white cashmere
shawl appeared to play a prominent part. Mysterious ! Ah ! her object evidently was to wrap
the shawl in question round the resisting form of
the young lady — evidently. There ! she had
carried her point, and now, of course, she would
go. Not a bit of it. Some officious wretch
brought her a light garden-chair, and she sat
down, again right in front; and all that the
telescope could now report was a new aspect of
the blue serge body, and, above and beyond it,
the upper half of the demon in stripes, who had
moved round to the back of Esmè's chair. Nothing of the fair girl was visible but fitful glimpses

of the top of her hat, for these two people seemed to heave forward against each other, like opposing waves, and obscured the treasure which lay in the intervening trough. It was sickening! He turned the telescope impatiently on other members of the party, and became aware of a neat lilac figure, which seemed to flit about among the rest, like a thing of joy. All the ladies he addressed appeared to be at once agitated with laughter; while the men doubled themselves up, smote their knees, and retired, convulsed and tottering. "What a buffoon!" sneered Cosmo; and then, "Of course! *just* as I expected! Tom Wyedale!"

Cosmo observed his friend's proceedings with rather a grim expression, which was by no means mollified when the "thing of joy," flitting past Esmè's group, was suddenly absorbed into it, and added another and decidedly aggressive element to the obscuring sea.

Matters continued to go on in this way for a long time; for, though game after game took place, and the players were constantly relieved, Esmè played no more, and the attendant group remained constant to her, and all in the same regrettable positions. "If they ONLY knew," thought Cosmo, "how ridiculous they look!"

And yet a disinterested person would hardly have agreed with him; for they were all decidedly good-looking, and their gestures, however aggravating, were the gestures of well-bred and graceful people. At last a couple of empty carriages drove up to the door, and a "powdered menial" came forth, and solemnly tolled a great booming bell which hung in one of the turrets. Whereupon, like a dog infected by the barking of other dogs, Lord Germistoune immediately began to wave his hat with great impetuosity (no doubt shouting lustily the while) to the group below, which must have been well disciplined, for the games were at once discontinued, and players and spectators moved promptly towards the house. Esmè was thus again visible for a little — but very slightly: for the waves were true to their mission, and floated about her without intermission; the devoted lady leaning upon her arm; the man of stripes moving, tall and graceful, on her other side (much too close, Cosmo thought); while Tom Wyedale hovered promiscuously round the group, whose lively gestures told that his quips and cranks were numerous and effective. Nothing could be more joyous than the *ensemble* of the whole party, which now disappeared, leaving Cosmo gazing into vacancy. The pageant had come and gone like the episode of a dream, wherein Lord Germistoune had been a magician that had set the revellers in order with a wave of his hand, and then dispersed them, as abruptly as Prospero's voice dismissed from their " country footing " his airy band of " fresh nymphs and sun-burnt sicklemen." Cosmo remained gazing abstractedly into vacancy, perplexed like one half roused from sleep, and doubting between illusion and reality. Very presently, however, this was succeeded by a vivid and painful sense of the reality of all he had seen. Painful ? He had seen Esmè, and surely that was bliss ? Where, then, was his gratitude ? where his ecstasy ? Yes, he had seen her, and the first glimpse of her, indeed, had electrified him ; but ecstasy had been shortly suppressed by supervening circumstances, and gradually replaced by emotions far removed from the ecstatic. The mere mechanical difficulties of contemplation had been damping, the physical obstructions irritating, and the persistence of the obstructionists enraging. But these were by no means all. Through force of his transcendental musings, and by the intense sympathy which an intense passion produces, Esmè had become to him, in some degree (if we may be permitted to soar so high for a parallel), what Beatrice was to Dante —ever present to him, and ever present in a halo of gracious attributes, which daily grew more and more real and familiar; so that her idea came to be linked with every association of the ethereal and the beautiful and the good which touched his consciousness. To - day, as he wandered up the glen, her spirit had seemed to come forth from all its beauties, and to hold commune with his own.

> " She stooped to him
> From all high places, lived in all fair lights."

And at this exalted level of sentiment he had been confronted with the scene just described.

The antithesis was obviously grotesque; but it was not its grotesqueness which struck Cosmo. A certain shock, to be sure, is involved in the idea of Psyche engaging in a boisterous sport with the full-fleshed children of men; and it may possibly have been a slight shock to Cosmo to behold the heroine of his day-dreams translated to similar conditions. But our modern Psyche is muscular. It is a wholesome fact with which we are all familiarised; so that he could not have been seriously affected by that consideration. What really affected him was, that she who had moved through his reveries in a halo of perfections had been there contemplated only in relation to *himself.* There were but two inhabitants in his psychical paradise —Esmè and himself. No other individuality intruded itself between them; she was there for him alone. Whereas here, dreamland dissolving, she was beheld as the joyous central figure of a bright and joyous life—beheld in a hundred new aspects and connections, not one of which had any relation to *him.* How complete was his nothingness to her! how wide the gulf which yawned between them! how remote and insignificant the orbit in which his life circled around hers !—such were the immediate convictions which displaced in his mind the fair fabric woven, through many a week, by the dreams of fancy and hope. Nor was this the worst. It was sufficiently desolating, indeed, to feel that he was nothing to her; it was even distressing to be convinced that she must be much to others; but a far keener anguish was involved in the suspicion that another might be much to her. The egotism of his love, aroused and wounded, was not likely to leave unused against itself certain suggestive incidents in the little drama which had passed before his eyes. There was an eclipse in his mind of all the morning's brightness; wintry twilight reigned instead; harsh discords rent the melodious flow of his thoughts; the outer world was transfigured, the light seemed to fade in the valley, and all the voices of nature jarred together, like sweet bells jangled out of tune. Sadly he addressed himself to his journey; his step was heavy on the hill; the heather had lost all its spring; and in this sad plight he approached his solitary abode.

CHAPTER XXII.

THE shooting-lodge of Finmore was charmingly situated : it stood high on a breezy plateau ; no neighbouring hill overtopped it, nor was it stifled by surrounding woods. Behind and around, and far and near, the eye could range over glowing undulations of moorland, reaching at one point a distant range of hills, whence the river which watered Glenerlacht streamed down through the heather tracts, passing below Finmore, and in view of the house, till lost in the pine-woods which closed around it, as it approached the tragedy of its career, at the great fall above the castle. When next visible, its ordeal was past, and it was gliding through the lower glen where we first made its acquaintance, so that the castle and its sacred precincts were not to be seen from Finmore. The lodge —originally a farmhouse—had been added to in such a way as to make it commodious and comfortable as well as picturesque; and, altogether, it was as cheery and enviable a shooting-quarter as man need wish for. Cosmo had already spent many happy days there, but this afternoon there was no happy recognition in his eye as he approached it. After all, the lodge and the shooting were now mere pretexts, which had no interest apart from the real object that had brought him here; and, since gloom and darkness enshrouded that object at present, he could see nothing in the place but a centre of desolation. Even the sportsman's instinct—so hard to suppress—failed to assert itself. The "muir-cock" gabbled its ineffable music, as he passed over the muir; covey after covey whirled up from his very feet, and deployed their rich brown phalanxes before his eyes; the black-cock *vedette* rolled his burnished plumage leisurely against the sun,—but Cosmo's pulses were unstirred. A flight of wild duck sailed over his head, so close that he could plainly see the green neck of the leading mallard, and almost catch its eye; yet even this supreme incident failed to rouse him. A mallard, and within shot! What stronger evidence could be given of morbid and unnatural apathy? Grange, his confidential servant and *factotum* of many years' standing, who had accompanied him on his many travels, and "understood him" better than most people, met him at the door as he arrived, and was vexed to see that the air of listless depression which he had latterly shaken off had returned. Philipson, his *shikari*, who had never seen him in such a mood before, was at his wits' end to account for such gloom on the eve of the shooting season; and when he strolled round to the kennels, old Davidson, the keeper, was perplexed, mortified, and outraged by the callousness of his tone in dealing with topics of the sacredest interest.

Davidson was a Lowlander transplanted to the Highlands by his absentee master, with some idea that in the "antagonism of races" he might find a safeguard against spoliation. He was a long-headed, persistent old fellow, with a keen eye to the main chance, and a foible for getting his own way, and of wearing out opposition by a sometimes maddening prolixity; but he was eager about sport, and, if dishonest, was too clever to let one have the annoyance of detecting him, so that he was, to a very fair extent, the right man in the right place, as far as the tenant was concerned.

"How mony guns wull there be the morn,

sir?" he inquired, after he and Cosmo had exchanged greetings.

"Only my own," said Cosmo.

Davidson gave a start of surprise and disapprobation, and said, "We wus reckonin' on fower."

"Were you? I really don't know why you should."

"Weel, sir, ye see, wi' nae mair than ae gun, there's nae sort o' justice can be dune the muir ava'."

"We'll try it, at all events."

"Maybe some ither jantleman will be expeckit sune?"

"No; I don't expect any one, this season."

"Peety me! That's bad, that's dayspret bad. Ye see, sir, the muir's big, and the birds is plenty; but, if we dinna tak them sune, we'll mibbee no' get them ava'. They're gey strong, the year, and a wee thing wild a'ready; and if so be as the wather comes to brak—— whoosh! it's a' bye. Ye'll no' win within twa perishes o' them. Ye may as weel gang grouse-shuting in Loch Lomond. Ae gun's no' fit to dae mair than kittle this muir. Beggin' your paurdon, sir, it's clean wastry. Mr Pheelipson, your ain sportman, wus geein' his opeenyun this mornin' that we suld begin wi' sax guns at the laist—that's what *he* thinks. 'It's ma opeen-yun,' says he, 'that——' "

" Never mind Philipson's opinion ; I must do the best I can with my own gun. There will be all the more birds for next year; that's one thing."

But a plethora of birds next year had no bearing on the "tips" of the present season, which, at this rate, promised to be a minus quantity ; so Davidson returned to the charge.

" Weel, sir, excaize me ; it's no' the birds o' this year, or the next, or the next afterhin', that I'm thinkin' o'. What I aye like is, to contant the jantleman wha is ma maister for the time so bein' — as ye hae been yersel, sir, and sae may ken. And I'll jist exactlee mak sae bauld as to say that ae gun *is* no' fit——"

" How do you find the dogs this year, David-son ? "

" Brawly, sir; the dugs is jist in what I may ca' extra fine condeetion. Eh ! puir beesties ! it'll be a hard job to fin' aixerceese for them a', let alane wark, the year. Wi' ae gun it's clean impossible. What's to come o't, I dinna ken; unless, indeed, ye was tae tak the thocht o' gettin' twa or three, or mibbee fower, jantlemen ower frae the caustle, frae time to time. There's a heap o' company there, I'm tell't; and Mr Pheelipson thinks he saw Mr Whydal at the station—Mr Whydal, sir; that's him that was here ance afore. Dod! he's a gran' shot, him!—and—weel, sir, that's the haill chance that I can see for the muir and the dugs and a'" ("keeper's pocket" being substituted for "a'," Mr Davidson's drift and pertinacity are explained); "and that's no' ma ain thocht alane, sir—it's the opeenyun o' yer ain body-sportman, Mr Pheelipson, wha said——"

"Confound Mr Philipson, and you too! Why do you keep bother, bother, bothering about the moor? I suppose I may be allowed to judge for myself?" cried Cosmo, whose exhausted patience was not reinforced by this allusion to the castle and its male inhabitants.

"Aweel, sir, ye maun excaize me; it was for yer ain pleesure I was thinkin', and naethin' else. Ye'll tak a look at the dugs, sir?"

"No; hang the dogs!"

"Aweel, aweel. Beggin' your paurdon, sir, what'na pairt was ye thinkin' o' takin' the morn, sir?"

"Any part; I don't care; it's all one to me."

"If so be as we wus takin' Craig Rona side,

sir, I bude to sen' the dugs awa' airly, ye see, sir ; an' ye'd hae to stairt braw an' airly yersel."

"Then we'll not take Craig Rona to-morrow."

"It wad be the maist feesablest kin' o' beat for the morn, sir."

"I tell you, I won't go there."

"Weel, sir, there's the 'Three Kimmers'—a tarable heap o' birds thereawa', the year."

"Well, I don't know. I won't decide to-night. Have everything ready to start at ten o'clock to-morrow morning, and I'll make up my mind in the meantime."

"Ten o'clock, sir ! and it ' the Twalft' ! "

"I said 'ten,' didn't I ? Have everything ready at that hour ; and when I give an order, obey it, and don't discuss it." So saying, Cosmo turned angrily on his heel, and left the pawky old keeper much marvelling at the change which had come over his once urbane and enthusiastic master.

"I tall ye, Lauchie," he afterwards explained to one of his subs, "the man's clean cheinged. He cam' roun' to the kannels for naethin' ava' that I could see ; glowerin' and fuffin' up at ilka word ; and naethin' wad please and naethin' wad sairve him—deein' and dammin' a'thing, frae Mr Pheelipson hissel doon to the dugs,

puir beesties—him that was aye sae douce and
ceevil ; and nae kin' o' hert in the sport, and
nae kin' o' respek for the day itsel—him that
was aye sae keen.   Dod ! it's maist tar'ble the
cheinge that's com'd ower him.   Ae gun, too !
Niver heed, Lauchie !   Wait a wee, ma man !
That Mr Whydal 'll be ower to halp us, or I'm
muckle mistaen.   He's an awfie notion o' the
'Three Kimmers,' that Mr Whydal. 'Davidson,'
says he to me when he gaed awa' the last time
(he gied me five pun', mair be token), 'aye keep
the 'Three Kimmers' for me,' says he, 'when ye
hear that I'm in thae pairts,' says he.   Dod ! an'
I wull."

CHAPTER XXIII.

WRITERS whose aim it is to insist upon the tearful aspects of humanity, have made large use of the pathos which associates itself with the abandonment of cherished habits and pleasures, when bereavement has dislocated a life, and taken the savour away from everything that once delighted it. But mankind are capricious in the bestowal of their sympathy; and though they extend it eagerly to the sorrows of the heart, where death has intervened, have little or none to spare for the sufferings of the lover, however true and poignant they may be. Therefore we shall not attempt the hopeless task of touching the reader's sense of the pathetic, by describing the melancholy evening which Cosmo passed in his lodge on this 11th of August; nor dwell upon that happier time when for him the eve of " the Twelfth " was a vigil, when he watched the stars grow pale and the dawn approach, eager to rush afield with the first practicable light. Suffice it to say that he passed the evening in sore discontent, and that, if his night was sleepless, the fever of sport had nothing to do with it; for he was better than his word, and, to Davidson's great disgust, was not even ready at ten next morning, but kept, what that worthy called "the haill apothek" (including, perhaps, keepers, dogs, and birds impatient for annihilation) waiting, for a solid hour.

The day was perfect; and to a sportsman in full possession of his senses, such tardiness would have appeared an impossible crime. With no symptom of conscious guilt, however, though with a sad eye and a heavy step, Cosmo at last made his appearance.

"Good morning, Davidson; a fine day it seems."

"A fine day it *wus*, sir; but I'm dootin' the best o' it's gane by. They've been bleezin' awa' on the caustle muir this five hours."

"Ah, well! they've got half their fun over, and mine is all before me,"—a bit of philosophy which Davidson could only meet with the remark—

"Ov coorse, if a jantleman thinks naething ava' o' the bag, ae hour may be as gude as anither."

With the view of pointing the moral that a large establishment was criminally wasted upon a single gun, he had paraded a preposterous number of gillies and dogs, and, with fine satire, had even produced a couple of hill-ponies, duly equipped with panniers.

"What the deuce is the meaning of all this?" cried Cosmo, when his eye fell upon the imposing force.

Davidson gave a well-acted start of sudden recollection. "Ach, dod! I clean forgot, sir! Ye see, it's jist whaat's usual here on 'the Twalft,' wi' fower or five, or mibbee sax guns; and it fair escapit me that we wus gaun to attempt the muir wi' ae gun. Hae, Lauchie; tak hame thae pownies, and—— How mony dugs will ye be wantin', sir?"

"Two couple will do, and another man besides yourself."

"Vara weel, sir. Tak yont thae pownies, Lauchie; and ye'll stay wi' me and the Captin, Aunra, and keep the black setter and the livert pinter, and thae twa young anes, and Rock; and see you, Donald, tak hame thae ither dugs; and a' you men, ye may gang and hag peats, or howk tawties, or whaat ye please. There's nae wark here for *you*, the day; mibbee the year, wha kens ?" he added, *sotto voce* ; and having thus made his dispositions with an air of being injured, yet resigned, he relapsed into a sulky silence. Cosmo, all unconscious of the poor keeper's wrath, and with a mind occupied with very different subjects, mechanically took his gun and some cartridges, and, followed by the other men, sauntered slowly on to them oor. His eyes turned in the direction of Glenerlacht, and his steps followed his gaze. "We'll haud wast a wee, Captin," suggested Davidson ; but his remark was unheeded.

"Wull I lowse the dugs, sir ?" he presently asked.

"Yes, yes ; of course."

"But we're gaun strecht doon win', sir."

"Never mind."

The dogs were being uncoupled, when a covey rose beside them — a splendid strong covey. Cosmo mechanically cocked his gun, levelled, and drew trigger. Click ! He was unloaded.

Davidson's red beard and whiskers bristled with indignation. "Dod ! that's maist notawrious," he cried, when he recovered breath; and then, as another covey, startled by the music of the first, rose and swept away down wind—

"See till them! jist see till them! Ganging awa' in thoosands! poasiteevly in thoosands! and a' doon to his lordship's grun'. Ae gun's bad eneuch, but ae unlodden' gun——"

"Hold your tongue, Davidson; don't make such an infernal noise." And on they went steadily down the wind—steadily down towards the glen which was magnetising Cosmo. The dogs, hunting on a side wind, got occasional points, which Cosmo negotiated; but sometimes the scent drew them far away back, up wind, upon which occasions he steadily declined to pay any attention to them. Davidson was in despair. "Hae, Captin! Juno's pintin'," he would cry.

"Where?"

"Jist aboot a mile ahint" (bitterly).

"Let her point, then, or call her off. I'm not going back all that distance. Why don't you keep your dogs in hand?"

Then, after a little—"It's the young dug this time, sir."

"Hang the young dog!"

"It'll clean ruin that young dug, if he gets nae nottice taen o' his pints."

But neither Davidson's remarks nor the dog obtained the slightest attention.

"He's clean daft," whispered the keeper to his sub.

At last they reached the boundary between Finmore and Dunerlacht; and at last Cosmo was obliged to "tak wast;" but he did so in the most unsatisfactory manner, for he kept close to the boundary wall, and his head was turned constantly in the direction of the glen, and all the more constantly when the smoke of the castle became visible, rising above the woods.

"Deil's i' the man!" muttered Davidson, "he'll no tak his ain birds. What wye will he be aye keekin' and glowerin' efter his lord-ship's?"

A fine sunny slope of heather, however, where the birds lay thick, here intervened, and Cosmo's great skill as a shot enabled him to run his score up tidily, notwithstanding his preoccupation, and Davidson was temporarily appeased.

Presently the sound of guns on the Duner-lacht side became audible.

"We'll gang sooth a wee, Captin," suggested the keeper. "The castle folk is comin' this way, and mibbee they'll be thinkin' that we're on the watch for their birds, if we hing sae nigh the march; we'll get the win' brawly, mair be token."

Again the voice of the charmer charmed in vain. A turret of the castle now became visible. Cosmo halted, and had a good long stare at it, indifferent to the fact that Juno was turning imploring eyes backward from the steadiest of points, and that the young dog was "backing," but with every symptom of impatience. Davidson called the dogs off, "took them up," and remained standing motionless—the picture of petrified indignation. Cosmo had his look, and went on again without a remark. The dogs were again uncoupled, and presently Cosmo had another halt and another stare, accompanied by the same manœuvres on the part of the keeper, who was now beyond the power of speech. Thus matters went on, time after time, till, when it was quite two o'clock, Cosmo turned from one of his long contemplations and said ("just as if naething was wrang ava'")—

"I think it's about time for luncheon now, Davidson. Let's see what you've got in that basket."

He was leaning against the march dyke, with his face away from Dunerlacht, when suddenly something that sounded like the war-cry of Red

Indians was bellowed into his ear, and he sustained a shock on the back which shot him forward almost on to the top of the kneeling keepers. Staggering back, he beheld Davidson's upturned face wreathed in grins of delight, and heard him say—

"Maister Whydal! I'm prood to see ye, sir, the day."

"Aha, Mr Cosmo! unearthed you at last; sly old fox! This is what you call the islands of the Ægean, is it? Oh, you miscreant! as soon as you think I'm planted for the autumn, you stand in for Finmore! Shabby, upon my life! too shabby! a great deal too shabby!"

"It was quite a sudden thought," said Cosmo, with some confusion, when he had shaken hands with his friend, whose prodigious vitality and *quasi* geniality had a sort of charm, when in his company, which softened Cosmo's harsher thoughts of him, in spite of himself.

"That's no excuse," replied Tom. "I always measure the merit of an impulse by its opportuneness. Now, to make this impulse of yours a good one, it ought to have exploded in May, down at Como. Never mind. We may be happy yet. I say, Davidson, how are the 'Three Kimmers'?"

"Hech! hech! hech!" chuckled the keeper, in great delight. "The vara words—the vara eedaintical words — I was expeckin'! The 'Three Kimmers,' sir, is brawly; jist smoored wi' grouse, the year."

"You'll have me over one of these fine days to give them a toozling."

"Weel, sir, they'll waant a' the toozlin' they can get; and I'm share we'll be prood to see ye, sir (beggin' the Captin's paurdon), for ye can see yersel, Mr Whydal, that we're short-handed; and you that kens 'The Kimmers,' kens brawly that wi' nae mair than ae gun——"

"Get the lunch out, Davidson, and don't stand chattering there all day. You'll lunch with me, Tom?"

"Well, I don't know; let's see what you've got."

"Oh! something quite simple—sandwiches, probably, and sherry and cold tea. Is that it, Davidson?"

"That's the apothek, sir; naythur mair nur less."

"I can't say I think much of 'the apothek,' then. No, Cosmo, I won't lunch with you to-day. By the by, I have an invitation for you to join our lunch-party; indeed that's what I came for. Lord Germistoune (I'm with him, of course) asked the keeper a few minutes ago who that was platooning away on Finmore, and we heard for the first time that you were here; and the old gentleman presents his compliments, and hopes, &c. &c. They're close by. We'd better go at once. There's a *pâté*, but it's not large; and Jack Ruggles, who eats for ten, had his eye on it before I left. Let us go."

"But am I really invited?"

"Of course."

"Then how on earth did you think of staying to lunch here?"

"Oh, if you had had anything really very eatable, I wouldn't have let the other lunch stand in my way. A reindeer's tongue, perhaps. Yes, I think, for a reindeer's tongue, in peace and quietness, I would have let his lordship slide."

"Well, you *are* a cool hand."

"I am; it's the secret of my success in the face of interminable difficulties; cool, sagacious, prompt. Come on."

Cosmo got over the wall and accompanied his friend.

"Good sport, Tom?" he asked.

"Very fair, indeed, I think; but the guns

hadn't all come in. My pal and I certainly have done well; but the score wasn't made up when I left. 'We have eight guns out, including the old man, who won't go for much, and a French Marquis, who is more likely to bag a pony or a gillie than anything else, from what I saw of his start. But it's really a great moor. By the by, when I've taken the cream off it, I'll come and have a look at your 'Kimmers'— seriously, I will."

"That's most kind of you."

"Oh, you may sneer as much as ever you please, but I will."

"All right, Tom—all right; you shall;" and then, with an effort to appear unconcerned, but conscious of a tremor in his voice, he said, "Have you a pleasant party in the house?"

"Ye-es; on the whole, pretty decent. Too many people, though—we dine twenty-five. I hate that. Too many women too; bothering all over the place; won't let you alone for a moment — billiards, lawn-tennis, everything. They're all up here to-day; jolted up in carts, by George! Even that old hag Lady Bugles has come. She will certainly never get *all* her patent teeth, and the whole of her complexion, back to the castle. That's one comfort."

"What do you mean by 'all up here'?" faltered Cosmo, who had turned very pale.

"Exactly what I say. They've come up here with the luncheon, to bother us over it; and they've brought us all the way down to this corner, right away from the afternoon beats, just to suit their own convenience. Women *are* so infernally selfish! It's all owing to that abominable Mrs Crock, who has her eye on Lord Ribston, and is always scheming things of the sort. She might save herself the trouble, for Ribston's on another tack altogether—Miss Douglas, you know, *my* heiress,—ha! ha! I say, do you remember how you flared up about her, that night you had the blues, at Cadenabbia? ha! ha! ha! Well, Ribston is 'on' in that quarter; perhaps *he* might save himself the trouble too. *Nous verrons.* And here they are; and just as I thought, old Ruggles *has* collared the *pâté*. Look at him! the cormorant!"

CHAPTER XXIV.

THEY had turned the shoulder of a little knoll, and came quite suddenly upon the party, who were disposed in every variety of picnic attitude, in a sheltered hollow. Cosmo was vaguely conscious of a large concourse of people; of a blaze of colour; of a loud hum of talk and laughter, and of the clatter of knives and plates. But he saw nothing distinctly, and paused at the edge of the circle, in a state of complete bewilderment. Then he heard a voice cry, " Unearthed him, you see, Lord Germistoune! caught him in the very act of a sulky luncheon!" And then he was aware of a quaint green shooting-coat, ridiculously puckered up at the shoulders; and of a preposterous grey sugar-loaf hat, decked with a black-cock's tail; and of a pair of shepherd-plaid trousers and yellow gaiters; and of a long bony hand which touched his own icily with two of its fingers; and lastly, of a harsh and metallic voice which recalled him to himself, like a *douche*, and proclaimed that the *ensemble* made up Lord Germistoune.

"How do you do, sir? how do you do?" said his lordship, pompously. "Be seated here. Ronald! a game-bag for the gentleman. There is a pasty and a *mayonaise*, and a recommendable *galantine*. Let me help you to something."

His dislike for Cosmo was cordial; but the instincts of heather hospitality are strong, and the resultant of these two forces was a manner in which austerity and fussiness were rather uncomfortably blended.

"And for wine," he went on, "which I never drink on the moor, there is sherry and light bordeaux. These heretics, as you see, drink champagne. I am too much of a sportsman to do that, or even to recommend the heresy; still, if you *will* be heretical," &c. &c.; and having made superficial arrangements for Cosmo's nourishment, he turned his back upon him frankly, and resumed his conversation with an eager-looking French gentleman, which Cosmo's arrival had interrupted.

Left thus to himself, and with his self-possession somewhat restored, he cast a rapid glance over the party, and at once encountered Esmè's eyes, who greeted him with a gracious bow and a kindly smile, and, as he was staggering up to go and pay formal respects, cried, " Pray don't think of rising just now, Mr Glencairn; pray don't. I am sure you must be dreadfully hungry, after your morning's work. I hope you have had very good sport."

Hungry! sport! what did the words mean? Cosmo, blushing and stammering like an idiot schoolboy, replied *à tort et à travers*, but was generally understood to intimate that, having eaten thirteen and a half brace of grouse that forenoon, he now felt himself pretty much in the humour for sport—a statement which roused the interest of his neighbours, so that he was conscious of a slight titter, followed by a short silence of curious observation ; under which circumstances, he devoted himself to his luncheon with a false air of appetite and absorption, but tingling all over, and feeling that the merest worm which crawls this earth occupies a high place in the scale of creation compared with his ; also, that it would be a capital thing if the hill above would kindly flow down, and overwhelm him and all the rest, and so blot out for ever the history of this accursed moment.

But the silence was not of long duration ; for this picnic was unlike the normal picnic, that most *triste* and sodden of festivities. It was really gay. Whether it was owing to the air, or the heather, or the champagne heresy, or what not, Cosmo thought he had never been among people who so laughed and talked, and seemed so generally to enjoy themselves ; and when he had long sunk into well-earned oblivion, he began to look about him, and take stock of the party, which, as Tom had said, was large. Though Cosmo had, yesterday, bestowed most of his attention on one group, he recognised a good many of the people who had taken part in what to him was a pantomime, on the lawn-tennis ground : with a good many faces, too, he was familiar, as a town-frequenter, but he saw no personal acquaintance. There were many of the types, male and female, usually to be met with at such, and indeed most, social gatherings, at a certain social level : the London " young man of the day," with his fine *physique* and comely features, and that look of hard immobility and indifference, in which our cynics read the selfishness and irreverence of his nature ; and the London " young lady of the day," with her eternal gleesomeness, which bears (according to our cynics) the same relation to the fresh joy of youth which her premature pearl-powder bears to its bloom; and that maturer hawk-like lady (inevitable, wherever two or three are gathered together for the *cultus* of Pleasure and Mammon), with her restless look of craning, which suggests that she is hungry for something——, for some one to love perhaps, but much more likely (if she is single) for some one to marry, or in any case to toady; and the shaggy man of distinction, who stands upon his own merits, and is here and everywhere, and indeed in the most incongruous places, because he is a "topic of the day;" and the plump, comely young matron, just under middle age, well dressed, popular, all things to all men (to their faces, that is), but nothing to *any one* man (having chosen the safer paths of gastronomy), except her husband, and not very much to him, who is also here, young-looking, gentleman-like, easy, indifferent, fond of a rubber and a good run, but on the whole merely an appendage to the pleasant selfish humbug who is his helpmate; and the iron-grey club man, whose face is to be seen framed in some window of almost any club in St James's Street or Pall Mall, who "abominates this sort of thing," but braves it, in consideration of the cook and the cellar, and because his doctor has prescribed ozone; and a sprinkling of neutrals, only remarkable as being God's creatures; and—and all the rest of them: except, by the by (and this is a large and important exception), those sprightly matrons who have histories, whether preserved by oral tradition in clubs, or entered in the chronicles of the law courts; except, too, those gay dogs who have helped them to compile their biographies, and have the misfortune to be, for the moment, notorious as their *collaborateurs*. These were quite unrepresented; for Lord Germistoune, independently of the fact that he loved his daughter, was, as we have seen, full of antique prejudice, and belonged to that stale old epoch, when a cracked or dusky reputation was socially as disqualifying as dirty hands or doubtful linen. There were some "locals" too, not so easily to be classed, except in the rough-and-ready way in which Tom Wyedale told them off, as "fellows with the air of having their coats made by their bootmakers, and of cherishing earnest convictions about police rates and the Colorado beetle."

The business part of the entertainment was over, except in so far as concerned Mr Ruggles, who was still in position in front of the *pâté*, appearing to be somewhat swollen and jaded, but with a look in his eye of "die but never surrender." The variegated party had shifted and shuffled themselves into congenial groups or couples. The men, cigarette in mouth, were sprawling, nineteenth-century fashion, among the ladies, at every angle and in every attitude suggested by ease rather than grace, and were languidly accepting the attentions of surrounding nymphs, who did their best to solace and divert "the poor, tired, worn-out unfortunates."

The liveliest group was typical; it displayed a *parterre* of ravishing female heads, and, cropping up in the midst of them, a pair of feet and calves, encased in nailed shooting-boots and knickerbocker stockings, round which the fair heads swayed and bobbed with little screams and cacklings of delight, responsive to certain growling monosyllables which came up from the heather, and intimated that the unseen "balance" of the feet and legs was a humorist, or person "who is *such* fun." Other groups were "in the same fancy," and mirth reigned over all.

Cosmo, although almost crushed into callousness, still felt a relief that Esmè was not one of the devotees of the boots and stockings. She remained with the discreet group who had been about her at luncheon—consisting of a shaggy-looking elderly gentleman, an unattractive young lady, and the lady who had played such an obscuring part on the previous day, and in whom he now recognised Mrs Ravenhall. None of them faced his way, and they were earnestly listening to the shaggy man, who appeared to prose, or at least to lecture, for he was not within ordinary ear-shot. The commonest civility and manners ought now to have taken Cosmo round to pay his respects to his young hostess, and to the only other lady whom he knew in the party. He felt this only too well; but he was rooted to the spot, and not merely sensible of his *gaucherie*, but also of the almost grotesque isolation in which he sat, attempting to carry it off by a ghastly semblance of interest in the structure of a blue-bell, which he peered into and held up to the light, as if its calyx were pregnant with botanical mystery. Lord Germistoune, with his back turned to him, still hammered away to the French gentleman, a good deal in the vein of our Transatlantic cousins when on their favourite theme of "American institutions." But his conversation came to an end at last, and with it some commencement of relief for Cosmo.

Lord Germistoune's "finish" was in this way: "Vous savez, M. le Marquis, que chez nous— chez les Ecossais—il y a des—des—chose!—je prétends qu'il existe, entre le seigneur Ecossais et ses vassaux, un certain lien qu'on ne trouve nullement d'ailleurs. Moi, par exemple, j'aime mon peuple, comme père, comme roi. Mon peuple, de leur part, entretient, à mon égard, une espèce de fanatisme; il me regarde comme un être tout-puissant, illustre, et fier. En même temps ils trouvent, ces pauvres gens, que pour eux, je suis d'une tendresse tout-à-fait paternelle. Je le suis. Ils ont raison, ces pauvres gens. Mais——what the d—l is that man M'Ardle about? What are you about, you great blundering jackass? Go away, sir! Get out of my sight. Where's Hammond? How often have I told him to bring up a proper number of footmen on these occasions! The idea of an infernal savage, like you, tumbling about here, among ladies and valuable china! Be off, sir! Why do you stand staring there? Where the d—l is Hammond?" Hammond not putting in an appearance, his lordship jumped up, and hastily introducing Cosmo to the Marquis, went off to deal with him who was answerable for the appearance of poor M'Ardle—a gillie who, acting as an improvised waiter, had walked into a *mayonaise* with one foot, and, with the other, finally subdued the fortress which had made so stout a resistance to the impact of Mr Ruggles. The Marquis was a good deal mystified by this discrepancy between the theory of the patriarchal relation and its development in practice; but he was too polite to show his feelings, and merely said, with a smile, as he looked after the angry old gentleman, " C'est une plaisanterie—un petit jeu de Papa—*one jock,* n'est ce pas, monsieur?" to which Cosmo assented, and, relieved to have some one to talk to at last, at once entered on the subject of the day's sport. This was the Marquis's first experience of grouse-shooting, and he had enjoyed it very much; he had exploded, he said, many *cartouches,* and felt pretty confident that he had severely wounded several birds, though none had exactly fallen. But he confided to Cosmo that the actual nature of the grouse involved a disappointment. He had expected to see in it an aggravated sort of eagle—larger and more ferocious than the ordinary type; and when he belted on his *couteau de chasse* in the morning, had regarded that weapon as the possible instrument of his deliverance, in a death-struggle with the awful bird of prey.

This kind of *chasse*, therefore, he found to be deficient in the element of glory, and so far disappointing, though, in other respects, entitled to rank respectably among the sports with which he was familiar—including the pursuit of the *merle* and the *alouette*, which latter he described as "une espèce de gibier fort difficile;" and then he prattled on with amazing zest and volubility, which so many Frenchmen bestow on *le sport* in all its developments, and which often makes one wonder at the small amount of wool which is connected with all this vociferous cry. To Cosmo, the Marquis was a real relief, and at first he gave him all the attention which he had bestowed on the blue-bell; but presently certain movements took place in the party which caused his attention to flag, and soon drew it off, definitively, to other objects.

The "humorist," who, as far as the general public were concerned, had been for a long time represented by his boots and stockings alone, at last finished his cigar, and rose lazily to a sitting posture, displaying, among the fair damsels who encompassed him, a yawning indifference which suggested the idea of a sultan bored in the zenana, or the "herald of the morn" getting under way for his morning stroll, or, what the humorist actually was, a great *parti*, carelessly dispensing with attentions always at his disposal, and therefore cheap as the cigar-butt which he had just flung away. Cosmo beheld his resurrection, and recognised the individual whose striped raiment and general objectionableness had attracted his anxious attention on the previous day. This was Lord Ribston, of whom Tom Wyedale had spoken. Cosmo did not know him, but shrewdly connected Tom's remarks with what he had himself observed on the terrace and what he now saw, and felt that he beheld the peer who was "schemed for" by Mrs Crock, but vainly, his noble aspirations being otherwise directed. He was very good-looking, though deficient of that "weary look about the eyes," without which we feel that a high-born and much-hunted *parti* is scarcely justified in intruding himself into the pages of a novel. There was nothing of this sort about Lord Ribston, who was a fine animal, of tall stature, with broad shoulders and a fine healthy complexion, and rich, dark, curly hair, and full of that kind of vigour of well-fed youth,

when digestion is unimpeded by a single care.
He was, moreover, a man who, being pretty confident of having his own way, and when, and
how he liked it—particularly among women—
was, naturally enough, in the habit of consulting
nothing but his own convenience or caprice, in
regulating his actions. Thus, though it may at
once be admitted that he was smitten with Esmè,
and though, therefore, he might naturally have
been expected to devote himself to her on the
present occasion, he yet, as we have seen, did
nothing of the sort. He had a philosophical
conviction that one pleasure at a time is better
than two or three commingled. He was also
excessively fond of eating; and thus he had felt
that he would be unable to enjoy his luncheon
satisfactorily were his attention distracted by the
immediate presence of his lady-love. Similarly,
he had decided that the cigar of digestion would
be more comfortably smoked in the attitude of
the worshipped, than in that of the worshipper.
Hence his separation from Esmè during the
meal; hence, too, the tableau of boot and stock-
ing which had supervened. But the pleasures
of the table being exhausted, and the pleasant
addenda of smoke and incense having had their
share of attention, his mind reverted to Esmè,

but not, by any means, with the anxiety of a
lover who fears that his absence may involve
forgetfulness, or another's opportunity. Lord
Ribston was superior to any vulgar tremors of
that sort; it simply now occurred to him that it
would be a pleasant thing to go and look at
Esmè's pretty face, and that the artless music
of her voice would soothe him, after the harsh
fanfares of forced laughter. Therefore he arose,
regardless of the frank remonstrances of his satel-
lites, and rolled his fine bulk leisurely over to
the group which was still hanging upon the
utterances of the shaggy senior.

This gentleman, who represented the "man of
distinction" or "topic of the day" element, was
purring away about fossiliferous strata and the
Cambrian schists, and was listened to by Esmè,
because she was amiable and his hostess, by Mrs
Ravenhall as Esmè's body-guard, and by Miss
Milkington—the complementary young lady—
because, being dreary and unattractive, and,
generally speaking, "out of the swim," she had
nothing else to do. He was a bore, however,
and perhaps, therefore, deserved extinction,
though scarcely in the abrupt manner in which
it was administered by Lord Ribston.

"If," the *savant* was saying—"if we hold,

with Sir Roderick, and argue from the condition
of these schists——" when his lordship plumped
down in the middle of the group, and remarked—

"What's a schist? anything good to eat?
By the by, Miss Douglas, let me congratulate
you on the luncheon,—best done thing I've seen
for ages. How we're to shoot after it, I don't
know." To which Esmè made a suitable reply,
and then said to the discomfited "topic of the
day"—

"You were telling us, Dr Pentacle, that Sir
Roderick Murchison——"

"I was simply going to remark, that if we
hold, with Sir Roderick, that the phenomena
exhibited by these schists——"

But the word "schist" was intolerable to Lord
Ribston; he put his foot down upon it. "For
heaven's sake, Dr Pentacle!" he cried, "let us
off the schists till the smoking-room to-night.
I don't think violent language of that sort ought
to be used before ladies. Do you, Mrs Ravenhall?"

"How rude you are, Lord Ribston!" said
Mrs Ravenhall, with an appearance of sup-
pressing laughter which wounded the *savant*
more than Ribston's brutality, so that he rose

and left them, saying meekly that they must forgive an old pedagogue for boring them with his unseasonable lore.

"Got his back up," said Lord Ribston.

"Cruel of you!" said Mrs Ravenhall.

"Serves him right for boring Miss Douglas," quoth my lord.

"I shall go," said Esmè, rising, "and beg him to tell me about Sir Roderick's theory; it is *most* interesting;" and, in this way, having snubbed the snubber, she was going to leave them, when Lord Germistoune — who had returned from worrying Hammond—was observed to meet the Professor, and to take him by the arm, and to carry him off towards the top of the knoll, no doubt giving him plenty of new ideas about the Old Red Sandstone, &c. &c.,— for Lord Germistoune was many-sided, had an opinion upon every subject, and was always right.

"You must postpone *that* pleasure, Miss Douglas," said Lord Ribston, ignoring the fact that Esmè was displeased; "but seriously, do you care to know about schist, and that kind of thing?"

"I think it is always interesting to hear a man talk about a subject which he really understands."

" Ah! now I shall know how to interest you;
what I've always wished to do. But do you
know, Miss Douglas, I think it *is* rather difficult
to interest you."

" Do you find me *blasée* ? " laughed Esmè.

" No, no, not that ; but you don't seem to care
about things—*you* know what I mean."

" Not quite, Lord Ribston ; because I do care
about a great many things."

" One can interest these others " (with a wave
of his hand in the direction of his recent dis-
ciples) " about anything ; but it's different with
you. Yet, somehow, I like your way best ; only
I *should* like to interest you. Help me, Mrs
Ravenhall, with an idea. How can I interest
Miss Douglas ? "

" Perhaps Tom can help us. Here, Tom !
Tom ! " to her brother, who was hovering about
from group to group.

" Well, what's the matter ? "

" Come and sit down here. We are in com-
mittee ; we want an idea, and you must help us."

" I'll give you an idea ; without sitting down,
though, because I'm going to see the keeper
about my afternoon beat."

" Well, what is it ? "

" It's quite frank, I warn you."

"Well?"

"It is simply this, that the Twelfth of August is sacred to grouse, and not to small-talk, and that it is high time for us to be taking the hill."

Esmè laughed. "How deliciously in earnest you are, Mr Wyedale!" she said.

"I am, you know," cried Tom, in his eager, aggrieved sort of way; "but don't you think I am right? I know you do, because you believe in earnestness. I look at it in this way, don't you see: I can't well have more than thirty-five or forty 'Twelfths,' at best. Half of these, at least, will be wet, and the other half will be eaten into by illness, the want of a moor, and other accidents. Altogether, it's extremely improbable that I shall have more than two or three such anniversaries of the day as this, in the course of my life. So I'm all for a start. Come, Ribston, here's my idea—you get up and help me to agitate for a move. You are a swell, and will be listened to. Come, *carpe diem!*"

"Carp it yourself, old fellow."

"Tom, you positively *are* a savage," cried his sister. "What you really mean is to drive us all home."

"Not a bit of it; I should recommend you to stay here and enjoy the mountain air."

"All by ourselves?"

"There are no bandits about; besides, you'll have old Spectacles or Binnacles, or whatever he calls himself, and all the other cripples, to look after you."

"A tempting programme, indeed! Come, Tom, sit down."

"I'll move in twenty minutes, Wyedale," said Lord Ribston.

"You shall," cried Tom; "and in the meantime, I'll go and see the keeper."

"No, no, Tom," urged his sister; "sit down and amuse us. We were getting rather *triste.* Come."

"No, I can't; but I'll find a substitute. There's poor Glencairn being bored to death by the Marquis. Look at his wistful glances! Quite a charity to release him. Hi! Cosmo! Wanted! Come here! Ladies want you!"

So Tom went off, and so, at last, there was nothing left for Cosmo but to harden his heart, and go across to the spot at which he had been steadily glaring, ever since Lord Ribston had flung his free-and-easy form into the group. Most embarrassing at best to meet Esmè! but to meet her now, thus, covered with the ignominy of demonstrated clownishness, was too overpowering. How he got across he could never have told you. Suffice it that the feat *was* performed, and that he presently found himself sitting pretty calmly beside Esmè, and opposite to Mrs Ravenhall, who greeted him with effusion, and opposite Lord Ribston, who, not knowing him, scanned him all over with that look of disapproving inquiry which the youth of the day bestows upon a stranger. There was a certain repose, and, at the same time, a frank unself consciousness in Esmè's manner, which were charming and reassuring even to a wretch in Cosmo's condition; and though there were tones in her voice (for it *is* the *voice* of the charmer which is her most potent charm), which, now and then, set his pulses galloping, its ordinary flow was melodiously sedative.

Esmè made no remark upon his tardy homage, but said, very heartily, that she was glad he had made up his mind to come to the Highlands, after all.

"It must have been *quite* a surprise for Mr Wyedale," she said, "for he was only yesterday talking about Finmore, and about you; and he said,—didn't your brother say, Mrs Ravenhall, that Mr Glencairn had gone to Melbourne to observe the transit of Venus?"

“Oh! Tom says anything that comes into his head, as I am sure you know, Mr Glencairn.”

“Yes,” said Cosmo, laughing, “Tom deals very largely in metaphors and hyperboles.”

“But I *really* believed him,” cried Esmè, “because——” she was thinking of the moonlight interview at the Villa Bianca, but paused and finished her sentence otherwise than she had intended, saying, “because he *did* appear quite grave and positive. I am sure,” she added, smiling, “that this is a much better place to be in than Melbourne.”

“Ah, indeed it is!” cried Cosmo.

“You liked Finmore when you had it last, did you not?” How pleasantly she seemed to remember things!

“I liked it extremely,” said Cosmo; “and,” plucking up spirit, “I mean to like it still more this time.”

“I hope you will; but are you alone?”

“Yes; the fact is, I took it quite on an impulse, and had no time to get up a party, even if I had wished to do so.”

“I think you are very much given to impulses, Mr Glencairn,” she said, with a smile.

“I—I don’t know that I am.”

“You were in an impulse of departure when

I last saw you, and now that I meet you again, you have just arrived by impulse."

"Ah yes," stammered Cosmo. "Of course— yes, to be sure—Cadenabbia—business—London —ahem! ahem!—things that very decidedly— yes——" and lost his head and broke down; and Esmè also became rather confused, recalling all the revelations which had preceded his announcement of departure, and fearing that he might suspect her of insinuating some banter concerning them.

This pause was taken advantage of by Lord Ribston, who by this time had decided that Cosmo wasn't "his form," and that he hated the sight of him.

"Did you like Cadenabbia, Miss Douglas?" he asked.

"Oh yes, so very much!"

"I suppose there was plenty of schist there?" and this being a joke and also a sarcasm, his lordship laughed inordinately.

"We had plenty to amuse and occupy us without schist," said Mrs Ravenhall. "We had something new to do almost every day—Miss Douglas and Lord Germistoune, and Tom and I."

"How did Wyedale stand it?" asked Lord Ribston, lazily.

"'Stand it!'" cried Mrs Ravenhall, with a look full of meaning. "Tom felt his good fortune in being there, I can assure you. I never saw Tom so happy, *never*; and *so* sorry to come away, although I must say we all enjoyed the Engadine very much—quite as much, indeed, I think."

"What! have you all been caravaning about together, the whole summer?" cried Lord Ribston.

"Yes; we have been *quite* inseparable, have we not, dear Esmè?"

"Yes, I am glad to say that we have. It has been delightful being with you."

"It could not be more so to you than it has been to *us*," with another look at Lord Ribston which was meant to express, "so you needn't hope to upset what you can see is a cosey little family arrangement—nearly as good as settled."

And his lordship did look a little reflective, and pondered over Tom's relations with the family, which were certainly a little puzzling, and to some minds might have been suggestive. Cosmo, too, did not *quite* like the ring of Mrs Ravenhall's voice, but was in too pure an atmosphere of bliss, thus seated beside Esmè, after all these months of absence and longing, to be disturbed at present, though probably Mrs Ravenhall's words might come back to him in the lonely evening, and not exactly as a soporific.

For some ten minutes the conversation went on in the same sort of vein, principally in dialogue between Esmè and Cosmo, relieved by occasional flashes of humour from Lord Ribston, who sprawled at Esmè's feet, and gazed into her face with looks of the frankest admiration; while Mrs Ravenhall "watched the case" for her brother, interpolating such occasional remarks as she thought might tend to his interests, or to the discomfiture and disadvantage of the two other men. It was brought to a close at last by the arrival of Lord Germistoune, whom Tom had got hold of and brought over to his way of thinking.

"Now, Mrs Ravenhall," he cried, "you know it is 'the Twelfth,'—that is to say, the only day in the year which has not for its motto 'Place aux dames;' so I hope you will not think me a bear, when I tell you that the carts are ready for you, and that *we* must be starting, which we can't do till we have packed you comfortably, and seen you off."

Whereupon Mrs Ravenhall jumped up with the greatest alacrity, vowing that, for the last hour, his lordship's extraordinary kindness in allowing them to remain so long, had been a marvel to her; and then they moved towards the carts, Esmè detaining her father for a moment, to say—

"Poor Mr Glencairn is all alone at Finmore, papa; wouldn't it be kind to ask him to dinner?"

"Tut! tut! tut! impossible; we shan't be home till nine. No compliment to ask him to dine on a day like this."

"Ah! I forgot; perhaps not. But you might ask him for to-morrow, and then he would see the gillies' ball too."

"Ahem! well, there is no positive objection to that—no *positive* objection, that I can see. Yes, I'll ask him. He's no addition to a party, though—silent and stupid. He hadn't a word for *me* at luncheon to-day."

So, when they overtook the party, Lord Germistoune tendered his invitation, and it is needless to say that Cosmo joyfully accepted it, notwithstanding the fussy austerity of manner with which it was offered. Then Lord Ribston, true to his system of one joy at a time, left the ladies' departure to be superintended by others, and went away to see about his beat, with the parting injunction to Esmè to take old Pentacle in the cart with her, and, if possible, work out the Cambrian schists before dinner, so as to give him the chance of an evening's innings; and Lord Germistoune having detached Mrs Ravenhall, Cosmo had five minutes in heavenly *tête-à-tête* with Esmè.

"I am so glad you can come to-morrow," said the latter, "although it is an uncomfortable hour for dinner. You must know that to-morrow is my birthday, and the people always have a dance to celebrate that great occasion; and as we like to go and see them for a little, we are obliged to dine early. I am afraid the shooters will grumble dreadfully."

"What! on YOUR birthday?" cried Cosmo.

"I fear that will scarcely console them; and, indeed, it is rather a pity that we must have it on that night; but it would not do to disappoint the poor people, for they have been accustomed to have their annual dance ever since I was born."

Cosmo made a terribly buckram speech, which sounded, even in his own ears, exactly like an extract from 'Pamela,' to the effect that "the man who, on such a day, could grudge," &c. &c.

Esmè laughed, and said, "Then I may count

upon your gallantry, at all events, to support me against the grumblers. I shall be glad of an ally against Lord Ribston and Mr Wyedale— they will be the most formidable——" and, before Cosmo could cry out that these men must be soulless, and worthy of the tormentors, she changed the subject, and said, " I hope you can dance reels. We are all expected to perform once at least—even papa, who goes through the trial most heroically."

" I don't think I have ever *quite* danced a reel," said Cosmo ; but to-morrow night I am sure I shall be inspired. I shall succeed by one of those impulses you accuse me of."

" Oh Mr Glencairn ! " cried Esmè, with a quick change of manner, "I want to say to you that I hope you did not think me rude when I spoke about—about—your going away from Cadenabbia on an impulse. If I had remembered, at the time, all you said to me that night in the garden, it would have been both rude and unkind ; but I did not think of it at the moment — not till I fancied you were annoyed——"

" Annoyed, Miss Douglas ? with *you* ? "

" I thought so ; and you might have been so, very reasonably ; but I really spoke without thinking—not that I have ever forgotten what you told me that night, because," and she spoke warmly and earnestly, "I was very, very sorry for you — you were so unhappy, and for such an honourable reason" (honourable indeed!); "but now, I hope, you quite understand that I did not mean to be rude."

Cosmo looked at her and smiled, and his smile was the great charm of his face—smiled dreamily, tenderly, worshippingly, and murmured some half-articulate commonplace, which had no meaning at all, being entirely lost in the eloquence of the look and the smile which accompanied it. Esmè did not at once withdraw her eyes from that mysterious regard. She could not. She felt a strange fascination, something between curiosity and some other emotion altogether new, which held her gaze and made the delicate colour waver and come and go in her fair face. Silence followed for a few moments. Then Cosmo, who seemed to feel the value of time and opportunity, went back to the subject of the garden scene at the Villa Bianca, and said—

"I have often thought, Miss Douglas, with shame, of the infliction to which I subjected you that night." (The serpent!)

"But I told you not to be ashamed; I told you that I was very much interested."

"You must have thought me so forward and eccentric," cried Cosmo, pressing the case against himself.

"I did think that you might have found a better *confidant*, but I said exactly what I meant. I said that I felt very much for your perplexities, which were so uncommon—at least they seemed so to me—and—and——" (here she made an effort to say what she could have said *without* an effort ten minutes ago, and she made the effort, as if determined not to admit the existence of any obstacle), "and I have often wondered since, what you would decide upon."

Cosmo felt that this was beatitude.

"You gave me your good wishes," he said, in a voice full of tremulous music; "and I felt, at the time, that that was an omen for good. I hope, now, that I have found the solution I was in quest of."

"Oh, I am so glad! May I know—may I be allowed to know what it is?"

"If you care to hear about it, it will be the greatest happiness to me to tell you."

But here they approached the rest of the party, and Esmè said—

"You will tell me to-morrow evening, perhaps."

"If you will listen to me, Miss Douglas. And oh, may I make one petition?—that you will sing me again that song which you were singing on that same night when I came up, like an evil spirit, as you said, out of the lake to listen? It has been ringing in my ears ever since; for I always seem to hear it when I think of you."

Cosmo was certainly not losing much time. Esmè looked shyly up, and again met that indescribable gaze which puzzled and confused her, but which yet left some impression that was not akin to pain, and said, "If you can tell me what it was—what song you wished me to sing—I will gladly sing it for you;" and when she had said this, and received Cosmo's thanks, their eyes parted; but before they did so, the lynx-vision of Mrs Ravenhall detected the love-light which shone in Cosmo's, and she said to herself, bitterly, "Another of these *abominable* fortune-hunters!" Then the ladies were carefully assorted, and packed into their vehicles, and despatched — rather a sombre and silent party; for all the Euphrosynes suffered from reaction, and, indeed, every one must feel that old Pentacle and his brother cripples were rather a bathos, after the boots and knickerbockers and intellectual charms of Lord Ribston. Esmè herself was silent and almost *distraite*. "You are tired, darling," said Mrs Ravenhall. Esmè disclaimed fatigue. "I can see it," Mrs Ravenhall insisted ; "and it is not to be wondered at. You have been sacrificing yourself all day to the worst bores of the party. Just like your goodness; but your strength is not equal to it. Only fancy, dear Lady Bugles, after giving an hour to Miss Milkington, and at least an hour to Professor Pentacle, this sweet child must needs take pity on that dreary Mr Glencairn, who must have been quite the *coup de grâce*, I should imagine."

"He looks dreary," said Lady Bugles—"very dreary. Who is he ?"

"Who is he ? Well, now you ask me, I don't think I quite know. Let me see. He used to live, as a youth, when he and Tom were at Eton and Cambridge together, with Colonel Wildgrave. You remember the Wildgraves who had a house in Grosvenor Square ? I think, but I am not positive, he used to be *called* Colonel Wildgrave's nephew. He succeeded to his fortune, certainly ; but I have a hazy sort of impression that there

was a mystery about him.   Don't say I said it ;
but I almost fancy there was an idea that he was
a foundling."

" He looks like a foundling," said Lady Bugles
—" *exactly* like a foundling."   Her ladyship's
patent teeth were becoming rather obstreperous,
from the motion of the cart, and warned her
that brevity, if not total silence, was advisable.
Esmè made no comment upon these remarks
about Cosmo, but simply repeated that she was
not fatigued, had enjoyed the day immensely,
and found no one a bore.   Mrs Ravenhall intimated her disbelief of this by a compassionate
smile, confidentially imparted to Lady Bugles,
and let the subject drop.

The reader will not have failed to observe that
these protracted operations were undermining
Mrs Ravenhall's *morale*, and upsetting the principles upon which her social success was built.
Convinced of the imbecility and risk of indulging in backbiting as a pastime, which is inevitably to rouse against one's own reputation secret,
and therefore incalculable, forces of retaliation
and injury, she would have been incapable, two
months ago, of committing herself to such reckless remarks as she had now made about Cosmo.
But the continuousness of the strain was becom-

ing severe; and it must be owned that the way in which new aspirants kept cropping up was trying. In two months there had been Count Fori and Lord Ribston, besides a shoal of smaller fry who had been eyed down or otherwise summarily dealt with. And now, here, evidently, was Cosmo, who, her instinct told her, was the most dangerous of all, and therefore to be counteracted by the strongest measures. Hence the "foundling" myth.

How she found herself at Dunerlacht, by the by, requires explanation. She and Tom had remained with the Germistounes at Pontresina till the last days of July, and had come home with them to London, where the party had broken up with many mutual regrets. But their separation was of the briefest duration. On arriving at Ravenhall, she found that her husband, resenting his long deprivation of conjugal solace and observance, had accepted, by way of reprisal, a bachelor invitation to shoot grouse and stalk deer in the Highlands for a month, and that he was on the very eve of departure for the north.

" What," she had asked, " is to become of me?" and had received, by way of reply, a generous permission to remain at home and " look after matters." But this was not her idea of the fitness of things ; and, by a happy inspiration, she had written a charming little comico-pathetic letter to Lord Germistoune, describing her forlorn situation—made doubly desolating by the too, too happy days she had recently passed in his lordship's society, and "quite frankly" begging him to allow her to accompany Tom, and inflict herself upon Dunerlacht for a few days, until "her other engagements in the north fell due." She said nothing about all this to Mr Ravenhall, who went away in a fool's paradise, chuckling over his wife's impending incarceration at home ; and he had not been gone much more than a day when a letter arrived from Lord Germistoune, backed by one from Esmè, welcoming Mrs Ravenhall's invasion with the most satisfactory cordiality. The results of which were, that Tom received the same afternoon, in town, a telegram which caused his countenance to fall, and drew from him the remark, " That woman's horrible energy will be the death of me ! By heavens ! she's becoming a regular Old Man of the Sea ; " and that, the same night, he and his adroit incubus were dashing away northwards together in the "Flying Scotsman."

Thus was Mrs Ravenhall again in the field,

facing, as she felt, severe odds, and not likely to stick at a trifle, either in word or deed. A pursuit of the sort, to an intriguing nature, increases in interest and excitement as it progresses, and even as difficulties multiply ; and success comes to be valued in the abstract as the triumph of skill and endurance, independently of the solid advantages which it represents.

CHAPTER XXV.

Old Davidson was at once struck with a change which had come over his master, when he rejoined him at the "march." With his head in the air, and a light step, Cosmo came swinging over the heather, and greeted the old keeper with a genial smile and a playful apology for his long absence. "Never mind, Davidson," he cried, "give me my gun, and we'll see if we can't make up for lost time. I don't mean to let many of them off, this afternoon, I promise you." And he was as good as his word. What a pace he walked at! The dogs ranged wide and covered a deal of ground, but he was up to the points like lightning. Juno had no anxieties. The fleet foot and the unerring barrels were always "there." The bag swelled perceptibly.

"We'll hae to ca' canny wi' thae hares, Captin, if me and Aunra's to get a'thing hame oorsels. An' ye gang on at this rate, sir, we'll hae to send for ane o' the pownies."

"Oh, I don't mean that you and Andrew shall be able to carry the bags home. You must make a depot somewhere, soon, and send back for the stuff. I'm only just beginning."

Master and men were in the highest glee; and not till the sun had well set, and the dogs were dead beat, was the sport abandoned.

"What's the bag, Davidson?" Cosmo asked, when the keeper came in, at night, for orders.

Davidson's admiration of his master's afternoon performance was so sincere, that he was generous enough to suspend, temporarily, his disapprobation of his single-handed escapade. "'Deed, sir, it's a tremendyus birds—jist tremendyus. Fufty-sax brace grouse, acht blue hares, three snipe, and a juke!"

"After all, not so bad for 'ae gun,' eh, Davidson?"

"It's a tremendyus birds to ae gun. There's naebody fit to tak and contradick that—that's conseederin' a' things—maist feck o' hauf the day lost, and your hert' no' in it (beggin' your paurdon, sir) the fore pert o' the day. Stull and with a', I maun say that to dae justice to this muir——"

"Yes, yes, Davidson, I know all about that. We'll get your friend, Mr Wyedale, over to help us one of these days, and I've decided to ask a friend to come down from London to join me immediately. We'll shoot early to-morrow — start at eight sharp. I shall have to knock off at four. Good-night."

So Davidson went away greatly comforted. "Dod!" he confided to an underling, "he was clean sully in the mornin', but he bruskit up brawly afterhin'. I doot they maun hae gien him something ower by at his lordship's — sh'mpeen, mibbee."

On his way home, Cosmo, inspired with a magical delight which it would have been hard to analyse, but which excluded all considerations of prudence, policy, and so forth, glowed with philanthropy and all good-fellowship, and, in this happy frame, decided that it would be a kind thing to give poor Phil Denwick a chance of some fresh air and a run on the hills, before he settled down to the routine of office life in London; and he now sat down and wrote, inviting him to come at once. "Bring your 'Ready Reckoner' with you," he said, "and other commercial implements, as well as your gun, and in this quiet place, you will be able to mingle business with pleasure." Then he went to bed and slept the sleep of the blessed, and all night long through the world of his dreams, this refrain seemed to echo—

> " I strove against the stream, but all in vain ;
> Let the great river bear me to the main."

Another splendid day. From roseate dreams Cosmo awoke to behold the hills again blooming under an unclouded sky, and also to find that the sudden fabric of his own mysterious happiness had not been absorbed into some kindred vision of the night, and had not departed along with it. As yet there was no reaction. Again to-day his vigour and energy on the moor were great, — somewhat feverish indeed ; but if the rapidity of his movements symbolised his impatience to overpass the interval which separated him from Esmè, rather than the enthusiasm of sport, the material results were highly satisfactory ; and when the hour for "knocking off" arrived, old Davidson's disapprobation of "anither o' thae hauf days" was softened by a bag of really imposing dimensions.

A full hour before it was necessary, Cosmo returned to the lodge to dress for dinner, and though he did his best, as he thought, not to be premature, he reached the castle some time before any one appeared in the drawing-room. It was a fine old house, in all respects worthy to be the seat of an ancient and historical family. There were arms and armour enough in the entrance-hall and wainscoted gallery, to equip a clan of fighting men, and above these weapons quite a clan of portraits—of the warriors, doubtless, who had borne them, intermingled with those of the fair ladies who had inspired their deeds of chivalry. In the drawing-room, some of the best of the family pictures were hung; and Cosmo amused himself for a quarter of an hour in inspecting them, and tracing the origin, development, and recurrence of this and that peculiarity of feature which formed, as one so often sees, a connecting-link between many generations. By one of these pictures his attention was strongly arrested. Strange to say, it was not the portrait of a peerless dame whose features had been reproduced in her latest female descendant. We feel that this is what it ought to have been ; but it was quite otherwise, being the representation of a rather grim and haughty-looking cavalier—neither young nor specially handsome, but with a remarkable expression of concentration, and power, and purpose, which, independently of the great merits of the picture, arrested the attention. Cosmo was impressed by all this, but by something more; for the moment he looked at it, he was struck with a feeling that he was familiar with the face, and must have seen the picture before. He walked from side to side, and got it into a variety of lights, trying to stimulate his memory. The cold, straightforward eyes of the cavalier followed him, with that look of vital movement which pictures borrow from the movements of the beholder. Cosmo could by no means remember where he had seen it before, but he was more and more convinced of his familiarity with the face. He could almost have sworn that he had seen the eyes, and, indeed, all the features, at some former time, and when they were animated in conversation. Vivid, however, as the impression was, the antique dress of the figure told him at once that the recognition was purely fanciful. A movement took place in the room behind him; but as he was engaged in shifting his position, he did not observe it.

"I seem to know you, my friend," he said aloud, and looking at the picture; "and, indeed, you almost look as if you knew me. Who are you ? "   He approached nearer, and read on the lower part of the frame—

"Sir Alan Douglas—slain at the battle of Philiphaugh.
Anno 1645."

"A little before my time," he said, with a smile.

There was a musical laugh behind him, and a voice said, "And I fear I am a little behind mine, Mr Glencairn."   He turned and saw Esmè, looking, he thought, lovelier than he had ever seen her before—dressed, as he had never seen her before, for the evening, which enhanced, if possible, her beauty, and developed new charms.   The little incident that he had been overheard in a whimsical soliloquy, gave a certain pretext for his confusion at meeting her, and he soon recovered his self-possession.

"I fancied," he said, "that I had found an old acquaintance ; but I have never been in this room before, and it is not likely, I suppose, that this picture has been elsewhere ? "

"No," said Esmè ; " I don't think it is likely that it has ever left this house ; but it is considered a very good picture, and attracts every one's attention."

"I suppose, then," said Cosmo, "I have been

merely experiencing the 'sentiment of pre-existence.' There are some very fine pictures here."

"Nothing but family pictures. Some of them *are* said to be good, and, of course, they are all interesting to us; but I suspect that the whole collection would scarcely bear the inspection of a critic like you. I have not forgotten our conversation at Cadenabbia."

"If I pretended to be a critic, Miss Douglas, I was an impostor, and now denounce myself. By the by, I have not been able in any of these pictures to trace a resemblance to you. I see Lord Germistoune, more or less, in several generations; but *you* are quite original."

"That ought to be gratifying, I suppose," laughed Esmè.

"There *is*, however, a picture—I have seen it often—which was recalled to my mind the moment I saw you at Cadenabbia. It has been a great favourite of mine for years. It is by Sassoferrato—a Madonna—and you might have sat for it. So that you see, after all, you are not quite original."

"Where is this picture?"

"In a collection—rather misplaced—in a village named Montestretto, in Italy. I have made various pilgrimages to see it. It took a great possession of my imagination. I used to amuse myself by putting together the characteristics which I thought would be suitable to such a face."

"And I am so very like it?"

"It is your portrait."

"And the characteristics? But, of course, you don't know me well enough to answer that question."

"Oh, indeed I do!"

"You must be a wizard then, Mr Glencairn, or at least a *clairvoyant*," laughed Esmè.

"Not at all; but I am convinced that you have exactly the same characteristics as I gave to the picture."

"But how?"

"I cannot exactly tell; partly from what I have seen of you, perhaps, and partly by instinct."

"I hope——" but Esmè stopped, blushing as she met Cosmo's gaze, and was perhaps rather relieved when Lord Germistoune stalked into the room with his pompous "How do you do, sir? how do you do?"

There was no fussiness in his manner now, it was pure austerity.

"I have been admiring that picture of your ancestor, Sir Alan Douglas, Lord Germistoune," said Cosmo.

"It is a good picture. We have always thought highly of it. Ah! my dear Mrs Crock, here you are! I am glad to see that you are still alive. I was watching you in that last game of tennis with Lord Ribston. Your agility is marvellous—distinctly marvellous. I almost think you are one too many for Ribston."

Mrs Crock devoutly hoped that, in another sphere, she might prove to be so, but disclaimed athletic superiority, and announced that she was perfectly fresh, and meant to dance any quantity of reels that evening.

" They are so inspiriting and picturesque and delightful," said Mrs Ravenhall, who now flowed into the room ; "we must all dance them."

" Any dance which Mrs Ravenhall dances must be picturesque and delightful," said Lord Germistoune. Mrs Ravenhall dropped a playful curtsey, and challenged his lordship to be her partner. This privilege, however, could not be conceded. Lord Germistoune explained that his reel-dancing was rather an affair of state, and that the honour of his partnership was, by a sort of feudal arrangement, always conferred upon the wife of the oldest tenant on the estate —a certain Mrs M'Haffie. Mrs Ravenhall affected to pout; Mrs Crock vowed she should be consumed with jealousy of the farmer's wife; and even Lady Bugles, who had now arrived, was understood, by a sort of whistling sound (for two of the incisors *had* gone), to convey that Mrs M'Haffie's monopoly was afflictive to her.

The rest of the party arrived by degrees; dinner was announced, and Lord Germistoune marched off with a very deaf dowager, notifying to Mrs Ravenhall that he *insisted* upon having her support on his other hand at table, with a slight imploring gesture which seemed to place her in a delightful antithesis, not merely to the deaf dowager, but also to the rest of the party. Yet, though this was a distinction which might well have preoccupied a head less cool, it did not prevent Mrs Ravenhall (who had studied the order of march and precedence with Esmè) from whispering to the young lady to whom Cosmo had been assigned, "Remember that Mr Glencairn is *quite* worth your attention; ten thousand a - year; matrimonially inclined; a score of people dying to marry him. I advise you to make the most of the opportunity." And thus incited, Miss Hungerford - Snapsley "went for" the "foundling" (which *sobriquet*, born of Mrs Ravenhall's reckless speech in the cart, had been adopted as appropriate by the young ladies in divan assembled) with the skill and determination which seven seasons of sedulous practice supply; and tried him all round, and in every vein, and in every class of topic, beginning with religious æsthetics and ending with riskier subjects, such as modern stage millinery. She give him of her fulness, but nothing from her cornucopia seemed to interest the "foundling." He was *distrait*, for ever answering at random, and often at cross-purposes.

"Anticipated! the wretch is in love!" this astute maiden said to herself, and promptly gave him up, and consoled herself by "having a round," for practice' sake, with a very young Oxford lad, son of the deaf dowager to whom Lord Germistoune was in thrall. Cosmo could scarcely help being *distrait*, considering all things; for, though far away, Esmè was in full view, and his eyes were turned in her direction as often as was permissible, within the limits of a not very vigilant prudence. The classic grace of her small head, with its rich auburn hair whose luxuriance could not be concealed by the severest simplicity of arrangement; the brightness and kindliness of her smile; the patrician grace of her fair neck; and a hundred charms of movement, pose, and expression — all so artless, but so full of unstudied harmony,—might well fascinate the gaze of artistic perception quickened by the power of love. No wonder Miss Snapsley found herself, as she afterwards complained to Mrs Ravenhall, "quite out in the cold."

Lord Ribston sat beside Esmè, but seemed rather sluggish and sleepy (which was just as well), and most of her conversation was given to the gentleman on her other hand, whom Cosmo could not see, but knew to be delightfully old and infirm, so that there was little to disturb his pleasant waking dream, albeit carried on in the midst of twenty - five banqueters. The dinner passed off like other dinners of the sort, the only public incident being the arrival of Tom Wyedale when it was half over. He had, of course, been unable to tear himself away from the grouse at the proper time, and now arrived, hurried but *nonchalant*, and marched up to make his apologies to Esmè, " as if," Lord Ribston thought, " the whole place belonged to him." In his hand he bore a bouquet of wild-flowers, to which he smelt jauntily as he marched up the room. These (a collection made that afternoon by Mrs Ravenhall) he presented to Esmè with a comic air of reverence, and cried—

"It is shocking, Miss Douglas, to be late upon your natal day, but it would have been shockinger to be in time, yet without a birthday offering. Deign to accept these humble flowerets. Let them plead my excuse."

"Oh Mr Wyedale, how kind of you! how beautiful they are! how very, very good of you to think of getting them for me, and actually to sacrifice some of your shooting to gather them! I know what the sacrifice *must* have been, and therefore understand the full value of the offering. Thank you, so very much! It is a most appropriate bouquet for a Highland ball!"

And then Tom went gaily to his seat with a grin of suppressed meaning, but was presently damped by finding that his sister's eyes were pouring upon him the lava of burning wrath and contempt. Was it for this public exhibition, this travesty, that she had furtively toiled and over-fatigued herself in the glen that afternoon? Tom was, to use the mildest expression, a hopeless marplot.

The ladies had not very long left the dining-room, when Lord Germistoune rose, and said he must go to see the factor about some arrangements which he had forgotten; the gentlemen might, however, do exactly as they pleased. Those who wished to join the ladies might now do so, while those who desired more wine might remain. "It is Liberty Hall," said his lordship; "and since that *viveur* Wyedale will stick to the bottles as long as he can, I leave him in command here," and so departed.

Then Cosmo displayed real generalship; for, finding Professor Pentacle (who now sat next him) to be in a rapture of prose about a Roman urn which had been recently dug up somewhere, and was to be seen in one of the public rooms of the castle, he encouraged the *savant*, by a fraudulent show of interest, to enlarge on the theme, and at last vowed that he was possessed with a burning desire to see the vessel in question—and at once; and did Dr Pentacle know, exactly, where the treasure was? The Doctor did; and since neither he nor Cosmo wanted any more wine, they most naturally went to inspect it. It was found in a glass cabinet in an octagon room which formed the interior of one of the flanking towers, and terminated a suite of drawing-rooms opening one from another. Here there was an organ as well as a piano; and these and other symptoms announced that the room was sacred to music. It was now, however, empty; and the Professor, getting hold of the urn, and opening a lecture which promised to be formidable, Cosmo began to feel that he was in for a bad time of it. But (was there ever anything like the luck of this fortunate fellow?) Lady Bugles and another dame had expressed a wish to see the music-room, just at the proper moment, and, when Pentacle was in full and ardent cry, entered the room, followed by their young hostess.

"What is going on here?" whistled Lady Bugles; "a lecture?"

"Yes," cried Cosmo, "a most interesting one;" and, when he had manœuvred Lady Bugles and the other lady into the position of an audience, he manifested the sincerity of his interest by at once dropping from the circle and joining Esmè, who had gone to pick up some music which lay on the floor, at the other side of the room.

"This is the music-room, of course?" said Cosmo.

"Yes; and it is a very good room for it, and very easy to sing in."

"May I venture to remind you of a promise which you made to me yesterday?"

"What is it? Oh! the song? Certainly. I will perform my promise, if you wish; but have we time? And shan't we disturb the Professor?"

"Nothing disturbs the Professor," said Cosmo, confidently; "and there is an hour to spare before the ball, or nearly so."

"I wonder if the others are all amused? I must just go and see first."

She went, and returned, bringing with her the dreary Miss Milkington, who, gravitating naturally to the dreary, at once joined the Pentacle group.

"They are all very good," said Esmè, "and quite to be trusted in my absence; so now, if you can tell me which song you wish, I will sing it."

Cosmo described the first song she had sung on that enchanting evening by the lake. Then she sang it; and with its first notes, all the scene, where he had first heard it, came back to him, and with it the recollection of that wild and stormy burst of revelation which had swept over his mind, evoked by the sound of her artless voice, as she sang this simple little lay—

Spring breathed on Winter's ice and rime,
  And free'd the flowers from Winter's thrall,
And woo'd them on, that Summer prime
  Might deck her bowers withal.

Spring gave the song-bird back the song
  That late in wintry durance lay;
Shall I, then, after waiting long,
  My heart, again be gay?

Alack! there is no Spring for thee—
  Song died because the flowers were ta'en,
And all the wild-wood minstrelsie
  Came with the flowers again.

But to give back *thy* music lost,
  It is not Spring that has the power;
Spring cannot touch the bitter frost
  That holds thy captive flower.*

When she ceased, Cosmo remained silent. Esmè looked up and saw in his face a look of strange intensity which puzzled her.

"It does not bear repetition, I fear," she said; "and besides, it is too melancholy. I know that you like melancholy songs *sometimes;* but not always, I hope."

"Oh, this song is beautiful! it is not melancholy; it is altogether delightful," and with great earnestness he begged her to sing it again,

* The music, by Miss Catharine Eliott-Lockhart, will be found at the end of this volume.

which she eventually did, though rather under
protest, and, when she had finished it, she remarked—

"I cannot understand, Mr Glencairn, how you
can say it is not melancholy."

"Whatever the air may be," cried Cosmo, "it
touches me with associations—mysterious, perhaps, and strange as it may sound to you—
which have nothing at all to do with sadness,
but with everything that is delightful."

"Not gay, surely?" laughed Esmè.

"No, not gay; but gaiety and happiness have
not much to do with each other. I *must* get
this song.   What is its name?"

"It has no name; it is not published."

"Do you think I can get a copy anyhow?"

"I don't know whether there is a copy in
existence.   There never was more than one."

"How?" cried Cosmo.

"In fact," said Esmè, "I am afraid your approval is making me very conceited. I am
going to make a confession which I have never
made before; but you must keep my secret.   I
am afraid I composed the air myself."

Then, when Cosmo's raptures threatened to
get beyond the bounds of discretion, Esmè
checked him by saying, "So, you see, Mr Glen-

cairn, that, as I composed it for sad words, my feelings as a composer are not gratified when you insist that the air is not melancholy."

"Ah, but I fall back upon my associations! and, since the song is so much to me, will you think me too bold and too troublesome if I ask the composer to make me a copy?"

"Oh," cried Esmè, "I shall be delighted! I am too vain of your approval not to be delighted to copy it for you, if you *really* think it worth having. But you must keep my secret."

Worth having! her song and her secret! Two gifts in one too blessed day! Surely his cup of happiness was running over! For the present, at all events, it was to receive no farther drops of bliss.

"Ah, my dear child, *here* you are. We have been looking for you *everywhere*. I had no idea that you had retired to the music-room for a *duet*, ha, ha!" Cosmo and Esmè now, for the first time, observed that the Pentacle group had disappeared.

"Lord Germistoune is rather in a fuss, dear. He says we ought to be with the people by this time. I think you really *must* come now. He seemed quite to vex himself when he found you were not in the drawing-room with the others;

and of course no one could *divine* where you were. I really think, darling, that you had better come."

"I am quite sure I had, dear Mrs Ravenhall, if papa has begun to fuss. But where are the Professor and Lady Bugles and Miss Milkington? They were here just now."

"Time flies fast on young birthdays, dearest. They have been in the drawing-room for half an hour; and indeed it was from them that I heard you *had* been here, *ever* so long ago—so I came to look, quite as a forlorn hope, I confess. I certainly did not expect to find you *still* here. Well, dear, do let us go. I suppose a gillie's ball is scarcely in your line, Mr Glencairn. Are we to say good night?"

Cosmo laughed rather heartily at Mrs Ravenhall's very palpable ill-humour, knowing so well its cause, and replied—

"By no means. I really don't know, Mrs Ravenhall, why a gillie's ball should not be in my line! I hope, on the contrary, to enjoy it extremely."

Mrs Ravenhall looked unlovingly at him. He met her glance without anxiety; yet she was not the sort of woman one would choose as an enemy.

CHAPTER XXVI.

At the conclusion of our last chapter, Mrs Ravenhall had just broken up, with a considerable display of animation, a *tête-à-tête* between Esmè
and Cosmo, which had been pleasantly progress-
ing in the music-room of Dunerlacht Castle.
When she and they rejoined the rest of the
party in the drawing-room, Lord Germistoune
was not present, but returned shortly afterwards, with many suave apologies for detaining
them all. It would thus almost appear that
Mrs Ravenhall had drawn, to a considerable
extent, on her imagination in describing his
lordship's extreme vexation at Esmè's prolonged
absence. Be that as it may, he certainly made
no unpleasant remarks, but led the way to the
grand function of the evening, in the blandest
of moods.

The visit to the tenantry and gillies, on that
annual occasion, was timed so as to take place

at the conclusion of the supper, which formed part of the evening's entertainment; or, to speak more correctly, the supper did not technically terminate until the visit had been paid, and until, the healths of Esmè and her father having been toasted in their presence, a speech from the latter, acknowledging the compliment, had terminated with a formal invitation to commence the revels; for all the arrangements at Dunerlacht were as liturgical as possible.

The dance was to take place in a spacious barn forming part of the offices, which were close to the house, and had, at one time, been connected with it; the supper was served within the castle, in an ancient stone-hall of imposing dimensions, which had stood, in the olden time, for the baronial hall of banquet. In a corridor in the vicinity of this apartment the party were met by Mr M'Kenzie, the factor—a plethoric, red-faced man, with a very important manner— who, acting as a sort of marshal, formed them into a regular procession; and at the head of this, Lord Germistoune, who loved all sorts of pomp and ritual, placed himself, and gave his arm to Esmè, apologising to the other ladies for this selection, on the ground that the entire proceedings were feudal, and therefore exempt from the social ordinances of modern life. A couple of pipers were then, after a good deal of tugging and jostling, got into their due position in front of his lordship, and, all being ready, Mr M'Kenzie placed himself in front of the minstrelsy, and gave a guttural shriek (echoed from the rear of the column by a miniature view-halloo from Tom Wyedale), and hereupon, in a storm of pipe-music, the procession started. As it entered the hall, another shriek from the factor brought the assembled guests—who, to the number of about a hundred, were ranged round two long tables—to their feet, and the party advanced, with immense solemnity, half-way down the hall, to a low platform, which was opposite the great central fireplace. The pipers marched on round the hall till they faced this *estrade*, when they halted, continuing to play while the party took their places on it. This done, the music was silenced by a signal from the factor, who then cried out, in Gaelic—

"You will give three great strong cheers for his lordship, and three more for Miss Esmè, and three more for the ladies and gentlemen—that is nine altogether; and let there be no mistakes."

"Suas i ! suas i ! suas i ! Hurrah ! &c.
A rithist ! à rithist ! sa rithist ! Hurrah ! &c.
Aon uair eile ! Hurrah ! &c." *

The cheers were loud and hearty, and executed with only a few irregularities on the part of the females, noted by Mr M'Kenzie, and brought home to the offenders by menacing gestures on his part, which seemed to produce a profound impression, the factor being evidently terrible and autocratic, as is the way of those who wield delegated authority. The people were then commanded to sit down, and a silence ensued—a silence of expectation—which lasted so long as to suggest that a hitch had taken place. And this was indeed the case ; for it turned out that Mr M'Haffie, the senior tenant, whose duty it now was to let off the speech of the evening, was so overwhelmed by the terrors of the situation, that he had subsided into a state of partial coma, from which neither the remonstrances of his friends nor divers small "exhibitions" of whisky had been as yet able to recover him.

"Mr M'Haffie !" shouted the factor sternly, but without effect. "Mr M'Haffie!" he repeated

---

* "Up with it ! up with it ! up with it !
Again ! again ! again !
Once more !"

in a still more dangerous voice; and when this also was unavailing, he descended into the body of the house, and, after a good deal of moral, and even physical, hustling, succeeded in getting the old fellow on to his legs, who at last, in a quavering voice, contrived to deliver himself as follows :—

" My lord and Miss Esmè, and my lord and all the ither gentry—and—and Mr M'Kenzie too—and the tinantry and ither folk. Miss Esmè was born to-day; and I do not mean that she was born this ferry day, but some years back: and it was a ferry good day for us that day when Miss Esmè was born " (cheers started by M'Kenzie) ; " and I will say, and we will aal be saying always in this glens, that she is the Flower of this Glens, and that is not a great deal, to be sure; but then I will say more, and say that she is the Flower of aal Scotland, for I suppose there is not annybody annywhere into this whole world, that is like to Miss Esmè, and we aal love her, and we would aal die for her ferry gladly,—and that is true, and iverybody kens that that is true " (loud uninspired cheers). " Miss Esmè, I am drinking to Miss Esmè's health and to her happiness, and may God bless you, Miss Esmè. My lord, his lordship was not born to-day, but it is a good day for us when we see you" (cheers led by factor), "and it is a ferry great honour to me to be his tinantry, and to every one here to be it; and I do not mean the leddies and gentlemen, because they are not the tinantry, but the tinantry; and he has been ferry good to us when the big spates was, and ——" (here a long pause, no doubt of fruitless effort to recall other good deeds on the part of his lordship, interrupted at last by an impatient cheer from Mr M'Kenzie, which sent the old fellow on with a jerk)—" and that was ferry good for us; and I hope, and we aal hope, that his lordship will live for a great long time; and when he is taken away—because I am afraid even his lordship himsel will have to be taken away some day" (pursings of the factor's mouth and elevations of his eyebrows, as though this position were, perhaps, debatable, but in any case offensive)—" I hope that Miss Esmè will take a good nobleman for her husband; and it is ferry certain that aal the nobeelity will be trying to get her, so that she will be able to pick the best out of it, and bring a fine lord to be the lord at Dunerlacht; and I am drinking his lordship's health, and I do not mean Miss Esmè's husband, because it is too soon to be drinking at *him* to-night; but I mean our own lordship that is still alive and here to-night; and I could have said all this readier in the Gaelic, because I am an old man, and have not got anny book-learning, but that would not do, because it is not a genteel kind of langidge to be talking before the leddies and gentry; so I will say no more to them, but I am drinking aal their healths, and Mr M'Kenzie's too. Here is Miss Esmè and his lordship, and the ither leddies and gentry—and Mr M'Kenzie too. Suas i! suas i! suas i! hurrah!" &c. &c. When the cheering had subsided, Lord Germistoune stood forth, looking awfully feudal, and though one might have heard a pin drop, Mr M'Kenzie shouted for silence in a terrible voice, and his lordship began, and spoke words stately and sonorous, being about as intelligible to the majority of his audience as if he had addressed them in Arabic.

"My good tenantry and friends, I am always glad to meet you on these annual occasions, and to receive these evidences of your loyalty and gratitude, which are as creditable to you as they are agreeable to me. It ought to be the wish of the lords of the soil to see their dependants happy. It is the duty of those dependants to be happy and grateful. I am distinctly anxious that my people should be contented and prosperous, and I am glad to say that you, my people, recognising this, show yourselves to be happy, grateful, and obedient. To such seemly relations existing between us, are due many of the blessings enjoyed on these estates. We have to be thankful that Radicalism is unknown in this district; we have to rejoice that the upas-tree of dissent has been uprooted here; we have to congratulate ourselves upon a head of game which shows proudly in the statistics of northern sport; nor is it indifferent to me that the noble red deer descend into the arable parts of the property, with perfect confidence, and in enormous numbers, for this shows that my people welcome their presence, and regard them as a picturesque adjunct to our unrivalled scenery. This is as it ought to be; this is worthy of a humane and enlightened tenantry." (At this point the cheering being a little languid, Mr M'Kenzie descended into the body of the hall and resolved himself into a sort of patrol of observation.) His lordship went on : " The feeling on these estates has always been, that what is good for the landlord is best for the tenant. It is this sentiment which guarantees the harmony of a community like ours, and I am glad to say that it continues unabated. While this is so, the voice of controversy and discontent will not disturb us; and while in other districts we have to deplore the progress of selfishness and disloyalty among the lower classes, here all will be peace, happiness, and contentment.

"My good tenantry, I am touched by the enthusiasm of your personal affection for Miss Douglas and myself. Miss Douglas, I may venture to assure you, is also touched.

"Mr M'Haffie has permitted himself to indulge in certain rather irrelevant speculations as to the duration of my life, and as to certain arrangements for Miss Douglas, into which it may or may not be thought expedient to enter at some future time. I feel bound to say that Mr M'Haffie did not display his usual discretion in making these remarks." (Here the factor "moved into position" near M'Haffie, and opened on him with a battery of indignant and scornful looks.) "I may say that they were wanting in that good taste and reverence which I have a right to expect from the oldest tenant on these estates." (Hear! hear! hear! from the factor.) "Mr M'Haffie ought to remember that my life is in the hands of the Almighty, and that Miss Douglas's future destiny is not a subject which should be approached in a spirit of reckless levity, at any time, and least of all in my presence. Mr M'Haffie has distinctly disappointed me to-night. I am willing, however, to forget the incident, in the expectation that he will problaby refrain from such ebullitions for the future."

There was very little doubt that Mr M'Haffie would. The poor old man, though he but half understood his lordship's tremendous sentences, was horribly aware that he was, so to speak, in the dock; and sat, the picture of conscious guilt, rolling his eyes fearfully from his lord to the factor, who was glaring and puffing at him, like a cobra about to strike.

"And now, my friends," his lordship concluded, "you will do me the favour to go and spend a happy evening in the ball-room which has been prepared for you, and where I shall have the satisfaction of visiting you in a few minutes. Mr M'Kenzie, have the goodness to conduct the tenantry at once to the ball-room."

The factor, with the assistance of some of his subordinates, got the people away with great promptitude, moving them off in single file by successive benches, and when all had departed, Lord Germistoune led his guests round the hall, and explained it to them, architecturally and historically.

Mrs Ravenhall thought it was "quite too delightfully medieval." "I can see," she exclaimed, "the knights in armour ranged around these tables."

"I can distinctly see them," said Lady Bugles.

"How are they looking?" cried Lord Ribston—"pretty jolly?"

"Do sit down, Lord Ribston," murmured Mrs Crock, "and then I shall know exactly how the knights looked."

"Am I your idea of a 'knight of old,' Mrs Crock?" laughed Lord Ribston.

"Don't fish for compliments, Lord Ribston," replied the widow, with a glance which made any sort of fishing superfluous.

"This hall," said Lord Germistoune, "served also as the baronial court of justice, and the 'tree of dule,' or 'hanging tree,' is close at hand; so that my ancestors were able to adjust any little difficulties with their people, very conveniently."

This was duly explained in French to the Marquis, who, however, continued to be very dense about the patriarchal system, and rose freely to Tom Wyedale's suggestion, that what he called the "affaire M'Hafiz" might probably have disastrous consequences for the aged vassal.

Presently the thunder of a cannon shook the castle. "That," said Lord Germistoune, "indicates that the bonfire on Dunerlacht is lighted, and that they are ready for us in the ball-room. Let us go."

They moved out into the courtyard, and halted there to admire the bonfire, which had blazed up into sudden maturity on the neighbouring height, illuminating the woods and the fall with a splendid effect, and casting a weird light upon the castle walls. As they looked, there shot up, in rapid succession, and apparently from the heart of the fire, nineteen rockets of various colours. The sound of distant cheering followed.

"My clock has struck," said Esmè. "I never feel that my birthday has really come, until the rockets have gone up."

"Why is that?" said Ribston.

"Oh, don't you know? Because there is a rocket for each year of my life. So that now all the great world of Glenerlacht knows what a formidable age I have reached. Nineteen! It *does* feel formidable!"

"I had no conception that there was so much difference between our ages," simpered Mrs Crock.

"Are you younger, or older, Mrs Crock?" asked Tom Wyedale, with profound gravity.

"Oh! ever so much older. Five years, at least."

"So that Mrs Crock," Lady Bugles whispered to Lord Ribston—"so that Mrs Crock must have married at eleven, and become a widow at thirteen! Astonishing precocity!"

Whereat Lord Ribston laughed out with hearty frankness, after his kind.

"It is a pretty fancy," said Mrs Ravenhall, "recording your age in this way, darling Esmè; but, by-and-by, you will shrink from such public admissions."

"Some of us here would do so to-night, I am *very* sure," says Mrs Crock, with a withering glance at Lady Bugles, whose whisper she had pretty fairly interpreted by Lord Ribston's mirth.

"If we were honest enough to send up the right number of rockets, which surely *you* would never recommend, dear Mrs Crock," replied her ladyship.

"I have not yet offered my congratulations,"

said Cosmo, who now joined the group. "I hope all the future years of your life will be as bright as the rockets which chronicle them when they are past."

Mrs Ravenhall's sharp ears caught the words. "That is another pretty fancy!" she cried, with a ring of sarcasm in her voice, and closing in upon Esmè.

"Let us now go and see the people," said Lord Germistoune, who had just concluded a long mystifying statement to the Marquis concerning Highland war-beacons and the fiery cross.

"Allons! marchons! partons! marchons!" sang the gay Frenchman.

The pipers struck up "Lord Dunerlacht's March," and a few paces brought them to the scene of the revel, where they were received with the same liturgical salute, under the fugledom of Mr M'Kenzie, "Ni sibh iolach tri uairean—ard agus ladair—airson a mhoralachd," &c.

The barn was large and brilliantly lighted; it had an excellent wooden floor, and the walls were ornamented with such simple yet picturesque decorations as hills and glens afford. Each light, with its sconce, formed the centre of some floral device, in which heather and broom played prominent parts ; and, every here and there, Esmè's monogram was displayed, or the crowned heart of the Douglases, woven in heather, white and purple, and inclosed in wreaths of bog-myrtle—the family badge of Dunerlacht. The company assembled included many who had not been present at the supper —" old established people " from neighbouring estates, and others, who had no feudal title to sit at meat in the baronial hall. In all, not less than two hundred men, women, and children were present, many of them in the Highland garb ; so that, what with the brilliant light, and the colours on the walls, and the bright hues of the tartan, the *coup d'œil* of the room was most striking and effective.

At its upper end there was an *estrade* similar to that in the hall, upon which chairs were arranged, and over it, all the decorations in the room culminated in a tremendous work of art, wherein claymore, dirk, and spear formed a glory round the word " ESMÈ," which blazed colossal in variegated lights.

At the opposite end, three or four fiddlers seemed to cower apologetically, dwarfed, as it were, by the splendid swagger and general efflorescence of a good many brother minstrels of the pipe, who had congregated from near and far, to support Lord Germistoune's piper, old Hector Douglas, a magnificent patriarch, who wore countless medals, trophies won at every " gathering " in Scotland, and wore them with an air which would have done credit to the insignia of the Garter.

The castle party moved up to the *estrade*, Esmè stopping now and then to shake hands with, or say a kind word to, some special favourite; and when they were established in their places, eight pipers, under the leadership of the great Hector, swept round the room with that combination of *élan*, grace, and dignity, distinctive of first-rate pipers, in rapid march. They played the " Dunerlacht Gathering," and after three circuits of the room, wheeled up, with military precision, and, fronting the *estrade*, changed the measure to that of a strathspey. The *morceau* was Hector's own production; it had been inspired by Esmè's twelfth birthday, and was known to more than local fame as " Miss Douglas's Favourite." The music was most spirited, and nothing could be more admirable than its execution, for the performers were together like one man. The effect on the company was electric—literally electric; for, on three-fourths of the people, some kind of spasm was observable,—some twitching of the hands, or movement of the feet, or vibration of the head, obedient to the irresistible rhythm of the pipes. Obviously, but for the awful presence of the magnates, the dance would have burst forth spontaneously all over the room, like the eruption of a volcano. Nor were they unaffected by it. The most benighted Sassenachs on the *estrade* owned its spell.

"It sounds like devil's music," said Tom Wyedale; "but it would make an oyster dance. Hector must be own brother to the 'pied piper of Hamelin.'" The Marquis, who had stopped his ears at the first blast, presently uncorked them, and fell into a state of dangerous ecstasy.

"I must *dance; I must* dance," cried Mrs Ravenhall.

"I *positively* must dance," echoed Lady Bugles, whose desire to ditto Mrs Ravenhall occasionally ran away with her discretion.

"If every one is so impetuous," said Lord Germistoune, "we had better begin at once;" and he made a signal to the pipers, who stopped abruptly, and, scooping the atmosphere away from their faces with their right hands, by way of salute, faced to the right about, and retired down the hall.

"M'Kenzie!" cried his lordship, "Meester M'Ken-see," echoed a score of voices, and the factor came up and got his orders. "We are ready now. Form the sets in the usual way, and when all is prepared bring up Mrs M'Haffie. You will dance opposite Miss Douglas, as usual." Then he explained to the circle that this dance also was hedged in with feudal restrictions, so that no one could participate in it, save himself, his daughter, and immediate dependants. "I am afraid, therefore, ladies, that you will have to repress your ardour for a little." Whereupon Mrs Ravenhall assured him that she had been only joking, and had no thought of dancing, which naturally evoked from Lady Bugles the confession that her dancing project was also but the figment of a sportive fancy. The Marquis, however, announced his firm resolution to assist in the second dance; "À la guerre!" he cried; "comme à la guerre!"

The factor seemed to have got the people into a marvellous state of drill. All eyes followed his movements, and as he turned from the *estrade*, he gave a slight signal. Whereupon, without any hunting for partners or other confusion, twenty sets of four at once fell regularly into their places, and when this was done, the factor lifted up his voice and cried " Mrs M'Haffie !" " Meestriss M'Haffee !" echoed the room. " Maintenant," murmured the Marquis, " l'affaire M'Haffiz va se dénouer !" But he was again cast back into the mists, when a little elderly, respectable-looking woman made her appearance on the floor, and advanced timidly, with downcast eyes, towards the factor. Mr M'Kenzie awaited her, looking very awful and uncompromising, as though it were now his duty to pinion Mrs M'Haffie, before conducting her to "the drop;" and, indeed, the poor woman looked every inch the terror-stricken criminal, her nervous agitation being evidenced by the trembling of her lips, the twitching of her fingers, and the quivering of a perfect forest of wholly unreasonable spikes and pendicles of ribbon which garnished her head-gear. When Mr M'Kenzie had, so to speak, taken Mrs M'Haffie's body over, he conveyed it to the *estrade*, on the edge of which Lord Germistoune stood, looking still more awful and uncompromising than the factor.

" How do you do, Mrs M'Haffie ? how do you do ? " said his lordship. " You will do me

the favour to dance in the reel with me.   Esmè,
we are ready ; M'Kenzie, take your place, and
give the signal to the pipers."

M'Kenzie obeyed and clapped his hands; the
sets sprang to "attention ;" "Miss Esmè's
Favourite" burst from the pipes with tremendous volume; the spell of restraint which hung
over the party vanished as by magic; the
delirium of the dance seized every one at once,
and, in an instant, the room was alive with
rhythmic motion.   There were many fine performers on the floor, and every style had its
representative, from the "orgiastic" dancer,
who danced with all his body, and waved his
arms, and shouted like a bacchanalian, to the
disciple of a chaster school, who kept his body
rigid, and with thoughtful eyes watched the
movements of his own feet, as though each
dainty step and twitch and twirl expressed
some *nuance* of an artistic conception.   But
varied as the styles were, all the dancers were
"together" as far as time went; and what
with this, and the music of eight pipers, and the
thudding and shouting of eighty performers, all
"going like steam," and the swinging and fluttering of kilts and plaids, and the flashing eyes
and animated faces, it would have been difficult

to find a scene more infectiously gay and exhilarating. The ladies and gentlemen were all enthusiastic, and on the *estrade* there were cries of " Bravo ! " and little view-halloos, and clappings of hands, responsive to the tumult of the dancers.

The Marquis gradually worked himself into a state of terrific excitement, and was for beginning at once.

" Maintenant j'y suis ! " he cried. " Madame de Bugells—Miladi Bugells! il faut commencer ! allons donc ! allons ! commençons ! " And he would have haled her ladyship to the floor had she not beaten him off with her fan. In front of the *estrade* Lord Germistoune's set had its station, and notwithstanding that Esmè's fairy form adorned it, no dispassionate observer could have beheld it with gravity. Lord Germistoune, stiff as a ramrod, his left hand on his left haunch, his right perpendicularly aloft in the air, in the attitude of a fakir under a vow, shuffled his feet about, with no reference to the music, but like, as the Scotch saying is, " a hen on a het girdle ; " while, opposite to him, Mrs M'Haffie, with her gown " kilted " so as to afford a liberal view of a pair of white woollen pasterns, and all the sensitive paraphernalia of her head in the wildest tumult, let loose her nervous excitement in a perfect cataract of nimble steps, astounding in a person of her years and demeanour. On the other side, Esmè's ethereal movements were in fine contrast to the performances of Mr M'Kenzie, who danced in the most apoplectic manner, with both his arms held straight above his head, his eyes fixed and protruding, and his feet hammering away without variation of step, like the feet of a man going through the treadmill at "the double."

The strathspey turned into the reel proper, and, with the change, the spirit of the dance became, as usual, faster and more furious; and when his lordship shouted for the " Hoolichan," and the music changed to that most frenzied of all the measures, it seemed as though every one had suddenly acquired a new lease of fire and vigour. "Hoolichan ! Hoolichan !" shouted the dancers. "Ouragan ! Ouragan !" shrieked the Marquis; and, no longer able to restrain his ardour, he dived into the very centre of Lord Germistoune's set, and, reckless of the feudal system, cut in between him and Mrs M'Haffie, whose performances had excited his liveliest admiration. "À moi, Madame M'Haffiz !" he cried; "à moi ! Ouragan ! Ouragan!" and proceeded to execute, in front of the bewildered woman, a frantic combination of the "Tarantella," "Cancan," and other dances of ecstasy. There was a shout of laughter on the dais. Lord Germistoune halted, looking black as thunder. "M. le Marquis!" he cried, sternly. "Ha! ha! ha! Ouragan! Ouragan!" screamed the Marquis; and seizing Mrs M'Haffie, in the turning figure, swung her off her feet, and round and round and round, till her white woollen extremities colliding frankly with his lordship's legs, all but levelled that awful potentate with the floor. "M'Kenzie! M'Kenzie!" cried his lordship, with a gesture of rage and despair. Whereupon M'Kenzie shouted and waved to the pipers, and, with the sudden collapse of a tropical hurricane, the hurly-burly closed.

Lord Germistoune, ascending gloomily to the dais, was met with a torrent of congratulations. The dance had been either "soul-stirring" or "fetching" to the last degree; while his lordship's share in the transaction had, of course, been worthy of himself and of a great nation.

"But I think," said Ribston, who had no reverence—not even for Lord Germistoune, "the Marquis has the highest score." The Marquis could, at this moment, be seen in the distance, adding to his score by gallantly kissing Mrs M'Haffie's hand in the way of adieu.

"The Marquis," said his lordship, severely, "has certainly made himself conspicuous; but I should be sorry to hazard a repetition of his buffoonery, so I think it will be discreet if we now withdraw, and leave the people to themselves. M'Kenzie, we are going."

Way was at once made, the pipers formed, the march struck up, and the party moved out of the hall, under another salute of "three great strong cheers." In so far, however, as the repression of the Marquis's buffoonery was concerned, the move was not a success, for neither he nor Tom Wyedale retired with "the quality," but continued with the proletariat till far into the night, winning golden opinions, especially the Marquis, who, in peforming "The Flowers of Edinburgh," twice achieved the feat of throwing his right leg clean over Mrs M'Haffie's head, without disturbing a single pinnacle of the mysterious edifice which crowned it, and added about a foot or so to her legitimate stature.

"He's an awfu' man, yon!" was invariably the remark of Mrs M'Haffie for several years after, when this ball was alluded to.

CHAPTER XXVII.

THE abbreviation of the state visit to the people's ball left some part of the evening still to be disposed of, and when the party returned to the drawing-room, dancing was proposed. Mrs Ravenhall, always obliging, and an indefatigable player of dance-music, volunteered for the piano, and in a few minutes eight or nine couples were floating round the room in the dreamy rapture of the valse.

Cosmo, full of courage, would have entered the lists for Esmè's partnership, but Lord Ribston was too quick for him, and bore her off triumphantly just as he approached. He fell back, therefore, upon Mrs Crock, the only disengaged alternative being Lady Bugles, whose complex mechanism was not the sort of thing to involve one's self with unnecessarily.

"Only for a turn or two, of course," said Mrs Crock; "it is the fun of an impromptu that there are no formal partnerships, but that every one keeps changing about continually." Her eye rested upon Esmè and Lord Ribston as she spoke; and Cosmo, with *his* eye on the same couple, said that he quite understood the theory, inwardly hoping to carry it into practice with the smallest possible delay. Then he took Mrs Crock for a circuit of the room. She danced badly, and was a little cross, and inclined, as is the wont of bad dancers, to blame her partner, and soon intimated to Cosmo that she thought the moment had arrived for a change, which he promptly admitted, and left her gazing, with her eyes full of vain expectation, across the room to Lord Ribston. Cosmo had a turn or two with Miss Snapsley, and one with Miss Milkington, and one with another damsel; and still Lord Ribston monopolised Esmè, either dancing, or sitting apart, with her, in apparently confidential intercourse—still doing so, although the dancing had gone on so long that Mrs Ravenhall had already had an interval of rest. Mrs Crock and Cosmo were both afflicted; a common sorrow drew them together; or, to speak more correctly, Mrs Crock having no one else to dance with, signalled to Cosmo, and he went to her.

" Pray, give me another turn," she said ; "none of these wretches will look at me."

There was a straightforwardness about this which was irresistible, and Cosmo complied. When they stopped, his partner said, " I never saw anything like this before ; they are all as faithful to each other as if they were under a vow to dance with no one else. It spoils all the fun."

Cosmo fully sympathised with her complaint, though, as a matter of fact, the system of change, except in so far as Esmè and Lord Ribston were concerned, was carried out very regularly. They had another turn. At its conclusion, the situation was unaltered. Mrs Crock glared at the offending couple, and then said, with considerable venom, " Miss Douglas really ought to know better. It is her part to set the example. No doubt her present temptation *is* great ; still a girl in her position ought to know better. It is against all etiquette monopolising one man in this sort of way."

Cosmo felt that it was against all etiquette, monopolising one *woman* in this sort of way, but practically they were agreed.

" We really ought to break up that *tête-à-tête*," said the widow. " Let us go and look at them, and make them ashamed of themselves."

Cosmo made no objection, and they went and looked. The manœuvre was, however, on the whole, abortive. The couple were not ashamed; and though Mrs Crock took her partner twice past them, and delivered a broadside of meaning glances on each occasion, the only effect produced was that Ribston, on receiving the second volley, said, sleepily, "The widow looks as if she were on the war-path, don't she? She'll have her knife into some one soon, I expect."

Mrs Crock then changed her tactics. "After all," she said, "I daresay Miss Douglas is not to blame. I suppose she is too unsophisticated to know how to get away from Lord Ribston; and he is so lazy he will sit still for hours wherever he is planted. I do think it would be a kindness to her if you were to go and ask her to dance; besides, it will take the drag off the evening: it *is* dragging dismally now; don't you think so?"

Cosmo entirely agreed with her, and did as she suggested.

"Miss Douglas," he said, presenting himself in front of the couple, "will you have a turn with me now?"

"No, no, no!" cried Lord Ribston; "Miss

Douglas is engaged to me — is dancing with me."

"Has been," said Cosmo, laughing; "and I am told that there *are* no engagements, and that every one dances promiscuously with every one, change and change about; I have twice received my *congé* on this principle, and if I have been taken back, I quite felt that it was as a *pis aller*. The fact is humbling; still I am entitled to use it in my favour now."

"No, no!" cried Ribston, rather hotly; "my good sir, one don't argufy about such things. It's a matter of choice."

"Well, that is true, of course," said Cosmo; "and as I could hardly expect you to choose to give Miss Douglas up, I lay the matter before her. May I have one turn, Miss Douglas? Think," he added, laughing, "of Mrs Crock's disgust, if I have to inflict myself a third time upon her."

"I shall be delighted," said Esmè, rising. Whereupon Lord Ribston, unaccustomed to be thwarted, glared furiously at Cosmo, muttered something to the discredit of Mrs Crock, and, without so much as a glance at that lady, retired to sulk over a book at the other end of the room.

And then Cosmo, dancing with Esmè, had his first true experience of the poetry of motion, seeming to glide through some rare medium of existence and movement, apart from this gross earth, suspended above it, in an atmosphere of melody.

. . . . . .

After three circuits of the long room they stopped, and Cosmo, without speaking, looked into Esmè's eyes. There was no tumult or trouble in his gaze, only an expression of rapt serenity and love and happiness, which gave great beauty to his always noble but often too sombre face. Esmè did not turn away her eyes, in which there was a look of half-dreamy bewilderment and inquiry.

"Heavenly !" Still looking into her eyes, Cosmo uttered the word, so that, unconsciously perhaps to himself, it had the force of a double significance. Esmè made no reply for a moment; then she hurriedly withdrew her gaze, looked down, and said, with a manifest effort to return to the commonplace—

"Yes; I delight in the 'Doctrinen;' and does not Mrs Ravenhall play charmingly ?"

"Charmingly !" echoed Cosmo; and then there was an abrupt and lengthened pause in

the conversation. Presently the music changed.
Mrs Ravenhall now played the ' Geliebt und
Verloren,' and, at a certain passage of thrilling
pathos, which all who know that exquisite valse
will at once identify, Esmè and Cosmo turned to
each other, as if by a mutual instinct, and, without any words, again floated away together into
the mystical realms of beatified reverie.

.   .   .   .   .   .

They came back to the cold world of fact;
again, but intensified, there were the same
phenomena—looks of rapture meeting looks of
shy bewilderment, meaningless phrases merging
in silences full of meaning; all these things being
the outward and visible signs either of tumultuous thoughts, vague and indefinable as yet,
or of tumultuous thoughts fully comprehended,
but as yet unutterable. Mrs Ravenhall, playing
with her back towards the dancers, little knew
what spells she was helping to weave with her
deft fingers, little recked what irony for herself
there was in every note of the music which she
made.

She had looked round once and seen Esmè
and Cosmo dancing together; she had looked
round a second time, and observed them standing in apparently harmless silence; but, on the

third investigation, she beheld them at the moment of their arrival from dream-land, and detected the perfectly frank revelation, which to any interested on-looker could not have failed to be discernible in Cosmo's face. And then the plaint of the "Geliebt und Verloren" came to a sudden and rather spasmodic termination.

"Esmè!" cried Mrs Ravenhall, "I am *so* sorry to stop, but my right wrist is dreadfully cramped. Would you get some kind person to take my place? or will you take it yourself, dear, for a little? So sorry!"

Whereupon Esmè ran to the piano with an alacrity which rather pained Cosmo, and began to play with an energy that had something feverish in it. And now, if Cosmo had been discreet, he would probably have paid Mrs Ravenhall the cheap compliment of asking her to dance; or similarly mollified Mrs Crock, who, like a lioness bereft of her cub, was furious with everybody and everything; or even harnessed himself to the risky complexities of Lady Bugles; or, in fact, done anything rather than what he did—which was to go and stand at the piano and look at the fair performer, not wisely, but too well. For Mrs Ravenhall, sitting with the two other malcontents, saw it all, and pointed it out to them, and was ferociously merry at the expense of "The Foundling," and said epigrammatic things about him, which were too good not to be repeated; and, in short, being now thoroughly convinced that Cosmo meant mischief, and might be mischievous, began seriously to mobilise her forces of reprisal.

There was a pause in the music, and a conversation took place at the piano which *looked*, in the distance, far more serious than it sounded —and another pause, similarly occupied; and at last Mrs Ravenhall could stand it no longer.

"It is dreadfully late, I am sure," she exclaimed; "and it is quite evident that *that* man has no intention of going." So saying, she rose and went over to Lord Germistoune—who had just sustained a series of crushing defeats at "Gobang" from Dr Pentacle, his pupil in the game, and was rather cross in consequence— and said that it was dreadfully late, and that she, being much fatigued, would now say good night, and slip away, without a word to the others, so as not to disturb the revels. Lord Germistoune detested (as she knew) late hours, and he at once rose and said it was time for them all to be in bed.

"But," objected Mrs Ravenhall, "Mr Glencairn has not gone yet; and indeed he looks as if he had *very* little inclination to go."

"I suppose," said Lord Germistoune, "he can take a hint. Esmè! Esmè! I think, my dear, that will be enough of music. Every one is tired, and it is time for so many fair ladies with bright complexions to be in bed."

Upon this there was a general move; and Cosmo, at once making his adieus to Esmè, said hurriedly, and in a low voice—

"I have to thank you for the happiest evening in my life. You will not forget the song?"

"No. I will copy it for you to-morrow."

"And when may I hope to get it?"

"The next time you come here."

"I am afraid I am dreadfully impatient. When may I come?"

"Whenever you please, Mr Glencairn, of course. The song will be copied to-morrow morning."

"Good night; and I wish," he murmured, "I had words to thank you with." Then he turned away, concentrating, in one long look, all his gratitude and love and worship. The rest of his adieus were quickly made to a cold or hostile company, and he left the room accompanied by Lord Germistoune, who went, less

with the air of a host performing a hospitable
courtesy, than of a man uncertain of the honesty of his departing guest.

"I thought," said Mrs Ravenhall, rubbing her
hands and beaming on the company, as if in
congratulation on their relief from so terrible an
incubus — " I thought that *dreadful* man was
never going !"

"I confess I feared the stupid creature was
going to be a fixture," echoed Lady Bugles.

"And neither a useful nor an ornamental
one," added Mrs Crock ; " he talks like a stick,
and dances like a poker."

"A fellow of that sort is not meant to dance,"
said Lord Ribston ; " and he certainly doesn't
seem to know when he's in the way."

This sudden attack upon one absent—upon
one so quiet and inoffensive to others, so gentle
and chivalrous in manner (she put it thus) to
herself, so superior to these small people—she
felt at the moment, that they were very very
small—who were sneering at him, roused Esmè's
generous indignation so that her colour rose, and
there was a flash of dangerous light in her eyes.
Mrs Ravenhall continued the attack. "I would
have saved you from him if I could, dear Esmè,
but I really could not offer to take the piano

again, because of my stupid wrist. I felt for you, however, I assure you; I did, indeed — deeply; so did Lady Bugles."

"Deeply, deeply," moaned Lady Bugles. Whereupon all the conventionals sustained a shock to their moral and nervous systems, for Esmè answered, with much spirit—

"I am afraid you have been sadly wasting your compassion, Mrs Ravenhall. I was in no sort of distress, I assure you. Mr Glencairn is by far the best dancer I ever danced with in my life, to begin with; and *I* certainly think him the last person I ever met with who could be called stupid. Of course that may be because I am stupid myself. Still I think so; so I have no right to your compassion."

Mrs Ravenhall's countenance changed. Here she found herself, for the first time, confronted with those characteristics in Esmè of which, as she had told Tom in the early days of their association, she feared that she beheld the symptoms—her straightforwardness and self-reliance and independence of conventional considerations, when these interfered with what she thought was just and generous and true. Mrs Ravenhall's sense of the proprieties was, of course, terribly lacerated by what she inwardly called

" this exhibition ;" but she was far more affected
to find that she had made a grave tactical
blunder.

" Darling Esmè !" she replied, in cooing tones
of conciliation, " I *really* thought you looked
dismally bored ; but now that I know I was
mistaken, I am penitent for having, under a
misapprehension, depreciated your *new protégé*."
This little stab was also dealt with in the same
thorough style.

" Thanks, Mrs Ravenhall — I am sure you
are ; for I am sure you know me well enough to
know that I do not like to hear absent friends
run down—any more than you would yourself."

And now, Lord Germistoune returning, the
party broke up, and the ladies went to bed.

But Mrs Ravenhall entered Esmè's room with
her, and tried to retrieve the error in her tactics
by another little demonstration against Cosmo.

" You are not vexed with me, my love ?" she
said, sweetly.

" No, dear Mrs Ravenhall ; how can you think
so ? If I had any cause to be so, you have made
the *amende*."

Then they embraced.

" You see, darling," resumed Mrs Ravenhall, " I
naturally thought you must be bored with *him*."

"Why '*naturally*,' Mrs Ravenhall?"

"Well, *unnaturally*, dear," laughed Mrs Ravenhall, with another kiss; "and perhaps—though, of course, *here* it does not matter in the least, not in the very least—I was just a little annoyed to see you so conspicuous with so hopeless an ineligible,—so hopeless that I *need not*, of course, have worried myself, if I had only reflected; but if I spoke sharply of him, it was only out of my love for you. I am a silly old goose; but it's your own fault for being so lovable. Now, darling, good night."

"But what do you mean by 'conspicuous,' Mrs Ravenhall? I don't understand how one is to avoid being so, if it is 'conspicuous' to take two or three turns of a valse with one gentleman in the drawing-room of one's own home. At all events, I can't see that, if that sort of thing does make one conspicuous, it can do one any harm. I am sure I did the same thing with Mr Wyedale the other night, and to-night with Lord Ribston. Was I conspicuous with them, too? How often ought one to change partners so as to avoid this dreadful calamity?"

"The lady doth protest too much, methinks,"

thought Mrs Ravenhall; but she had shot her

bolt about Cosmo's ineligibility, which was all she intended, so she cried gaily, "You shall dance for a hundred or a thousand turns, darling, with one man and with the same man if you please, and I shall always vow that you are right. I had no idea that you could take things *au sérieux* like this, you silly child. Now I must go to bed;" and, with another silencing embrace, she escaped in flight from further discussion.

CHAPTER XXVIII.

If Esmè had been brought up with the advantages which so many girls conventionally educated enjoy—that is to say, of being surrounded by female mentors for ever (and often prematurely) inculcating the precepts of that diplomacy which concerns itself about the relations between the sexes,—for ever and often prematurely harping upon matrimony in all the ramifications of that important subject,—Mrs Ravenhall would not, perhaps, have had so much cause to complain of Esmè's lovableness, and Esmè herself would have been saved from many of the confusions in which she now found herself involved. For, in addition to the fine arts of "drawing on," "discouraging," "holding in suspense," and otherwise "playing" the suitor, in addition to a correct appreciation of the matrimonial tables of weights and measures, she would have had, codified, so to speak, and at her fingers' ends, the various symptoms, in all their *nuances,* which bespeak the presence of the tender passion. But Lord Germistoune was not a likely source from whence to derive lore of this sort, nor yet was the admirable lady who had brought her up from her earliest years, and who, in educating her young charge, had acted on the old-world principle that it was her duty to develop a rational being, rather than to construct a marrying automaton. And thus it befell that the events of to-day and yesterday, and a world of new emotions and problems arising from them, suddenly confronting this inexperienced young heart, overwhelmed it with a bewilderment inconceivable, perhaps, and certainly laughable, to girls her juniors in age, but moulded, which Esmè certainly was not, "to the fashion of these times."

Cosmo had interested her from the very first; so much will be remembered. There was something unusual about him, and his ways of life and thought, and even in his manner, which touched her imagination and her sense of the romantic. Then the strange revelation of his troubles had, in the very confession of his weakness, not only disclosed the nobleness of his aspirations, but thrown a bridge of sympathy over the distance which separated her from him, intellectually, as she believed. Nor could it fail to touch her that this man, whose somewhat proud reserve kept him apart from others, had unbent for *her;* that he had given to her the secret of his moral conflicts, and thereby interpreted to her much in him that was enigmatical, perhaps, to every one else. She had felt much interest in him during the brief period of their first acquaintanceship; she had constantly remembered him with interest during their separation, and perhaps it was not merely on Cosmo's part that the feeling of a *rapport* existing between them had grown in the interval. She was very happy to meet him again; but since they had met — in these two short days — what had happened to make him no longer the object of a tranquil, if of a warm, interest? This perplexed her. She did not consciously put the question to herself, but the perplexity which it represented was there. What had happened? What *had* happened was, that Cosmo had thrown into evidence before her the full volume of his unspoken passion; that, without restraint, he had expressed it in every look, and implied it in every tone, and, even involuntarily, conveyed its declaration through the mysterious medium of magnetic sympathy. What *had* happened and what *was* happening was naturally producing a change in the character of the interest which she felt for Cosmo Glencairn. But she was perplexed, knowing not the signs and symbols of these strange matters. She tried to formulate her impressions and her feelings. " He likes me very much, and I am glad that he likes me. I am sure that he likes me, because he looks as if he were very happy to be with me. He said that my song had been always ringing in his ears, and that he had thought of me very often. He thanked me for the happiest evening of his life. But why should he like me ? and why should he have been so happy? I only sang him that trifling little song. Could *that* make him happy? But I am sure that he likes me, and I am very happy that he likes me. And I am sure that I like him; and I am glad that I said he was my friend—because he *is* my friend,—and defended him against all these ill-natured people. What right had they to speak of him so ? They don't know what he is. If they only knew what I know of him, they could not speak so. I wonder why he likes me more than he did at

Como !—if he *does* like me more, and I think he does. Yet it is only two days ! And I wonder why I seem to know him so much better, and to like him more, I think — I *do* think—much more—and that is so strange, because it is only two days ! And I wonder if he likes many other people *much !* And—but surely I have thought enough about him."

"I wonder, and I wonder, and I wonder !"— to this refrain the innocent young heart explored a labyrinth without a clue; and through all her wonderings, the eyes of Cosmo haunted her bewilderingly, and his sweet, grave smile seemed to lead her on; and, though the eyes wore not the look of a *friend*, and though that sweet smile was not *friendship's* smile, yet was the ever-recurring conclusion of her guileless reverie only this, " I am sure that he likes me very much, and I am sure that I like him. And I wonder why it seems so strange to-night !" It will be seen that she was as ignorant of the philosophy of love, as she was unlettered in the science of matrimony; and that " ineligibles," " conspicuousness," and so forth, were terms of a language which had little meaning for her ear.

Was Cosmo acting heroically ? Was he true

to himself ?—to his principles ?—to his resolution ?   Let us remember that he had decided that the only condition on which any sort of hope of winning Esmè was admissible—even to himself—was the achievement of personal distinction so complete as to obliterate the stigma on his birth, which seemed at present to place a barrier between her and him.   How, then, could he reconcile with this his presence here ? or, if that were explained away, how could he reconcile with it his demeanour towards her, whom his every look and tone wooed with the fervour of a master-passion ? It must be admitted that he could not reconcile these things.   It must be further owned that he did not attempt to reconcile them. The casuistry of love had gradually levelled his pedestal, till now, heroic no more, but altogether human, he moved only in obedience to the dictates of the divine delirium, and not to those of reason.   The nearest approach to a compromise with his own resolve which he had made was this—and he soon saw and was ashamed of its selfishness, — that if, by any means short of an *éclaircissement*, he could assure himself of Esmè's love, then he would be satisfied ; then he would go silently away, and, strong in this inspiring certainty, achieve that renown whose alchemy, transmuting baseness to nobility, should entitle him to approach her worthily. But, when this was condemned, he sought no substitute; and though he was now following his father's advice, he did so unconsciously, abandoning himself upon no principle whatever to the swift rushing current of delight, concentrated on the present, reckless of the future, fearless of all the catastrophes to which he might be gliding.

Alas! there is no defence for him, although Esmè's surpassing charms might perhaps be admitted as extenuating circumstances of special force; no defence, save that contained in the trite old aphorism (old, probably, as Love itself) which levels the hero with the hind, and confounds the simple with the sage — "Love conquers all."

CHAPTER XXIX.

OLD DAVIDSON would have required the patience of Job to stand the various disappointments to which Cosmo subjected him. The morning after the ball at Dunerlacht was as fine as its two predecessors, and at last, the keeper thought, there would be an end of "nonsense" and half-measures. He had quite decided in his own mind that this morning he would take his master over one of the wilder and more distant beats, which would be less easily and productively shot after "the weather broke"—that contingency which hangs like a nightmare over Scotch keepers. Deep, then, was his disgust when, in reply to a suggestive message which he sent up to Cosmo's bedroom, and by which he craved to know "whether the Captain would take Craig-Rona that day, or content himself with the Kaims," he was informed that the Captain, for his content, required neither the one nor the other, nor *any* other beat, not being minded to go out at all that day. Davidson turned his face heavenwards, and raised both his arms high in the air, as if calling heaven to witness that he washed his hands of this squanderer of its bounty. " Maist notawrious ! " were his only words, as he went sadly away.

The idea of shooting had never crossed Cosmo's mind, because he assured himself that it was absolutely necessary that he should call at Dunerlacht that day, as the merest matter of etiquette ; but, independently of that, the song was to be ready that morning, and if he did not reclaim it at the earliest opportunity, would not his indifference be justly regarded as brutal ? There was but one obvious answer to this ; and, with difficulty restraining his impatience till something like the canonical hours of visitation had arrived, he went. He went on foot, and he had a delightful walk, albeit moving at speed ; for, buoyed up with blessed anticipations, he trod upon air, and beheld the outer world by a beautifying inner light which no cloud veiled.

The door is reached ; the bell is rung ; there appears to be a delay of about six calendar months; and at last a leisurely footman, who has obviously been disturbed at a meal, and is still in the act of mastication, appears. The insensate being seems to be a little aggrieved, and almost to take a malicious pleasure in delivering his overwhelming announcement. Not at home! No one : not even Lord Germistoune; not even Mrs Ravenhall, for whom actually, in his desperation, Cosmo asks! Most of the gentlemen have gone shooting, the rest, with *all* the ladies, have gone for a picnic.

" A picnic !—what! another picnic!" cried Cosmo, in a tone of such frank disapprobation, that it brought the rudiments of a grin to the footman's face; and after trying that official's patience by remaining for some time silent and motionless, he woke up, and saying that he would not leave cards, but return to-morrow, went away, moving with a crushed and bewildered air, in strange contrast to the energy and eagerness of his arrival. Slowly and purposeless he loitered down the glen. The progress of his life was virtually arrested for twenty-four hours. The only event worthy of the name, or which could advance his history by ever so short a stage, was postponed for that time, and the interval—that long and weary

interval—must be passed in a feverish middle
state, between dream-life and waking consciousness, monotonous but without repose,—monotonous from the domination of one idea, but
of an idea whose fierce activity reigned in
perpetual tumult. Slowly he went down the
glen, held by love's attraction within sight of
Esmè's home; lingering in the scene upon
which her beautiful eyes constantly rested;
making oracles of the hills and woods which had
mingled with her thoughts; seeking association
with her in every leaf and flower, and indulging
in all the wild and picturesque fantasies of a
poet-lover's pantheism.

Hours passed, and still he lingered—now
down by the river, now up among the woods.
At last, descending to the highroad, where it
was in the middle of an ascent, he heard the
distant sound of wheels, and turning, beheld a
large carriage slowly ascending towards him.
It was a brake, full of people, and blossoming
with the bright hues of ladies' hats and parasols.
There could be no doubt that this was the
Dunerlacht party, nor any that they would be
up with him in about three minutes—a limited
allowance of time wherein to recover one's
senses, after a descent from the visionary world;

and flight to the thickets was his first impulse.

But *she* must be of the company, so that flight was impossible; and feeling that it would not do to be found mooning and stationary on the highroad, he compromised the matter by turning back in the direction of the castle.

They gained on him; the sound of many voices grew more and more distinct; the breathing of the horses was audible above the beating of his heart; he drew aside; they were abreast; he looked round. And first he saw Lord Ribston, who took no notice of him; and then Mrs Ravenhall, who sweetly and silently bowed to him; and then—a lowered parasol; and then Lord Germistoune, who rolled out his usual formula, "How do you do, sir?—how do you do?" and this attracted the attention of all, and compelled the elevation of the parasol and the disclosure of Esmè's beautiful face, made all the more beautiful by a vivid blush, which it seems almost brutal to chronicle, but which, as a matter of fact, had been taking place for some little time, behind the parasol, indeed from the moment when her eyes (before all other eyes) had caught sight of Cosmo. He, keeping pace with the carriage, saluted the party comprehensively; and then, crossing to Esmè's side, made special inquiries as to her condition after the ball, also as to that of "the eternal Mrs Ravenhall," who sat beside her—all in orthodox form, astonishing in a man whose thoughts were the merest chaos.

"I called at the castle this forenoon," he said, after walking along for a little in silence; "but as I hope to do so again to-morrow, I did not leave my card."

"We shall be at home to-morrow, I think," said Esmè, "though most of the gentlemen will be, of course, on the hill."

"You cannot be such a devotee to sport as your friend Tom, Mr Glencairn. Two days away from the hill in succession! that sounds very lukewarm—quite *surprisingly* so!" said Mrs Ravenhall.

"Oh, I have had so much of it in my time —I am no longer a ravenous sportsman; but my keeper quite agrees with you, Mrs Raven-hall; he thinks me a monster of insensibility. By the by, would you kindly say to Tom that, if he cares to go, and will go and shoot at Finmore to - morrow, I shall be very much obliged to him. If some one doesn't shoot there, I don't know what will happen to old

Davidson: I believe he will shoot *himself*. But if Tom can go, he will be appeased. Tom is a great hero of his."

"It can't be a stratagem," thought Mrs Ravenhall; "for that wretch" (Tom had become "that wretch" since "the Twelfth") "could make no one take the trouble to scheme against him." Then she said aloud, "I will give him your message," speaking glumly, feeling how hard it was that this man should come and take so naturally to the part which all her skill and tactics could not get Tom to play with the slightest life or continuity.

"I suppose," she continued, "Tom is to go to your lodge? I suppose you will shoot the first part of the day with him?"

"Unfortunately," said Cosmo, "I expect that a friend will probably arrive from town to-morrow ‚forenoon, and I must be at home to receive him. If he should arrive, Miss Douglas, may I bring him over with me to the castle? He has not been in Scotland before, and I should like particularly to show him so very fine a specimen of the old Scotch architecture. He will be greatly interested in it."

"Pray bring him," said Esmè; "and won't you come to luncheon?"

"Thanks, I shall be delighted, if he arrives in time."

"And then," she said, "he can see all our lions outside and in. Papa," she continued, turning to her father, who always contrived to abstract himself aggressively, by alien conversation or otherwise, from any sort of intercourse with Cosmo — "papa, Mr Glencairn is perhaps going to bring a friend who is much interested in architecture" (Phil Denwick!) "to see the castle to-morrow, and perhaps they will be able to come to lunch. Shall you be at home?"

"You know, my dear, it is impossible for me, short of a definite engagement, to say that I shall certainly be at luncheon on any given day; but if Mr Glencairn does us the favour to visit the castle with his friend, there will be luncheon for him whether I am at home or not."

And with this somewhat ungracious ratification, delivered without a look at Cosmo, the summit of the ascent was reached, the horses broke into a trot, and Cosmo was again alone with the music of her "good-bye" ringing in his ears, and the ineffable witchery of her smile thrilling in every fibre of his heart.

"So much for the FOUNDLING!" said Mrs

Crock; whereat there was boisterous merriment, all over the party.

"Who?" said Lord Germistoune.

"The Foundling," repeated Mrs Crock, amid renewed mirth.

"And may I ask who the Foundling is?" said his lordship.

"That man we have just left behind. He still looks a little lost, doesn't he?"

"As if he would be the better of being found over again? Eh? ha! ha! ha!" cried Lord Ribston.

"But why do you call him 'the Foundling?'" asked Lord Germistoune.

"I? Oh, I don't know; because he is one, I suppose. Didn't some one say so?" said Mrs Crock.

"Mrs Ravenhall knew the people who found him, I believe," said Lady Bugles.

"My dear Lady Bugles, how *can* you say so?" said Mrs Ravenhall, aghast at being involved so far beyond what her diplomacy contemplated.

"In the cart, you know," suggested Lady Bugles; but this hazy *aide-mémoire* threw a fresh mist over the subject; for Lord Germistoune cried out, impatiently—

"Yes, yes; but *who* found him in the cart? that's what I want to know."

"Mrs Ravenhall——" began Lady Bugles; and the loud laughter of the whole party stopped the inquiry for a time.

"Indeed I didn't," laughed Mrs Ravenhall; "but I said—and it just shows how foolish one is to say things—that I *fancied* I had heard that there *was* a *sort* of suspicion, that there *was* some *little* mystery about Mr Glencairn's birth. If I used the word 'foundling,' it could, of course, have only been as a joke, for I know nothing about it."

"Hum!" said Lord Germistoune, delighted to scent something to Cosmo's disadvantage; "this is mysterious; you don't know what his origin is?"

"No," said Mrs Ravenhall; "I cannot say that I do."

"And your brother does not know?"

"I should suppose not."

"Oh, then, he may be a foundling after all. There is no smoke without fire. Now, Mrs Ravenhall, does it not occur to you that there is a slight recklessness in all this, on your brother's part—I think I may say, an unpardonable recklessness—in introducing, right and left, a

man he knows nothing of? Wyedale should
not have done this. I must speak to him about
it. I am distinctly disappointed in Wyedale."

"But, dear Lord Germistoune," said Mrs
Ravenhall, beginning to get alarmed, "*did*
Tom introduce him to you?"

"I—I apprehend so. Well, let me recollect;
perhaps not precisely, but practically, your brother was his voucher. Now Wyedale takes upon
himself a heavy responsibility. Wyedale doesn't
know what he may be answering for. At this
rate Wyedale may find himself standing sponsor
for crime, even,—what?"

But now the matter was getting much too
serious, and Mrs Ravenhall was obliged absolutely to dispel the mist, as far as in her lay,
not only for Tom's sake, but for her own, as the
launcher of the unfortunate epithet. "My dear
Lord Germistoune," she said, "you are altogether
mistaken; Tom and Mr Glencairn have been
friends since their childhood—at school, at col-
lege, and in society. Mr Glencairn is perfectly
well known in society. He has been in the army;
he is received everywhere. His uncle, Colonel
Wildgrave, was extremely well known in London. This nephew of his inherited his fortune
and his social position. You are really taking

the matter far, far too much *au grand sérieux;* and all because I can't say that I know Mr Glencairn's origin; or rather, because of this comical mistake of Lady Bugles."

There was really nothing to be said after this; but Lord Germistoune had taken kindly to the "foundling" theory, and parted with it unwillingly. Besides which, when he had boiled up to the pitch of the didactic and the awful, he could not be expected to boil down again all in a moment. He remarked, therefore, that that was, no doubt, all very satisfactory and very true, so far; but, for his part, he thought Wyedale was bound "to probe the mystery,"—for he adhered tenaciously to the existence of a mystery. Then, *apropos,* he related an anecdote of a ticket-of-leave man, who had been recently going about in London society as a foreign nobleman. "So," he concluded (and thus perversely suggesting a possible connection between Cosmo and the ticket-of-leave class), "we can never be too careful. I shall certainly speak to Wyedale."

This he accordingly did, in the drawing-room, before dinner.

"I wish, Wyedale, to ask you something."

"Not a conundrum, my lord, I hope?" said Tom, gaily.

"Not a conundrum," said his lordship, in a tone which discouraged levity, "though it concerns what appears to be somewhat enigmatical. There was a good deal of discussion to-day, in the carriage, about your friend Mr Glencairn, and my curiosity is piqued about him. Ahem! Lady Bugles and Mrs Crock appeared to have the impression that he was—ahem!—a foundling."

Here Tom burst into an extravagant fit of laughter, which could not be quenched for some time, and during which Lord Germistoune began to stiffen palpably about the neck, and to look dangerously aquiline.

"This seems to amuse you," he said, grimly.

"Oh yes, indeed it does; and I beg your pardon," gasped Tom, with the tears running down his cheeks. "I *must* tell Cosmo. It is the awful dignity of his face, when he hears his origin, that I am thinking of, and that kills me. A foundling! ha! ha! ha! Capital! Lady Bugles, you deserve a medal."

"But——" Lady Bugles began, in remonstrance.

"The whole thing, Tom," said Mrs Ravenhall, eagerly, "was simply a misunderstanding arising from my being unable to say exactly what Mr Glencairn's origin is; the word 'found-ling' was simply a little joke of Lady Bugles's — or — or some one else's — it doesn't matter who."

Lady Bugles was astounded to find herself being shoved deeper and deeper into the "found-ling" *imbroglio*; but she never could get a chance of righting herself.

"If you will allow me to say, Wyedale," said his lordship, with his ears well back, in resent-ment at having the word taken out of his mouth, —"if you will allow *me* to say—what I would have said some time ago, *if* I had been per-mitted,—there was no serious question as to his being a—ahem!—a foundling. That, I believe, was admitted to be a pleasantry which Lady Bugles allowed herself. But, leaving that aside, I venture to say, and I venture to repeat, that there is a certain recklessness in answering socially for a man about whom there is a mystery. You understand me?"

"Certainly; but where is the mystery?"

"About this friend of yours."

"There is no mystery about him."

"No!"

"None whatever. I have known him all my life."

"But his family?"

"Well, I knew his uncle—capital fellow his uncle! tipped Cosmo's friends with a catholic hand; and his aunt too—a capital specimen of the aunt—and——"

"Yes, yes, yes, Wyedale; but had your friend a father of his own? and if so, who was he?"

"You asked me that, I remember, once before, Lord Germistoune; and I can only say, what I said before, that he not only had, but has, a father, though I don't happen to know him. After all, there's nothing mysterious in that. I don't know everybody's father. Very glad I don't. Fathers, as a rule, are a mistake. Present company always honourably excepted."

"Then," said Lord Germistoune, "I suppose we must give him the benefit of the doubt. We must conclude that Lady Bugles's jest had no serious foundation."

"There's no doubt about Cosmo Glencairn," cried Tom, heartily; "and no mystery, except that he is a mysteriously good fellow to be going about loose nowadays; and Lady Bugles must have dreamt——"

"But," cried Lady Bugles, "I never——"

Here, however, dinner was announced, and the conversation was broken off, Lord Germistounc perversely nourishing a sort of hazy half-belief that there was something amiss about Cosmo's antecedents, and that Lady Bugles could unfold a tale, if she only chose to do so. So that this one little spiteful word of Mrs Ravenhall's, let slip in a moment of undiplomatic vexation, was near producing a dangerous commotion without doing anything to further her views—indeed, probably much the reverse. For the abuse of the absent—even of the absent unknown—is always distasteful to a generous nature; and Esmè was beginning to think that there was a general disposition to attack and decry Mr Glencairn, whom she knew and—and respected; and what the effect of this upon her feelings towards Cosmo might be, it is unnecessary to discuss. It may be mentioned, however, that the same evening, when Tom Wyedale was making one of his light cynical speeches as to the general inexpediency and hollowness of human friendship, she said to him with great warmth, "No, Mr Wyedale, I am sure you don't think so, because *you* don't turn your back upon absent friends; and I can easily forgive your theories when your practice is—is what I admire." Tom opened his eyes: he had forgotten all about the Cosmo episode, and merely said,

"I'm so glad you're glad I'm admirable;" but, after all, he was entitled to some credit for disappointing Lord Germistoune's palpable prejudice, when we recollect that the great bulk of the "mixed shooting" was still unexhausted, and that the "Three Kimmers" were a certainty for him, in any case.

CHAPTER XXX.

On his return home Cosmo found a telegram from Phil Denwick, announcing that he would leave town that night and be at Finmore on the following forenoon; and on the following fore-noon Phil made his appearance accordingly. He was a very different-looking individual from the shabby lounger whom his friend had so recently found on the brink of the abyss, and rescued with so much promptitude; and as Cosmo recognised that the true cheery ring had come back to his voice, and saw the old light sparkling again in his merry eyes, he felt a thrill of pure unselfish happiness, which, as he said to himself, was the best return his money had brought him for many a long day.

"Here you are, old Phil!" he cried heartily, as his friend drove up; "awfully good of you to come!"

"Here I am, Cosmo, with commercial promptitude and despatch—also as per invoice, wired. I didn't lose a single train, you see."

"No, that was right. The grouse want shooting, and the sooner they get it the better. Come in ; have you breakfasted, and can you hold on till luncheon ?"

"Breakfasted ! yes—and I can hold on till midnight. I say, what a glorious country ! what air ! what scenery !"

"Yes, and I am glad you have it so fine for your first experience."

"Fine ! it's heavenly." Then he went on with his old boyish eagerness. "And I've already seen grouse ! grouse upon the wing ! A covey of fourteen actually raced with the train—kept up with it too. It was a thrilling spectacle for a Cockney sportsman. It quite set me trembling all over. By the by, what queer fellows your Scotch second-class passengers seem to be ! I playfully confided my agitation about the grouse to a fellow-traveller. He looked me all over very carefully for about two minutes, and then said, judicially, 'A rack'n ye'll be easy fley't !' which, whatever he may have meant, seemed inconsequent, and to a foreign ear has a truculent sound, has it not ?"

"What did you say to him?" asked Cosmo, laughing.

"Say to him? Oh! I said, that for the matter of that, I fancied I was pretty well able to take care of my skin—which seemed to puzzle him, for he shut up. But then another fellow stood in, and shouted at me what might have been a war-cry, and which sounded like 'Whaur-i-ye-fae,' and kept shouting it at me over and over again, and louder each time, till at last it was a regular bellow, 'WHAUR-I-YE-FAE?' I told him that he might howl away till he was blue in the face, but that if he expected to get a rise out of me he was mistaken; and that choked *him* off too, but he seemed pretty savage. They appear to be a rum lot. I say, old boy, you're looking awfully thin. What have you been about? Taking it out of yourself on the hill?"

"No, not too much; haven't had time yet. But tell me all about yourself, Phil."

Then, as they walked about the garden, Phil gave his friend an account of his educational progress, and made him laugh with several funny stories about Mr Hopper in his capacity of commercial mentor, and the compliments which Mr Hopper paid his disciple, and the "prodigious trading instinct" which he had

discovered him to possess; and rattled away
in his exuberant vein till he had exhausted the
topic, and then said—

"Now, Cosmo, I'm not a bit tired. Is there
any just cause why we should not go out and
have a shoot this afternoon? Splendid day!
pity to waste it!"

Whereupon Cosmo blushed and explained
that they were engaged to lunch at Dunerlacht Castle, and looking at his watch, said
that they must start in twenty minutes; so
that if Phil wished to freshen himself up a
little after his journey, now was the time. Then
Phil's face fell as he begged off, swearing that
he abhorred castles, and abominated society, and
would rather stay behind, and enter himself with
the grouse. He was overruled, however, and of
course carried off.

"You are supposed," said Cosmo, as they
drove along, "to be going expressly to lionise
the castle, and to be deeply interested in architecture; so mind you be interested."

"All right," said Phil. "Who does the place
belong to?"

"Lord Germistoune."

"Never heard of him."

"You'd better not let him know that. He is

rather a dangerous old gentleman. In fact, generally speaking, you had better be very careful."

"Oh, hang it, Cosmo! you speak as if I were going into the witness - box. You'd better let me down, and I'll go back to the grouse. Remember I don't know the ways of the country."

"Don't be alarmed, Phil. All you've got to do, is to be very amiable—which comes natural to you."

"I see; employ the soothing system; agree with everything he says."

"That," said Cosmo, laughing, "will certainly be the safest plan."

"All right; even if he says 'whaur-i-ye-fae,' I shall say that that exactly represents my view of the matter, and that the sentiment does him credit. I would rather have tackled the grouse, though."

"You shall tackle them to-morrow, to your heart's content."

They arrived rather late, and luncheon was already in progress. The party was not in strong force. Some departures had taken place, and most of the gentlemen were on the hill. Lord Germistoune was, however, present, and his capricious temper appeared to be in unusually good order. Things looked promising. Cosmo found a seat near Esmè, and Phil was installed beside her father.

Phil was one of those lucky fellows who prepossess most people they come across, even the most dissimilar people. He had that frank simplicity of manner and expression, which is the charm of children, and irresistible in the grown up, when, as in Phil's case, combined with intelligence and geniality. At present he showed to great advantage, for he was brimming over with the happiness of reaction, and as fresh and eager as a schoolboy out for his holiday. Even Lord Germistoune, notwithstanding the auspices under which Phil was his guest, soon unbent, and became very civil and even cordial; and it was fortunate that Phil knew nothing of the relations between his introducer and his host, so that he was quite unconstrained, and had only a humorous recollection that it was his duty to coincide with his lordship's opinions upon things in general.

"Your first visit to Scotland, Mr Fenwick, I believe?" said Lord Germistoune, after he had quite thawed down.

"I am ashamed to say that it is," said Phil, " though I won't say that I am sorry, for I am enjoying all the pleasures of a first experience, and they are very great.   This is a glorious country!"

"I think that we may consider it a glorious country."

"I would give anything to have a property here."

"Ah! that is a different question: that is a very prevalent feeling.   Our land is very much sought after in the market,—offensively so."

"Indeed!"

"Hucksters from Manchester are always on the watch — the harpies! They bid anything for land in this quarter."

"Ah! I'm not surprised at that."

"They swoop on us like vultures, with their ill-gotten gains."

"And purchase the land?"

"And mob out people who are entitled to be landholders.   The whole of the neighbouring parish of Auchinfeoch has recently been acquired by a huckster."

"Really!   From Manchester?" asked Phil, sympathetically.

"From Manchester; of the name of Runnicles —which might account for almost anything.   I flatter myself Mr Runnicles knows very distinctly the view I take of *his* conduct."

"You resented the purchase as—as an intrusion?"

"I resented it, sir, as a scandalous abomination. How would you like to have German Jews walking about in kilts in your district?"

"It would be highly unpleasant, of course," said Phil, stifling his laughter with great difficulty.

"Unpleasant! It's enough to demoralise the whole district. You are comparatively exempt from such pests in the south. I presume, however, you are what in England is called from 'the North'? There is no mistaking your name; it has the true border ring."

"Still, Lord Germistoune, I am not a Borderer."

"Not perhaps immediately, but certainly of Border lineage." .

"I am not aware of it."

"Oh, but there is no question about it. I interest myself in family history, and your name is simply a corruption from 'Of Alnwick;' drop the 'O' and you get Falnwick and Fenwick."

"But you have mistaken my name, Lord Germistoune, which is not Fenwick, but Denwick."

"Ah, really! Well, but is it not obvious to you that they are the same?   Denwick is simply d'Alnwick, so that you don't get away from the Border, nor from the Fenwicks. It only · throws you a stage further back, and proves you to be a Fenwick and a Borderer of the oldest and most inveterate description. I am never at fault in such matters. Your family possessions are not in that district, however?"

"No," said Phil, thinking that, if anything, he was for the time a Highland proprietor, all his worldly possessions being contained in a battered old portmanteau now at Cosmo's lodge. "No, but I should be happy to re-establish that sort of connection with the Border." .

"There may be openings there.   I understand you are greatly interested in architecture. Any building projects in view at your own place?"

"The old fellow is determined to make a swell of me," thought Phil, as he laughed, and disclaimed both place and project.

"Only an abstract lover of the art? Well, I shall be happy to show you our old house. There is a bit which goes back certainly to the twelfth, some say the eleventh century. I shall be pleased to get the opinion of an expert."

Phil was a good deal puzzled by the unexpected consideration which he was receiving;
but the explanation was very simple. Lord
Germistoune was, as we have amply seen, a
man of sudden personal prejudices—violent and
unreasonable for, or against, their objects. Fair
examples of his system were to be found in the
cases of Cosmo Glencairn and Tom Wyedale
respectively; and Phil Denwick was fortunate
enough to share the happier experiences of the
latter. Hence this complaisant garrulity, and
this mysterious imputation of pedigree, property, and lore; which were merely so many
ways of expressing that his lordship fancied
him, and therefore assumed him to possess the
advantages to which a man thus distinguished
was entitled, according to the fitness of things.

Meantime, at the other end of the table, there
was no great flow of conversation. The talking
men of the party were on the moor; and many
of the ladies only took the trouble to talk when
the right men were present. Esmè was somewhat silent and constrained; conversation lan-
guished and flickered; and Cosmo felt a certain
chill creep over his spirit. He began to feel
that coming to luncheon had been a mistake—
the meal had better have been omitted. After

divers flashes of silence, Mrs Ravenhall, who had made gallant efforts to keep things going, at last said, pettishly—

"How deadly-lively we all are to-day! I wish these tiresome men would sometimes stay at home and amuse us."

"If it were *only* for a change," moaned Lady Bugles.

"Some of them are coming back early to play lawn-tennis," said Mrs Crock.

"I should be sorry to count upon *that*," said Lady Bugles, who watched for Mrs Crock.

"Oh, but it's a promise!"

"I wouldn't give much for their promises."

"Very likely not; but my faith is stronger than yours. I suppose faith depends a good deal upon experience." With which trump it was felt that Mrs Crock took the trick from her ladyship, who had not long ago figured disastrously in a rather racy breach of promise case.

"Well, what *are* we to do this afternoon?" said Miss Hungerford Snapsley.

"I'm going sketching," mewed Miss Milkington.

"'Sir, she said—sir, she said,'" hummed Miss Snapsley; "but that won't amuse *us*."

"And I shan't amuse you by writing letters, of

which I have a bushel to get through," said Mrs Ravenhall. "Why not play lawn-tennis *en attendant?* I daresay Mr Glencairn will help you."

She now saw the necessity of being more circumspect in her measures as to Cosmo; and besides, it is obvious that a man who means mischief can do less of it when panting at lawn-tennis than in quieter aspects.

" I shall be delighted," said Cosmo.

" *Till* the others come," said Mrs Crock, quickly, and added, " because when they do, it's a fixed match, you know. Perhaps your friend plays ? "

" Oh yes, he does."

" Very well, then, I will take you, and we'll challenge Miss Douglas and your friend."

When they went out, however, Lord Germistoune, finding Phil a sympathetic peg on which to hang his prose, claimed him for his prey, and carried him off for lionising purposes ; so one of the " cripples " was taken instead ; and another set was made up by Miss Snapsley, who had, however, to content herself with the same unsatisfactory *personnel.*

" I can't play very long," said Esmè, " because I have promised to take Miss Milkington to her sketching-ground."

"How you sacrifice yourself to that creature!" said Mrs Ravenhall, beaming approval, however.

Then the game took place, but it was a hollow affair, Cosmo and Mrs Crock being both experts, and Esmè unable to support the heavy handicapping of the "cripple."

Other games were played, the "cripple" being tried in every combination, but with the same results; and when it was beginning to get a little hopeless, joy suddenly flashed into the face of Mrs Crock, for Lord Ribston and two other "nice" men falsified the predictions of Lady Bugles by appearing on the scene.

"They sent whisky instead of brandy, and forgot the soda altogether," explained Ribston, with his usual candour, "so we were obliged to come home. But now that we've refreshed, we're on for a match. Miss Douglas, you and I against Mrs Crock and Berkeley."

"Oh, *that* isn't the match, Lord Ribston! it was you and I against Miss Snapsley and Captain Berkeley," said Mrs Crock.

"That isn't a law of the Swedes and Prussians, is it?"

"*I* can't play, Lord Ribston; I have another engagement," said Esmè.

Whereat the noble lord, who had descended the mountain partly for her sake, though mainly for the brandy, was mightily disgusted, and was not at all a pleasant partner for the widow Crock.

"I am afraid I must say 'good-bye' now, Mr Glencairn," said Esmè. "I have kept poor Miss Milkington waiting so very long."

This was terrible! Cosmo had hardly exchanged a word with her during the whole visit; so he took heart of grace, and said—"Will you think me too importunate?—but I daresay you have forgotten all about it—the song——"

"Oh, indeed I have not forgotten it; it is copied, and if you care to have it now, I will give it you. Will you come up to the house, or shall I send it down to you here?"

"Pray let me go to the house," said Cosmo, eagerly. "How very good of you to remember it!"

"Oh no," said Esmè. "I promised, and though I have rather repented of my promise, I am going to keep it, of course."

"But why have you repented?"

She did not answer for a moment, and then said, "I never meant any one to know anything about it, and—and I don't know why I told you

—and I think—you know there *is* really nothing in the song—and so it seems absurd to give it to any one."

Cosmo felt an indescribable restraint; and when he said that there was much in the song, and that he should value it very highly, the words sounded, even to himself, dry and chilly.

They walked to the house in silence; and when they reached the door, Esmè begged him to wait while she went up and fetched the copy. Presently she returned, accompanied by Miss Milkington, and presented him with the song, saying, " You will keep my secret," and then checked his raptures which threatened to break out, by adding, with a laugh, to Miss Milkington, " You don't know what a confession of guilt I have been making to Mr Glencairn !"

" Tell me about it," said Miss Milkington, lackadaisically; " I do so like to hear about guilt !"

And this made both Esmè and Cosmo laugh, and the cloud rose a little.

" I wonder where my friend has hidden himself ? " said Cosmo.

" I think," said Esmè, " it is quite certain that papa has taken him to the ruin. No one escapes the ruin."

"Are you going in that direction?"

"Yes, we are. Miss Milkington wishes to sketch the Fall from a point in that quarter."

"Then may I be allowed to place myself under your guidance, so far? I must go and look for Lord Germistoune and Denwick."

"Oh, certainly; but would you not rather stay and play lawn - tennis till your friend returns?"

"No," said Cosmo. "I can play tennis any day, but I can't walk with a composer and an artist any day."

"Hush!" said Esmè, laughing. "Remember!"

CHAPTER XXXI.

THEY wound up the hill-side, through the woods, by a path which was unfortunately so narrow that they were obliged to move in single file, in which formation, with the strong non-conductor of Miss Milkington's person interpolated between Esmè and himself, Cosmo felt that he might as well be promenading alone on the other side of the glen. But, after about ten minutes of silent pilgrimage, they diverged by another path to the right, and, again descending, came upon an open plateau, where they halted. Far beneath them, the river was just escaping from the eddies of the Fall; over against them, on a higher level, it made its first leap towards the abyss; and higher still, ivy-bound, and encircled by a few ancient and writhen trees, the venerable keep seemed mournfully to contemplate its impending doom in the anguish of the caldron down below.

The great and solemn sound of the waters lent a fitting voice to the weird sublimity of the scene.

For a moment they all contemplated the grand *coup d'œil* without speaking; but Miss Milkington, who was a sketcher, and not an artist, rather impatiently broke the silence, and clamoured for her "point of view"—*the* point of view whence as much as possible of the scene could be utilised, and condensed into her caricature.

Esmè took her away some little distance, placed her in position, set her to work, and then, returning to Cosmo, said—"If you think you have time, and don't object to a scramble, you can get down from here to the level of the river, where there is a splendid view of the Fall. But I warn you that the path, which is known as 'Jacob's Ladder,' is difficult; still, if you care to venture it, I will show you where to begin the descent."

As there seemed no prospect of angelic society on the descent, Cosmo felt that he had better adhere to the heavenward end of the "Ladder," so excused himself on the plea of time.

"How," he asked, "can I get round, and up, from this to the ruin?"

Esmè described the route, which *was* rather intricate, but Cosmo feigned stupidity with great success; and after many attempts to make him understand, she desisted, laughingly, and said—

"I see you have no bump of locality, and would inevitably lose yourself, so I will take you to a point, after which you can't make a mistake."

This was, of course, exactly what Cosmo had been scheming for, and they started. He was resolved to break down, from the first, the sort of constraint which seemed threatening to rise between them, so he forced himself, with an effort, to talk fluently.

"We seem destined," he said, "to meet 'on the heights,' and to meet in wonderful scenery."

"You are thinking of Lake Como, and that lovely walk behind the Villa Bianca?"

"Yes; I got quite a new view of the lake by that walk: I never *really* knew its beauties before."

"I think it *is* the most beautiful view I know of the lake."

"And I have got quite a new view of the Erlacht Fall to-day."

"I think here, too, we are fortunate, and have the best of it beside us."

"So that I have to thank you for twice 'lifting the veil.'"

"Or rather, for the humble fact of living behind the veil, in these two cases. What a different scene this is !"

"Yes," said Cosmo, "and how characteristic of the two countries ! There, there was nothing hard, or sharp, or obtrusive ; hundreds of beauties, of different kinds, lay around us, but diffused, and disposed in a sort of easy, languid grace, so that nothing was insisted upon. Here it is all concentration, eagerness, energy—like the national character. It is a battle. Look at the malignant fury of the waters ; the rocks are the very picture of stern and cruel resolution, and these sombre woods and that sad old ruin can be nothing but the grim spectators of the tragedy. Everything is forced upon you ; you can't forget it for an instant, for the roar of the water cries everlastingly, ' Come and see our combat !'"

"And which do you like best ? "

"Like you, I have my moods, and every mood has a different preference."

Esmè looked up and laughed. "How," she asked, "do you know that *I* have moods ?"

"Do you forget that I am a *clairvoyant ?*

Don't you remember our conversation about the picture the other night? or rather, do you think I forget our conversation on the last walk I had with you?"

"Oh, Mr Glencairn, do tell me more about the Sassoferrato picture!"

Cosmo, nothing loath, complied, and there ensued a long conversation of dialogue and dissertation which, lightly floating over a hundred subjects, extracted from each some subtle implication of Cosmo's love and homage.

Conversations of the sort are apt to be engrossing, so it is not wonderful that Miss Milkington came to be forgotten, and that, without observation on either side, Esmè ended in being Cosmo's guide all the way to the ruin. Recalled by reaching it, she was for hurrying back at once, but Cosmo suggested that, now she was here, a few minutes more or less could make no difference, and assured her laughingly that, since her father and Phil were not visible, he gravely mistrusted his unaided bump of locality to guide him back again. So she consented to remain for a few minutes, during which they explored the old castle and its precincts.

"This takes one very far back into the old world," said Cosmo.

"I think," replied Esmè, "about six hundred years."

"It has always been in your family, I suppose?"

"Yes," said Esmè; "or rather, it has always come back to us, for it has been confiscated four or five times—which shows that we have not been a well-conducted race, does it not?"

"Or rather, it shows that you have not been a neutral race. It shows that your ancestors have been mixed up (which every one knows) with the history of the country, and helped to make it. To me there is something most enviable in such a descent."

"Do you think it so very enviable?"

"Perhaps because I do not possess it."

Esmè, with all the innuendos about Cosmo's birth so fresh in her recollection, involuntarily betrayed her interest by something like a start.

"No," Cosmo continued, "I won't give that as my reason, for I am convinced of its real advantages. I think that ancient and honourable birth must be a great incitement to nobility of life, and a great help in reaching it. The man who possesses it must feel an inspiration when he looks into the past. The past must have a special voice for him, to encourage and warn him. It is impossible that he can forget that his fame or dis-fame affects a grand series of traditions and not merely himself. If he has any loyalty or reverence in his nature, he can't help feeling that he is the latest link in a chain of pure metal, and that *he* must not be the first to debase it."

"If every one felt so, how noble nobility would be!" said Esmè.

"But depend upon it, that if vast numbers did not feel so in some degree, nobility would be much less noble than it is. I do not possess it, but I can see its value. For a man like me, of brief and obscure pedigree, the past has no special voice appealing to the reverence or the romance of his character ; there is no accumulated force of traditions to propel him. He must rely on himself alone. Like the more fortunate, he has, of course, the *supreme* inducements to lead a noble life ; but they have a host of minor ones which touch human nature very attractively, and help it, and add something of the picturesque to duty." Cosmo paused for a moment, and then added—"Therefore, I envy the fortunate people who possess long and illustrious descent."

Esmè said, "No doubt, if looked on as you look on it, it would be a very ennobling thing; but if one does not require such incitements—and I am sure *you* do not—I do not see that there is much to regret in the want of a long pedigree; it is only a romantic sentiment—provided, of course, one is of gentle birth."

"And what constitutes that?"

"Mr Glencairn, surely you know better than I."

"No, I don't, Miss Douglas—indeed I don't. I wish I did. Do you suppose that *I* am of gentle birth?"

Esmè looked terribly confused, and changed colour and said—"Of course, Mr Glencairn. How can you ask such a question?"

"Because I have grave doubts about my own case. You shall have it before you. I am well-born—extremely well-born, on the mother's side; on the father's, my pedigree is untraceable after three generations. There may be surmises, but I have no right to think of my pedigree except as absolutely a blank beyond that limit. Now, how do I stand? Is that enough? Am I of gentle birth?"

Esmè half smiled at his vehemence. "I should think," she said, "that no one could deny it; for it cannot matter on which side the ancient descent is, and the worst side is—is" (she was thinking of its remoteness from the disgrace alleged by the foundling story) "respectable.   You must be very difficult to satisfy."

"It is enough?" repeated Cosmo—"you say that it is enough?"

"Of course I do, Mr Glencairn."

"Then, for myself, I am satisfied.   I require no higher patent."

"I fear," she said, smiling, "it is not a patent of much authority.   My father, for instance, always accuses me of being a Radical—ever since, in a rash moment, I quoted to him that 'kind hearts are more than coronets.'"

A change came over Cosmo's face, and he said, involuntarily, and almost with a groan, "I can well imagine it."

"Well," she said, as if defending herself against Cosmo himself, "I suspect I *am* a Radical, if that kind of sentiment makes a Radical.   I suppose the length of my pedigree entitles me to say what I think about the claims of long descent?"

"Undoubtedly so."

"Well, you have spoken of its advantages. I say nothing against what you say; I only doubt that they are used as you think (and *I* think) they ought to be, and might be used; but I retain my radical opinion."

"What?" said Cosmo; "'The rank is but the guinea stamp'?"

"I say nothing against the rank; it is a splendid thing—because it is a great power—if it is nobly used; but it is a pitiable thing—and still because it is a great power—if it is not nobly used. Do you agree with me?"

"Indeed I do."

"And I *do* believe in that kind of nobility and gentlemanhood which patents and pedigrees cannot make—of heart and actions and manners. I place them above the others. I *do* prefer the substance to the symbol. You shudder at me as an unromantic Radical. I can't help it."

"You forget, Miss Douglas, that I am not entitled to shudder at such sentiments; but, if I could be supposed to speak impartially, I should say that they were very generous and noble. As to their being unromantic, however, I am afraid that is the last description they would receive in the world you live in, and which I also—perhaps on sufferance, perhaps only because I have money—inhabit."

"Oh, money! that is a dreadful passport to depend upon!"

"Yes, it is—though it is the passport in this country, nowadays, to most things; and I find now, in that conviction—that it is a despicable, and, in my case, even an insufficient passport— the incitement, which I cannot derive from old traditions, to try to reach, by my own achievements, a standing-ground in the world which cannot be gainsaid."

"Of course I think it is admirable to wish to be great, to determine to be great; but if it is only to assure a position in society—which, after all, is quite assured already—that seems rather a small ending for a great beginning. But I am sure I have mistaken you; *you* cannot mean *that?*"

She looked quickly up at him at last; for in all this time there had been none of those strange meetings of the eyes which had filled her with so much bewilderment, — she had avoided them by a conscious effort,—and, looking up at him, she met his gaze, intensified beyond all its former intensity, so that it held her riveted with a power which she could not resist.

"You are right," said Cosmo, speaking in a

low and earnest voice which was full of music and pathos, "and you are wrong. I desire it, not for the petty advantages of social life, but as a means to an end—an end which I *must* reach, or life, with all its aspirations, and hopes, and promises, and possibilities, will become to me only a longer or shorter interval of pain or torpor,—it will be death in life."

He paused; they remained silent and motionless, rapt each on each; and to each it seemed that the beating of their own hearts was audible above the thunder of the waters shouting their battle-cry far below.

Silent and motionless, and desperately in earnest. What would he say? what would she say? who would speak first?

These problems were not solved. The irony of Fate brought an interruption.

CHAPTER XXXII.

"' Last May a braw wooer cam' doon the lang glen,
And sair wi' his love he did deave me ;
I said there was naething I hated like men—
The deil gae wi' him to believe me, believe me !
The deil gae wi' him to believe me !'

Blessin's on your bonny face, Miss Esmè ! it's a weary time ye've been awa' ; and here's auld Maggie at her post to gie ye welcome."

Thus singing, and thus speaking, a strange-looking woman suddenly presented herself before Esmè and Cosmo, as they stood in the critical situation described at the close of our last chapter. The noise of the waterfall, and their own deep abstraction, caused her approach to be unobserved ; and her presence, close beside them, was announced by the first high and harsh notes of her song.

She was old, and, though neat and clean in her appearance, had that restless light in the eye which proclaims an unsettled brain. The ordinary expression " half - witted " would be unjust, for Maggie had plenty of wits, only they were dishevelled, and exercised irresponsibly and at random. It was her privilege to act as *cicerone* to such stray tourists as came to visit the Fall; and, on the days when access to the castle side of it was permitted, she was always to be found lying in wait for her prey at the farther end of a light bridge which spanned the river a little above the ruin. Her discourse, on these occasions, was diversified by fragments of local legend and sudden digressions into song, and even dance, which in her wandering imagination, had probably some illustrative connection with her themes, and which, at all events, never failed to amuse her clients. From this description, old Maggie, who still lives and plies her vocation, will no doubt be recognised by some of our readers.

Opportune or inopportune, her sudden appearance rudely dissolved the spell which held Esmè and Cosmo in the silence of deep emotion. The former started from her abstraction in a confusion so deep that, at first, she could find no voice to return the eccentric salutation. The old woman gave her time, however, by breaking into another snatch of song, and when it was finished Esmè was able to speak.

"I am glad to see you again, Maggie," she said, offering her hand to the woman, who raised it to her lips with all love and reverence, "and happy to see you looking so well."

"My thanks to ye, Miss Esmè; I'm aye weel —praise be blessed!—when the simmer time comes and brings ye back, and," she added, with a twinkle in her eye, "the towrist bodies, wi' their saxpences and siclike. And wha's the bonny gentleman? he'll no be a towrist?"

"This is the gentleman who is living at Finmore, Maggie; and I've been doing your work for you. I've been showing him the ruins, and telling him some of the old stories."

"And maybe it was au auld story he was tellin' you, when I cam' ower the knowe. I'm no a spac-wife, Miss Esmè, and I haena the second sicht—weel, aweel—

<blockquote>
'My heart is sair—I daurna tell—
My heart is sair for Somebody!
I wad dae—what wad I not?
For the sake o' Somebody.'
</blockquote>

and aiblins the bonny gentleman will hae a saxpence in his pouch to gie auld Maggie, for a' he binna a towrist."

Cosmo at once took the hint, responding to it very liberally, in hopes of getting rid of the old woman, whose musical illustrations were so unpleasantly *apropos.*

"Eh ! thank ye kindly, sir !" she cried; "eh ! but this is nae towrist's fee !   Siller, and siller, and siller ! There's luck in three, and there's luck in nine !   I'm nae spae-wife, as my leddy kens, but I'm thinkin' ye'll be something great and gran' yersel—a belted earl maybe, or a baron bauld, mayhap ?"

"No, Maggie," said Cosmo, laughing, "I'm neither belted earl nor baron bold."

"Aweel, ye hae the look o't, my bonny lad; and whiles wha isna suld be, and wha suldna be, is ; and your time may come some day— wha kens ?

> 'Bide ye yet, and bide ye yet,
> Ye dinna ken what may betide ye yet.'

And I wuss ye weel, for if ye hae the heigh look ye hae the free han'; and that's no aye the way o't.   His lordship's sel's nane ower free wi' the bawbees.   Mony's the time I've tell't him *that.*   'The han' o' a Douglas,' quo' I, 'suld aye be tight on the sword, and slack on the purse,' quo' I.   Hoots ! he'll no heed me ; I'm jist daft auld Maggie, ye ken."

"Well, Maggie," said Esmè, "we must be going. I don't think there's anything more here that Mr Glencairn would care to see."

"Troth, Miss Esmè, ye'll be richt—naething mair that he wad care to see, if I ken him ava'—for it's no the ruins, and its no the Fa', that's brocht *him* here the day. Na, na! it's something else, as ye ken brawly, my winsome leddy.

'Oh, luve will venture in whaur it daurna weel be seen,
And luve will venture in whaur wisdom ance has been ;
But I will doon yon river rove, amang the woods sae green,
And a' to pu' a posie to my ain dear May.'

Hoots! ye'll no be heedin' me—I'm jist daft auld Maggie, ye ken." And here the old woman varied the entertainment by dancing a pretty long bout of the "Highland fling," humming the notes of a strathspey for music, and conducting the performance with a solemnity of expression in grotesque contrast with the wild vigour of her "footing."

"Bravo! bravo!" cried Cosmo, with rage and despair in his heart, when she came to a halt; "and now we must say good-bye."

"What's yer hurry?"

"Well, it's growing late, and I must be getting home. I'll come back another day and hear all your old stories."

"Wait a wee till I dance ye 'Gillie Callum.'"

"Not to-day, Maggie; we must really be going."

"Aweel, I'll see ye aff my ain domain. I couldna dae less, ye ken."

To be forestalled in your own declaration of love by a mad woman, who shouts your tender secret, in transparent parables of grotesque song, accompanied with crazy dancing! *Lugete Veneres Cupidinesque!* Could anything be more crushing to a transcendental lover? And, to a maiden for whose wondering eyes a doubtful light is just beginning to dawn upon the world of love, could anything be more overwhelming than an illumination so garish, brusquely flashed upon the mysterious region which her timid feet are in the act of entering? With a burning blush fixed in her fair cheek, Esmè, with downcast eyes, walked hurriedly and in silence; and Cosmo, by her side, moved also without a word, paralysed by his sudden drop from the pinnacle of high emotion, into the bathos wrought by Maggie's extravaganza. The old woman followed close behind them—now, fortunately, launched on an endless legend, shouted to ears which did not listen, and enlivened with bursts of song which rang, weird and shrill, above the water's roar.

In these unhappy circumstances they rejoined Miss Milkington, upon whom Maggie, mistaking her for a tourist, instantly pounced, dancing up to her and chanting her *cicerone's* formula: "Will ye see the Fa', bonny leddy? Will ye see the auld Douglas Castle, bonny leddy? and I'll sing ye a sang, and tell ye a tale, and dance ye 'Gillie Callum,' and a' for a thank-ye and a saxpence, or maybe twa, bonny leddy! Hae! gie me the satchel—I'll carry't for ye," and she was for possessing herself of Miss Milkington's drawing paraphernalia, but that young lady drew back, scared by the wild aspect of the old woman.

"Hoots!" cried Maggie, "what ails ye? I'm jist daft Maggie, ye ken. Hae! gie me the satchel," and she again closed with her victim, who again started back, piping tremulously—

"Go away! go away! you horrid, dreadful person!"

Maggie drew herself up in offended dignity.

"Dreadfu' person!" she exclaimed; "is it *me?* hard ye e'er the like o't? Afore my

leddy, too! and me a vassal o' Dunerlacht!
and you a towrist body frae Dundee, mayhap,
wha kens? wi' a face like soured sowans,
and——"

"Hush, hush, hush, Maggie!" cried Esmè;
"this lady is a friend of mine; and if you
say another word I shall be very angry. Go
away at once. I am ashamed of you."

"Dear heart, Miss Esmè! what wye was I
to ken? The gentles ne'er misca's me; but
I beg the bonny Miss's pardon; and aiblins
she'll hae a saxpence for auld Meg, jist to
show there's nae ill-wull atween us."

"You shall get nothing more to-day, Maggie.
Go away. I am extremely displeased with
you."

"Dinna say that, Miss Esmè — but I'll
gang: and good-bye to ye, my leddy; and
to you, my bonny Miss—I'm wae for sayin'
yon aboot the sowans; and to you, my bonny
gentleman. I wuss ye weel; and ye mauna
look sae dowie;—

> ' Ne'er break yer heart for ae rebute,
> But think upon it still, jo !
> Then gin the lassie winna do't,
> Ye'll fin' anither will, jo !'"

with which parting counsel, Maggie took her

departure, and went carolling away back to her "ain domain," having performed to perfection the functions of that awful social pest, the *enfant terrible*, and in his most favourite sphere of action.

And now, if Miss Milkington had been neutral and useless all her life, she was really serviceable at last; for, without her presence, what could Esmè and Cosmo have done? Could they have returned to the conditions in which the old woman had surprised them? Surely not; the sensitive delicacy of these conditions made that impossible, after Meg's interlude. No; they were both overwhelmed with embarrassment; and they must have either acknowledged this by a desperate silence, or betrayed it in a *fiasco* of commonplace talk— miserable expedients both of them; and to either would have attached this danger, that it might have developed a new point of departure for the relations between Cosmo and Esmè, which had now begun to move, pretty definitely, in a certain direction. Under these circumstances Miss Milkington was a godsend; and it was wonderful to see the sudden interest which both her companions displayed in her and her artistic performances, and the persistence with which their remarks were addressed exclusively to her on the homeward route. This circumstance, and a certain feverish loquacity which they displayed, might have been suggestive to the average female mind; but Miss Milkington's wits were rather below par, and her only emotion at the conclusion of the journey was one of relief at her escape from so unwonted a conversational strain.

Lord Germistoune and Phil Denwick had just returned from some other quarter, and were standing at the castle door when the party arrived. Esmè, with somewhat suspicious *empressement*, hastened to tell her father of their vain search for him at the ruins—even venturing to speak of it as a disappointment—and described the old woman's encounter with Miss Milkington as though it had been the prominent feature in the afternoon's adventures. Lord Germistoune, loftily unsuspecting, and glad of an occasion against old Maggie, whose freedom of speech, but for Esmè's intervention, would have long since procured her disestablishment, " extended " himself with some ardour on this matter, vowing that Maggie was a distinct pest, and that the cup of her abominations was now full to the brim.

"If Miss Milkington desires it," said his lordship, "the woman shall be cashiered at once."

"Oh yes, *please*," lisped Miss Milkington; "she is so dreadfully horrid."

"No, no, no!" cried Esmè; "I won't have her cashiered!   It was all from a mistake. Maggie mistook Miss Milkington for one of the tourists, whom she looks upon as her serfs. That was all; and I only mentioned it as a joke — not to get the poor old thing into trouble."

This was really magnanimous, considering the enormity of Maggie's unreported offences, and it prevailed, Lord Germistoune dropping the bone after a little further worrying over it.

"I greatly admired the Fall, from this side, Lord Germistoune," said Cosmo; "it is quite the best point of view I have seen."

"We have always considered it undeniably the best point of view," replied Lord Germistoune; "and if you, Mr Denwick, do me the favour to visit me again, I shall hope to introduce you to it."

Phil expressed his acknowledgments; and as their dog-cart now drove up, the young men made their adieux.

" Good-bye," said Cosmo to Esmè.

" Good-bye," she murmured: her eyes had not met his, since old Maggie's intervention at the Fall, and they were still cast down.

" Good-bye," he repeated, retaining her hand, so that she looked up involuntarily into his face, and there again read the earnest story of his love —legible, *now*, beyond any misinterpretation. A sudden blush flashed over her fair brow, and she drooped those beautiful eyes, in which there was trouble, but no longer any bewilderment.

CHAPTER XXXIII.

WHILE the afternoon had been occupied for Esmè and Cosmo by these strange events, Lord Germistoune and Phil had passed it together in a *tête-à-tête*, characterised by dreary monologue on his lordship's part, and the despairing attention of amiable docility on the part of his companion. They had thoroughly " done " the castle, within and without. Phil had had to pay dearly for his imputed cunning in architecture, by diving into many mouldy dungeons, and scaling the tortuous stairs of many a rickety turret; for everywhere there was an " object of interest," and on each Lord Germistoune descanted at length. Then there were the traditions of the place, complex and numerous; and from each section of the discourse an inference had to be drawn, to the personal glorification of his lordship, who, somehow, contrived to take credit for everything, from a gargoyle to a ghost.

Thus it took a considerable time to exhaust the castle; and when that was done, Lord Germistoune carried Phil off to see the bridge and gatehouse, which were modern, though in the ancient style, and on which the noble proprietor greatly prided himself, stating them to be from his own design. " I found that the architects were making a botch of the business, so I took it into my own hands, and did it myself, with, I venture to think, respectable results." This legend had been current for forty years, so that, by the law of prescription, at least, it was entitled to the honours of veracious history.

As they walked down from the castle, Phil, remarking on the beauty of the scenery, happened to say how grateful he felt to Cosmo for giving him the chance of visiting it; and Lord Germistoune, with " the mystery " still haunting his fancy, thought the present might be a good opportunity for probing it, and set about doing so accordingly.

" You are an old friend of his, I believe ?" he inquired.

" Yes, Glencairn is my oldest, and, I may certainly say, my best friend."

" School friendships are very binding."

" We were not school-fellows, but our friendship dates farther back than school days — in fact it is hereditary; our fathers, and even our grandfathers, were friends."

"Hum ! country neighbours, perhaps ?"

"No, not exactly that. They were very much connected in business, I believe, and my grandfather was guardian to Glencairn's father."

"Ah, indeed ! That naturally constitutes a tie."

"It has not made much of a tie between me and old Mr Glencairn," said Phil, laughing; "but, after all, that was probably due to my fault more than——"

"You catch a view of the bridge, here, Mr Denwick, which I think is effective."

"It is indeed," said Phil, "most effective;" and when it had been duly admired, Lord Germistoune resumed—"But I beg your pardon; I interrupted you. You were about to relate some facetious incident in connection with Mr Glencairn's father ?"

"Oh no ! I once rejected some advice of his, at which he was very angry, and I have not seen him since—that was all."

"It would appear that the gentleman is arbitrary."

"Yes, I believe he is rather an arbitrary man;

and when a man of that sort is consulted on a matter connected with his own speciality, he expects to have his advice taken."

" His speciality, you say ?"

" Yes, I consulted him about an investment; and I suppose Mr Glencairn is at the top of the tree in finance matters."

" May I ask who, and what, Mr Glencairn is?"

" Oh, don't you know ? "

" Is it very remarkable that I should not know ? "

" Not at all ; I merely fancied, somehow, that you did.   He was the head of an important firm in the iron trade, and is now principal share-holder of a company which took over the business ; besides which, he is a great — I don't exactly know what you call it; ' financial operator' is, I believe, the expression."

" Why ! " cried Lord Germistoune, in great astonishment, " you must mean Archibald Glencairn ? "

" Yes, I do.   The title of the company is ' Archibald Glencairn & Co. Limited.' "

" I have some reason to know about it ; but Archibald Glencairn — surely *he* is not your friend's father ? "

" Indeed he is."

"Some one distinctly assured me to the contrary; and besides, I always understood that the individual in question is a bachelor, and a kind of hermit, living alone in some remote quarter. I know it is next to impossible to get a personal interview with him,—a symptom I have never liked in the man—a distinctly suspicious symptom."

"Well, he is Glencairn's father; he lives as you say, and has been long a widower. But you know him, after all, Lord Germistoune?"

"In a business way, I do; but only in a business way. His firm had all my Ferniehall minerals, and my Welsh field into the bargain; and in consideration of this, on the formation of the company, I was induced to become a shareholder to a considerable extent. I trust my confidence was justified."

"I have full confidence in the company; and I speak as a prospective shareholder."

"Oh, indeed! Well, you know, the dividends have not been what we anticipated—there has been a continuous diminution."

"But we must consider the general stagnation of trade," cried Phil, who had heard Mr Hopper in apology a hundred times; "and then, there is a guaranteed minimum."

"Yes; that is to say, there is Mr Archibald Glencairn."

"Who is a tower of strength. His credit is most assured, and his integrity is proverbial."

"Integrity is a good thing, but it is not capital."

"Oh, but he has an immense capital."

"With which he 'operates financially.' I tell you frankly, the man did not impress me favourably, very much the reverse. I have only met him once. You can't meet him—he won't let you meet him. He skulks—by the Lord Harry, skulks! and if you *do* meet him, he insults you. My dealings with him have been, with one exception, by correspondence, and his tone on paper is never what it ought to be — curt and self-sufficient, and in addressing me, quite devoid of that recognition of my status in the world, not to say in his Company, which I have a right to expect; and I shall not soon forget the way he received me, on the one occasion when I succeeded in getting access to him. He didn't rise, he kept his hat on his head, he continued his writing, and actually motioned me — *me!* — to a chair, with his infernal pen, just as if I had been a—a huckster like himself! I at once stated roundly that my time was too valuable to be trifled with in that fashion; and what do you suppose the fellow replied, almost without looking up ? Why, that it was his rule (*his* rule !) to transact business by correspondence alone ; and that if I chose to force him out of his groove, to his great inconvenience, I must expect inconvenience to myself. Then when I began to remonstrate temperately, but firmly, he held up his hand !—to me !—to impose silence, by the Lord Harry ! Of course I at once left him, and you may be very sure I have not repeated the experiment of calling upon him. The man is arrogance personified, and arrogance is the parent of recklessness, a quality which is not reassuring in the chairman and guarantor of a company. I have my uneasy moments about the man, I can tell you. And so *he* is your friend's father ? Hum !"

" I have always heard the highest opinions of his honour and sagacity, but his manner is certainly brusque and disagreeable—so very unlike his son's."

"Hum ! The son is not connected with the business—with the company ?"

"Oh no, he has a large private fortune; though, by the by, indirectly through me, he is now becoming connected with the company."

And here true-hearted Phil, full of enthusiasm

for his friend's generosity, impulsively related what noble things Cosmo was doing for him. The narrative failed to evoke the admiration anticipated, on Lord Germistouue's part, who said drily, " When you have reached my time of life, Mr Denwick, you will know that there are many wheels within wheels in financial matters; and that in transactions like this—though I trust your case may be exceptional—a *quid pro quo* is invariably extracted."

" Impossible in my case. Glencairn knows only too well that he couldn't get a *quid* out of me. I feel certain he would have given me the money as an unconditional present, if he had thought it for my good—if I would have accepted it, that is to say."

" Ha ! hum ! indeed ! There now, take the whole effect of that bridge and gatehouse, and say what you think of an architect who would have placed the gate on this side ? "

Lord Germistoune had got the information he desired, and Cosmo's merits not being a congenial theme, he changed the subject abruptly. He had got the desired intelligence; and though the foundling theory lay in ruins, it afforded his prejudice some consolation to learn that Cosmo was the son of so objectionable a parent.

"Well, I have probed the mystery about this Mr Glencairn," he said that evening to Mrs Ravenhall.

"Have you *really*, Lord Germistoune? How clever of you! Now, *do* tell me. I suppose Lady Bugles was mistaken. I am afraid you are going to dissolve the little romance. There *is* something so divinely romantic about found lings! Well?"

"There is nothing romantic about his origin. Quite the reverse. His father is a City man of the most flagrant and offensive description — purse-proud, arrogant, a speculator."

"And vulgar, of course?"

"Vulgar! the man is distinctly a brute." Then he repeated the history of his cavalier reception by Mr Glencairn.

"Ah," said Mrs Ravenhall, "I felt there was something wrong."

"My instincts never deceive me. I always had my misgivings about the young man."

"How sly of him to conceal all this!"

"That is quite of a piece with the rest of the —ahem!—business."

"Now I think of it, there is something artificial and disingenuous in his manner and expression, though he is certainly well-bred enough.

Now everything is explained; the necessity for constant dissimulation puts a strain on the manner naturally."

"But what business has he to go dissimulating about in society?"

"It certainly leaves a painful impression on the mind. A lady, of course, feels it more keenly than a gentleman. She knows so well what hazards there are for her own sex in the devices of clever adventurers."

"Well, 'adventurer' is possibly too strong a word."

"Perhaps it is, but it is hard to find a milder substitute."

"You see the young man is wealthy, and 'adventurer' implies the reverse."

"True; but, dear Lord Germistoune, pardon me, a man may have designs unconnected with money which are still unjustifiable in his position; and if he conceals his position to carry out his projects, he is, in a certain sense, an adventurer, I think."

"Very true, very true."

"And I confess it always makes me tremble when I see persons of this sort brought into contact with girls in whom I feel interest."

"Conceivably they might be most dangerous;

but fortunately, in this case, our hero seems to have no attractions for the fair sex. I think they seem quite unanimous in making fun of him here. The fact is, a man so enamoured of himself as this gentleman appears to be, *is* devoid of attraction for women. I think," he added, with a dry laugh, "we need have no apprehensions for Lady Bugles's peace of mind."

"Oh, Lady Bugles! ha! ha! I wasn't thinking of *her*. If it were only Lady Bugles, I should be spared much anxiety."

"Trust an old man of the world, Mrs Ravenhall, and dismiss anxiety for any of your young *protégées*. This young man is not the stuff of which lady - killers are made; though possibly some of them might be attracted by his fortune; and, if that were so, I suppose neither you nor I need feel any affliction. But a lady-killer! No, no. I think I ought to know something on *that* subject."

"The less you encourage him to come here, Lord Germistoune, the safer it will be, I assure you," said Mrs Ravenhall, goaded on by his maddening obtuseness to all her hints.

"Encourage him, my dear lady! what are you talking off? I never fancied the fellow; and after these discoveries, you may be sure

I shall only have such intercourse with him as the claims of neighbourhood rigorously demand."

"I hope that will not amount to much."

"You may trust me, I think, to know exactly what is fit and proper in such matters," said his lordship, his crest palpably rising at Mrs Ravenhall's pertinacity.

"The egotism and vanity of this old imbecile make him simply impenetrable," she thought to herself; but not venturing on any broader hints for the present, she assured the old lord that his tact and discretion were infallible, and so dropped the subject.

CHAPTER XXXIV.

THE next day being Sunday, Mrs Ravenhall had one of her "tiresome headaches." In London she would not, for worlds, have been absent from her post in a certain fashionable sanctuary, where the *cultus* of the bonnet was very devoutly performed; but under circumstances like the present, where there was an absence of any real devotional inducement, the tiresome infliction usually supervened, and, as on this occasion, kept her away from church. The quiet and leisure secured to her by the absence of the party, she devoted, like a Ministry outvoted in the House, to the "consideration of her position," which she found to be very far indeed from satisfactory. For many a week, now, she had toiled and spun for her incorrigible brother; sacrifices innumerable she had made of time, convenience, and even money. In return he had amused her with false hopes

and endless postponements; and at last, when
the rival interest of sport had come into com-
petition, he appeared to have abandoned all
consideration of that which ought to have been
paramount. And while Tom thus remained
inactive, perils thickened from other quarters.
Lord Ribston was obviously in the field, and
would, doubtless, declare himself before long.
Possibly there was not much to be apprehended
in that fact; but Cosmo Glencairn was also in
the field, and her instinctive suspicion that he
was dangerous had now ripened into the firmest
conviction. All her manœuvres against him
had hitherto failed. She had done her best
to make him ridiculous with the party at the
castle, and so, indirectly, with Esmè; but her
principal aim had not been reached. Her innuendos about his birth had led to nothing but
a discovery of the truth, which had done no
good; for Lord Germistoune's dislike for Cosmo
was a foregone conclusion, which did not require to be quickened. Her hints to his lordship had missed fire; her direct action with
Esmè had only roused a spirit of championship
in the latter, which Mrs Ravenhall knew to
be full of peril. Miss Milkington had apprised
her of the excursion to the ruins, and she felt

that, if a few such opportunities were to recur, Cosmo, desperately in love and resolute, as he clearly was, might soon succeed in capturing the affections of the heiress.

The situation was discouraging in the extreme. She felt baffled and powerless; and Tom would not help her. She had but one hope, and it was this. Esmè had evidently the most cordial liking for Tom; she and he were on terms of the easiest intimacy. That, indeed, precluded the idea of *love* on her part. But might it not be possible—before she was thus affected from another quarter, before she knew the meaning of love at all—might it not be possible for Tom to succeed by a sort of *coup de main*, in which surprise on her part, and exceptional energy upon his, should extract from the warmth of her friendship and her inexperience and simplicity, the prize which he aimed at? If once her heart knew what love was, it would be too late. Possibly, not probably, however, it was already too late. In any case, this seemed the sole device remaining—a forlorn hope, perhaps, but the only one. But would Tom entertain it? Well, if he would not, she resolved to wash her hands of him. She dearly loved success for its own sake; and that passion had helped to support her in many trials: but she was growing weary of this long up-hill fight without allies; she was now very much inclined to own herself beaten, and abandon it; and her just resentment against her brother had no small influence in drawing her to this conclusion. "Well," she said, "I will give him this one more chance, and if he doesn't choose to take my view, I'll be done with him and his affairs."

In the midst of these meditations she was disturbed by a knock at the door. Hastily snatching up a Church Service, she invited the knocker to enter, when who but Tom himself should make his appearance. That worthy had also absented himself from church, by a not very remarkable coincidence; but as he had recently been shy of anything like a *tête-à-tête* with his sister, it *was* singular that he should have sought this interview, and timed it so opportunely. His face was excessively lugubrious, and he carried in his hand a bundle of papers, which his sister at once recognised as specimens of a kind of literature with which the post very frequently favoured him.

"Not at church?" said Mrs Ravenhall, very drily.

"No, Lucy, the devil is too sick even to be a monk to-day."

"Well, if you *will* sit up all night in the smoking-room——"

"Hang the smoking-room! that has nothing to do with it. I'm sick of life!" And he dashed his papers vehemently on to the floor.

"Pray don't litter my room; and please remember that I have a headache," said his sister.

"Headache! what is a headache compared with total collapse and .ruin?"

"I'm not in a position to judge; the headache is quite bad enough for me, I know."

"What selfish humbugs women are!" cried Tom, ferociously.

"I daresay you're right," said Mrs Ravenhall, languidly; "but don't you think you had better go and take a walk? I don't feel quite equal to tragedy this morning, and that seems to be your programme."

"Don't drive me mad, Lucy. You see before you a desperate man."

"And I invite him to relieve me of the spectacle, which has none of the charm of novelty. I really wish you would go. You can see that I am at my exercises; and besides, my headache is no trifle."

"Very well—good-bye; I'm off finally;" and he gathered up his papers. "You may sneer at my desperation as much as you please; but it's true *this* time. Good-bye; you may as well shake hands."

"Good-bye," said Mrs Ravenhall, and gave her hand with contemptuous indifference.

Tom went resolutely to the door and opened it; but before he disappeared, his sister called to him, "Tom!"

"Well?"

"What do you mean? where are you going to?"

"Out of this cursed country."

"But where?"

"I haven't quite decided. I'm going to emigrate; it may be to—to Paphlagonia—or—or—Otaheite. I don't know. I'm going, at all events."

"And why this sudden resolution?"

"Why! Just look at these letters."

"Oh no, no; please not."

"Then why on earth do you stop me?" and he turned his face again in the direction of Paphlagonia.

Mrs Ravenhall, recognising in his more than ordinary disturbance a possible basis of operations, again recalled him.

"I suppose," she said, "it is only the old story?"

"With a difference — for the worse. Just listen. I wrote to a whole lot of duns some time ago—when I was going to Italy—and said that, as I was obliged to be absent on a mission which involved uncertainty of address, for six months or so, they had better make any financial remarks which might occur to them in the interval to my solicitor. I wrote also to him, and said that I was off on a promiscuous cruise, and that I should feel obliged by his making the best fight he could with any creditors of mine who might apply to him during my absence. I also told him (which was quite true) that I had instructed my banker to pay to him any remittances which might come to his hands for my credit; and these funds I authorised him to administer, at his discretion, for the appeasement of my creditors.

"Well, to cut the matter short, the solicitor has proved to be lymphatic, and without breadth of view; unequal, in fact, to the strain. He writes—here is his contemptible effusion— that he must decline to have his offices mobbed, morn, noon, and night, by my creditors. He states that one man—a tobacconist, and a very turbulent fellow (I know the beast!)—may really be said to reside in his anteroom; and he can't stand it any longer. The banker, he says, derides (so like *him!*) the idea of remittances; there are four county court summonses out against me, and two judgments; and he adds that his life is made a burden to him; —as if that were a matter of the faintest interest to *me!* He suggests that I should remit to him at once, say five hundred pounds; and estimates that a farther large sum—say a thousand, roughly—will be necessary within the next few weeks or there will be what he calls 'grave complications.' But the sting of the letter is in its tail. If, he says, the named sum is not *at once* forthcoming, he will be obliged to divulge my address, and abandon his business connection with me. There! what do you think of that?"

"Think of it? it is simply disgraceful."

"Yes, it *does* show callousness; still we must remember that the fellow is a half-bred—not entitled by birth to chivalrous instincts."

"You know perfectly well that it is to *you* I am alluding."

"Me!"

" Of course.   Your conduct is absolutely revolting."

"I came here expecting sympathy, Lucy," said Tom, with mournful dignity, "and not insult, from you, at least. I shall now leave you."

"And may I ask how this five hundred pounds is to be paid ? "

"That, I think, is a problem which we may safely leave the expectant payees to solve among themselves, if they can. It no longer interests me,—not even as an abstract question. I propose to avoid any discussion of it with them, which could only lead to angry recriminations, and not impossibly to the curtailment of my personal liberty, which I could never brook. No ! I will escape from these annoyances, and seek an asylum, and a new point of departure, among simpler forms of life."

" In plain words, ' run away from your creditors ' ? "

"I can quite conceive that the ruffians might describe it in some such way."

"And so you are off, at once, on this reputable journey ? "

" Well, there seems to be nothing else for it. If I waited, you see, till Wednesday, or so, I should probably have to receive certain visitors here, whom I would rather avoid. One has a delicacy in receiving any visitors in another man's house; and in this case, it would be specially distasteful."

"Whom on earth do you mean?"

"Bailiffs."

"What! do you dare to bring such people about Lord Germistoune's house?"

"Ha! ha! 'Dare!' unfortunately they don't require 'bringing.' They will have no delicacy about coming uninvited."

"This is disgrace for all of us!"

"Yes, it is, you know; that's why I came here just now; but your unreasonable heat seems to make any business-like conversation impracticable; so no good purpose can be served by protracting the scene."

"These wretches will actually come here and arrest you?"

"No, they won't arrest *me*—I'll take care of *that*; but they will come here and look for me, and put a watch over the house; probably arrest Ribston or Berkeley, or some other fellow, by mistake, now and then—perhaps Lord Germistoune himself, if they fall in with him in the dark. Of course, I shall be on the friendly billows by that time. Ha! ha! now I think of it, there *is* something awfully funny in the idea of their arresting Ribby, or the old patriarch! Ha! ha! ha! how they *will* swear! The castle will be quite wakened up."

"Monster! have you no consideration for your family?"

"Frankly, no. There must be reciprocity in such matters, and my family have no consideration for me."

"I never heard of such ingratitude!"

"We should never agree about that; so, on the whole, I think I'll go now."

"Tell me why you came here just now?"

"My dear Lucy, because I thought it right so far to consider my family, though they don't consider me, as to let them know, through you, what is impending; so that, if they thought it worth their while, they might save themselves from this little scandal. It was the merest matter of courtesy on my part. The previous conduct of the family makes it evident that I could have no selfish hopes. Now I have discharged my duty, and may go."

"Even if the family were willing, I don't know where the money could come from—I don't know who has it?"

"No, no, of course not.   Let us drop the subject.   Lord Germistoune, to be sure, will blow
his bugle pretty loudly over the matter ; but after
all, that won't break any of the family's bones."

" And here, with this catastrophe staring you
in the face, you have been neglecting the only
obvious means of extricating yourself ! "

" If you refer to Miss Douglas, I deny the
neglect ; and even were I engaged to her at
this moment, pray reflect that I could not ask
her father for the money now."

" Ah ! in these circumstances we might have
come forward."

" You would then have discovered where the
money could come from !   Well, well, I forgive
you.   Poor human nature !   Go on."

" Well, then, as to not neglecting your opportunities——"

" Your whole view of me in this matter, Lucy,
is based on a misconception of my tactics, which
have been pursued with the dogged persistence
of a sleuth-hound."

" Really? they have been wonderfully masked."

" That's the art of the thing.   Listen.   You
wished me to carry on a thunder - and - lightning courtship ; well, I saw, almost at once,
that that was inexpedient for many reasons.   I

therefore changed front, and resolved to proceed by a slower method, but, I think, a surer one — and that was, gradually and almost imperceptibly, to make myself necessary to Miss Douglas's existence."

"By avoiding her persistently, and shooting grouse from morning to night?"

"The art of the thing again! Success has attended my procedure."

"You are necessary to her existence now, are you?"

"Very nearly; but I don't go quite so far as that. What I mean to say is, that she likes me immensely—more than any one else, in her own quiet way. You won't venture to deny that her liking is obvious?"

"Then why don't you persevere?"

"I *am* persevering, slowly and unostentatiously; but it takes time; and just as success seems within my grasp, this horrible explosion takes place, and my scheme is ruined."

"I should have said, 'Just as success was finally escaping your grasp.'"

"Yes, *you* would, I daresay. That's our point of divergence. I am only telling you what *my* view was, and what my scheme has been."

"Are you serious?"

"Is a man in my situation likely to jest?"

"You think she would accept you now, if you proposed?"

"Very likely; but it would be safer to give her more time. But, of course, that's out of the question now; so what's the good of talking? I say! only fancy if the bailiffs were to arrive just as Lord Germistoune had given me his blessing! Ha! ha! Something like a dramatic situation, eh? Did it ever occur to you, by the by, what a capital Sir Anthony Absolute his lordship would make?"

"Pray let us keep to the matter in hand. As you say, it is out of the question to give her more time. I don't mean because of these wretches who are coming to hunt you: I mean that there are other influences at work—some one else has got his designs upon her."

"Pooh, pooh! nonsense! Old Ribby! She laughs at him."

"Ah! I don't mean Lord Ribston; there is Mr Glencairn——"

"Ridiculous. He repudiated the idea altogether."

"——and others," added Mrs Ravenhall, deeming it hazardous to dwell too forcibly on Cosmo.

"Well, I don't care whom you mean. No one else has a chance."

"You are wonderfully confident."

"With a little more time."

"Which you can't have."

"If these bailiffs could be stopped!"

"I have my very strong opinion, that even if they could be stopped, your only chance would lie in instant action. Your only chance. Other influences are working, and working rapidly; take my word for it."

"Well, well, we needn't worry about it. I must go and see about my packing."

"And leave the family to be disgraced?"

"How *can* I help it?"

"Listen. Here is the very last effort I mean to make for you, and *I* will not make it without a most stringent condition. With the view I take of this affair with Miss Douglas, I say immediate action is absolutely necessary. I may be right or I may be wrong; that is my view, and I mean to make it the foundation of a proposal to you, which is this : If you will now promise me, upon your sacred honour as a gentleman, to propose to Miss Douglas within forty - eight hours, you shall have the money you require for these wretches. It will greatly hamper me, but I shall trust to being repaid, either by your brother or by yourself, when you are able. What do you say?"

"Lucy! Say! It's awfully sudden; it takes my breath away," stammered Tom, who had, of course, been playing for this stake all the time, but without these terrible conditions.

"That is *positively* the only condition on which I will move a hand to help you," continued Mrs Ravenhall.

"And the further sum—roughly, a thousand pounds—which will be required a few weeks later?"

"Well, I will promise to use my influence about that with your brother, if, after honestly carrying out your conditions, you honestly fail with Miss Douglas."

Tom walked to the window and mused. After all, he was in a terrible hole, and this would extricate him, and leave him something in hand —the sums "roughly" required by his solicitor being probably somewhere about three hundred and fifty, and eight hundred, rather than five hundred and a thousand, the respective balances representing, more or less, the little profit which Tom counted upon making on such cash transactions as his family undertook for his benefit.

Lax morality this for a man who could still respect his word of honour; but the continued pressure of money difficulties, and the perpetual shifts which they involved, had no doubt left their mark upon Tom, as they have constantly left it upon men of a higher stamp. And, besides, Tom had what he called "strong perceptions of the family tie," which involved the firm conviction that his family were, by the law of natural affection, bound to "see him through" his scrapes; and that, since they now pretty uniformly failed to recognise this duty, he was justified in levying on them, and taking any advantage of them which presented itself. Proceeding with his reflections, he felt that he had to face a refusal; he was confident that that was in store for him; but what of that? It happened to lots of fellows; and at this moment, he was by no means sure that it was not preferable to the alternative, with all its prospective advantages. The act of proposal was really the worst of it. While he thus reflected, Mrs Ravenhall arose, and, opening a despatch-box, took therefrom a cheque-book, and began leisurely to turn over the foils thereof. There was considerable art in this suggestive movement. Tom's eye kindled.

"Well, Lucy," he said, "I think it's a risk; but I'll close; I'll take the plunge."

"Upon your sacred word of honour, and within forty-eight hours?"

"Within that time; upon my sacred word of honour."

"Then I am satisfied."

"I daresay: but I'm not; no more are the bailiffs. This is distinctly a ready-money transaction."

"Oh! you require the cheque *now?*"

"Clearly, unless you wish the bailiffs to mix themselves up with my proposal."

Mrs Ravenhall took up a pen and detached a cheque, Tom standing over her.

"There are generally," he said, "some vexatious little law expenses in staying proceedings. I suspect it will be better to err on the safe side, and make the sum guineas. Five hundred guineas—in other words, five hundred and twenty-five pounds. There! that's it. Thanks!"

"Now remember! by this time on Tuesday."

"You have my word of honour, Lucy; but make it Tuesday midnight. You know one can't command one's time during the day here, and the evening opportunities will be more plentiful."

"Very well ; but it's the very last concession."

"All right. Now I feel quite faint with all this agitation. I must positively go and rub in a little sherry."

The thieves' compact being thus concluded, Mrs Ravenhall lay back on the sofa, and thought it over. On the whole it was her own scheme, with the slight difference that it was more expensive by five hundred and twenty-five pounds ; but she was not disposed to make much of that, every other road to success being absolutely barred. If he should succeed, what a *coup*, what a triumph it would be ! Such a brilliant match ! such wealth, *prestige*, and position, and all to be acquired by a spendthrift, younger son, through the *finesse* of his capable sister ! Besides the solid family advantages, there was reputation to accrue from that ; ay, that there was ! And then, from a minor point of view, Esmè in herself would be so excellent a wife for Tom !—a safe wife, upon whom, even in these risky days, one might certainly depend. Altogether it would be worth far more than all her trouble and sacrifice, if he should succeed. But could he ? He seemed strangely confident of his footing with Esmè ;

and they certainly appeared to be on the best of terms. But could he be trusted to play his cards? There was the main doubt. Ah! she must rehearse it with him, and send him to the trial equipped, *cap-à-pie*, with the armour of her worldly craft. The die would soon be cast. Forty-eight hours, and then — victory; or, if defeat, at least also a release from a long and harassing campaign.

CHAPTER XXXV.

IT took a good deal to damp Tom Wyedale's
spirits.   Blessed by nature with a very buoyant
temperament, neither dyspepsia, nor any sense
of the responsibilities of life, disturbed him ;
and familiarity with the only kind of difficulties
which constantly beset him, enabled him, as a
rule, to carry himself with cheerful *nonchalance*,
in circumstances which usually darken the faces
of most men.   In the circumstances, however,
which now confronted him, his past experience
could do nothing to help or reassure him ; and
as he contemplated them, on that Sunday afternoon, after leaving his sister, his courage gradually oozed away.   Sitting alone by the river, in
a remote part of the glen, he spent the long
hours between luncheon and dinner in revolving
various schemes and considerations in connection with the ordeal which lay before him.   He
felt that it was now absolutely inevitable.

Slippery though he was, the words "sacred honour of a gentleman" involved a pledge which he would not have dreamt of violating; and even if he would — (which we are far from asserting)—have attempted to fulfil his engagement in the letter, while practically evading it, by some such device as a burlesque proposal, it was obvious that nothing of the sort would escape detection by his sister, who was evidently in a determined and dangerous frame of mind. It must be fairly done—that was clear. But how? where? when? in what words? and with what results? He felt that he might put an acceptance out of the question; or, if so unlikely a thing were to happen, there would be plenty of time after its occurrence to consider the revolution in his life which would thereby be involved.

But the alternative? Refusal? The fact of being refused was only an essential episode in a drama which, from first to last, was horrible to contemplate; in itself, indeed, it was not half so bad as the act of proposal. For in Tom's soul there lingered certain sparks of chivalrous feeling; he had a strong regard and admiration for Esmè, and in his present rare mood of thoughtfulness, with the matter fairly before him—no longer vaguely and in the remote future — there did seem to him to be something very repulsive in the idea of mixing up this gentle and innocent lady with so coarse a transaction. Schooled, however, to repress his better emotions, and driven, as he felt, by necessity to the inevitable, he wrenched himself away, as best he might, from painful sentiment to practical considerations. The results of a refusal—what must they be? This reflection now occupied him; and a large portion of the afternoon was spent in considering how the catastrophe could in any way be brought to harmonise with his autumn plans — his shooting projects, and so forth.

His cogitations led him to no comfortable conclusion; and when he appeared at dinner, the total eclipse of his Yorick-like characteristics was patent to all, and dulled the tone of the whole party.

Mrs Ravenhall observed it with lively satisfaction. " It wants point, however," she said to herself. " Why can't he look at Esmè? and oh, if he *would* drink less of that champagne — it is so deplorably exhilarating !" On this latter head her anxieties were not realised. Tom's gloom and silence only seemed to deepen.

Lord Ribston drew Esmè's attention to it. "There are no great 'events' on just now," he said, " or I should fancy Wyedale had come to grief again. As it is, I suppose he's only grudging the grouse their day of rest."

When the ladies left the drawing-room, Mrs Ravenhall came up to her with great tragic eyes, and said in a tragic whisper, "Poor dear Tom! what a terrible state he is in! Do, pray, darling, try to find out what is the matter." Whereupon Esmè reported Lord Ribston's theory.

"Ah!" said Mrs Ravenhall, "this is no laughing matter—no joke. I know the play of his features too well. His face frightens me. Take an opportunity, dear, and ask him what has happened. He will tell you anything, I am sure. Do—to oblige me."

When Tom made his appearance, he still wore the same rueful aspect, and seated himself apart in the large drawing-room, resting his head mournfully upon his hand. And then, since there was no sort of reserve, but rather a frank *camaraderie* between Esmè and him, she, in passing him as if by accident, stopped and said kindly, "I fear you have a bad headache, Mr Wyedale."

"No," replied Tom, looking up without a smile—"no, I have no headache."

"What is the matter, then? You look very ill, as if you were in pain."

"I *am* in pain; but I am not ill; horribly unhappy, that's all."

"I am very sorry; but I am sure nothing very serious ever happens to you."

"Ah! but this *is* serious — vitally serious. I can't tell you about it now, but I will to-morrow, or some other time."

"Tell your sister, Mr Wyedale. She is very anxious about you."

"No, I certainly won't tell her. I'll tell you, if you'll listen to me. Will you, some other time?" And she assenting, left him in yet deeper gloom, from the step which he had taken in the direction of the abyss.

Innocent Esmè was quite grieved for the heavy affliction of her cheery friend. "He confesses," she said to Mrs Ravenhall, "that he is very unhappy, and wishes to tell me all about it. So, of course, I shall soon know; and, if he doesn't forbid it, I will tell you what he says."

"Thanks, darling; it will be *such* a relief: but please don't let him escape you. Find an opportunity as soon as possible. I will help you."

Having thus contrived to set the fowler and the prey mutually in quest of each other, Mrs Ravenhall felt that she had made assurance doubly sure, and that it would be hard indeed if the desired opportunity did not at once occur. Next day, however, the "fowler" finding himself in better spirits, or at least able to take more philosophical views of what was impending, thought the inevitable moment might be advantageously postponed in favour of another day's shooting—his last, perhaps, at Dunerlacht—and went forth, accordingly, *malgré* his sister's remonstrances.

The day was fine, and he had a good many hours of something like enjoyment : but with the shades of evening, the shadows fell again upon his spirit; so that his conduct at dinner and in the evening was, as Mrs Ravenhall admitted to herself, "almost beautiful."

"No better! even worse, I think!" she whispered to Esmè, shaking her head dolorously. "Has he spoken to you?"

"There has been no opportunity, as yet."

"Only twenty-four hours now," muttered Tom to himself, as he went to bed; "well, hang it! it will be all over by this time to-morrow — that's one consolation," and so turned in, and slept the sleep which blesses the last hours of condemned criminals.

The inevitable day—the last twelve hours —came at last. Tom, chained by his pledge, had to reject all sporting temptations, and, in every sense, envied the sportsmen, as he wistfully beheld them disappear in the direction of the moor. His sister invited him to come to her room, and receive certain hints as to his conduct in the impending trial; but he would none of this. "It would only confuse me and make me nervous," he said; "and, heaven knows, I'm shaky enough already!"

Then he went and mooned about in the flower-garden, awaiting Esmè's arrival; for he knew that it was her habit to go there, every morning, after breakfast.

Tom could not be said to wait impatiently; but as Esmé had not made her appearance in the garden long after her usual hour, he left it, and strolled down the avenue in the direction of the bridge, with a languid intention of seeing whether anything was stirring in a certain salmon-pool of which he knew. Arrived at his destination, he began to peer into the water, which was clear, though deep, and somewhat troubled with back swirls from the main current. Presently his eye caught the outline of what seemed to be a noble "fish," fitfully visible in the depths, and, with the sportsman's instinct at once aroused, he set to work, cautiously, to get himself into a better position for observing it, and estimating its proportions —an impulse with which keen lovers of the "gentle art" will perhaps sympathise. While thus earnestly employed, a voice from behind accosted him.

"What *are* you doing, Mr Wyedale?"

"Hush! hush!" whispered Tom, holding up his hand; and though on looking round he beheld Esmè, the salmon retained the position of paramount interest.

"If you come here, very carefully," he continued, "you will see him to perfection."

Esmè went over to him very carefully. "What is it?" she said, adapting herself to the situation, by also whispering.

"I'd almost stake my life, he's a thirty-pounder; clean as a whistle, too. Look at him!"

"I can't see anything."

"Why, there, *there* — just over that yellow stone. Oh, Miss Douglas!"

These last words were uttered in a tone of

bitterest reproach; for Esmè, in raising a hand to shade her eyes, caused some movement of her drapery which caught the mysteriously-angled vision of the fish, and he was off like a flash of lightning.

"I am so sorry!" she said.

"Oh, it doesn't matter," replied Tom, magnanimously; "we couldn't have caught him, you know. Now I wonder what *his* plans are! I *should* like to have a struggle with a fellow of that sort. He *must* be thirty pounds at least—probably more, perhaps thirty-five."

"Why don't you go and get a rod and try for it?"

"Oh, there would be no chance just now." And then it flashed upon Tom, still recumbent, that another kind of angling must occupy his immediate attention.

"I am going down to the lodge to take these papers to the old people there, and I must make haste," said Esmè.

"I'll walk with you, if I may," said Tom, rising from his post of observation; and they started.

"Tremendous, great, fine fish that!" he remarked, after they had walked a few paces in silence.

"I wish I had seen him," said Esmè.

"Another time you must remember that fish see round the corner, and hear with their tails."

"I don't think I shall forget *that*."

After this, Tom indulged in some reflections upon the caprices and general frowardness of the salmon tribe, speaking with a chastened vitality, though by no means languidly. When he had done, Esmè said, "I am glad to see you are better to-day, Mr Wyedale."

"Thanks," said Tom, nervously; "but I am not better, I'm worse; I've been getting worse daily for some time past."

"I should never have detected it."

"No, no, I daresay not; but the strain of concealment has been very trying. You know what Viola says about concealment, and her damask cheek—or somebody else's damask cheek —and the worm i' the bud, and that?"

"Oh yes," said Esmè, with a painful inclination to laugh, repressed in honour of Tom's lugubrious expression; "but why should you conceal your troubles? You have a most sympathetic friend in your sister; and I am sure you can have nothing to be ashamed of."

"Ashamed!" cried Tom; "quite the reverse —I'm very proud of it."

" Proud of what, Mr Wyedale ? "

" *It*, you know, the—ahem !—the trouble."

" Indeed ! " said Esmè, in deep bewilderment.

" Yes ; and you know sisters are all very well in their way, but one can't confide everything to one's sister."

" No, no, of course not ; but why not go to some gentleman friend ; Mr—Mr Glencairn, for instance, or my father ? I am sure my father would be only too happy to help you with his advice."

" I am sure he would," said Tom, thinking of the kind of advice his lordship would be likely to give under the circumstances ; " but I can't go to him in the first instance."

" Well, then, some one else. Pray, do. We are all so sorry to see you dull and sad."

" Are *you* really sorry ? " said Tom, halting.

" Mr Wyedale ! can you doubt it ? "

" Oh no. I thought you mightn't be, you know—that was all," said Tom, becoming perfectly incoherent ; and presently added, in the same vein, " and, indeed, I'd rather *you* weren't sorry."

" Mr Wyedale ! "

" I would rather you rejoiced in the whole

transaction, you know — that's the honest truth."

"Transaction! I confess you fairly puzzle me."

"I daresay I do. I know I puzzle myself. I'm an imbecile, an idiot; but you won't mind that, will you?"

"What? that you are an imbecile?"

"No; that I'm talking up and down, and across, and round the corner. The fact is, I'm as nervous as the——as can be. Don't you see, I'm trying to tell you all about it?"

"No, Mr Wyedale, I can't say I do. Do you mean about the—the trouble?"

"Certainly. You said you would listen to me, you know."

"And so I will, with pleasure."

"You're sure it won't bore you?"

"Oh, quite sure."

"Very well, then — ahem!— ahem!——" Tom had again halted, and he now came to a dead pause in his speech. Esmè was obliged to turn away her head to conceal her mirth. The preposterous gloom of his face quite over- powered her. "The fact is," Tom stammered, at last, "a dreadful thing has happened."

"To you, Mr Wyedale? to yourself?" cried Esmè.

"To me."

"Yes, but—but, pray, what is it?"

"It is a kind of thing which fortunately happens, I believe, only once or so in a man's lifetime. That's the only consolation; though it leaves its mark on him, they say, from—from the cradle to the grave."

"What *can* it be?"

"Well, to be perfectly frank with you, I have become a prey—a prey,—I say—a victim——"

"Oh! to what, Mr Wyedale? Please don't keep me in suspense."

"A victim, I repeat—of course, a willing victim; you clearly understand *that?*"

"Yes, now I do; but to what, or whom?"

"To emotions, Miss Douglas. I have conceived an aff—— I have contracted, that is to say, an attach—— Hang it! I'm in love! There! that's the long and short of the matter."

Esmè's eyes opened very wide.

"You, Mr Wyedale — *you!*" was all she could gasp; and then the torrent of her mirth could no longer be pent in, and she laughed till the tears ran down her cheeks. Tom regarded her in discomfited silence. When she had recovered a little, she said, "Can you ever forgive me? I am so ashamed, so sorry; but I could *not* help——" and then, catching another sight of her companion's woful visage, she had another relapse.

"I am sorry," said Tom, with sad dignity, "that you find an honest man's love so ridiculous."

"No, no, Mr Wyedale; it is not so, I assure you. It was the way you spoke, and the way you looked, that upset my gravity. You made such a tragedy of it, I was quite frightened; and then, when you told me what 'the trouble' really was, it seemed all so—so different," said Esmè, with symptoms of another break-down.

"I suppose," said Tom, "it *is* ridiculous?"

"No, indeed! why should it be so? But am I to know anything more?"

"Oh yes. I fear, however, that you will only laugh at me."

"No; I promise you I will not. May I ask who the—the lady is? I hope she is very nice."

"She is adorable."

"Do I know her?"

"Intimately."

"Really! Where is she? In Scotland?"

"Yes; she is in Glenerlacht."

"How very exciting! Why, you must mean one of the party at the castle?"

"Yes, certainly, and——"

"Let me guess. Not Miss Snapsley?"

"Very much the reverse; but listen——"

"Not possibly Miss Milkington?"

"You are sneering at me, Miss Douglas."

"No, no; I assure you not. *Can* it be Mrs Crock?"

"Why don't you say Lady Bugles at once?"

"Please don't be offended."

"Miss Douglas!—ahem! Esmè!—listen to me. I feel the madness—the presumption—the hopelessness of my love; but it will have utterance. For long months I have grappled with it—grappled, I say—like a man; but I am beaten now. I succumb. I throw up the sp—— ahem! I love you, and I offer you my love. A poor man's love is a very poor offering; but it is all I have to give, and it is yours, if you will condescend to accept it."

Esmè stared at Tom in complete stupefaction, and said nothing.

"You hesitate!" cried Tom, with some perturbation; "at least, you hesitate! Oh, say I need not abandon all hope!"

"Mr Wyedale," said Esmè, at last, "am I

dreaming ? or is it possible that you are talking to me in sober earnest ?"

" Nothing could be more solemn and sober. Be assured of that. All my—my peace of mind rests on your reply."

" I am distressed—I am infinitely distressed, Mr Wyedale, to hear you say so — if you are serious. But surely—what can it mean ?— surely I have done nothing to lead you to suppose that there was, or ever could be, any-thing between us but friendship ?"

" No," said Tom, " that is perfectly true. I said that I was mad and presumptuous."

" And surely—it *is* most mysterious !—surely it cannot really be true that you have been— have been entertaining such feelings all the time you speak of ? This must be some strange de-lusion."

" Not at all," said Tom, doggedly; " it is sadly and bitterly the truth."

" Then, Mr Wyedale, I can only say that I am deeply distressed."

" You can give me no hope ?"

" I am grieved to give you pain, and I don't require to tell you how warmly I regard your friendship ; but I can accept nothing more than it."

The conviction that it was all over afforded unbounded relief to Tom; but he was greatly at a loss what to say next—how, in fact, to finish off the little drama, *selon les règles.* He remained silent, therefore, looking discreetly woebegone, and waiting for an idea, or some further utterance on Esmè's part. They had turned—the visit to the lodge had been tacitly abandoned—and were now slowly walking back to the castle. A pretty long silence was at last broken by Esmè, who, looking at Tom's sad face, and thinking how bright it used always to be, said, with an impulse from her warm heart—"I am so sorry for what has happened, Mr Wyedale. I can't tell you how truly I am grieved."

"Oh, please, don't be distressed, Miss Douglas. It serves me right for my presumption; and besides, everything goes wrong with me; I never expect anything happy to come my way."

"Don't say so, Mr Wyedale; I am sure you are generally very happy, and make others very happy too; and I am sure this little illusion will very soon pass away. I hope we are always to be friends—true friends?"

"Always, and with all my heart," said Tom, heartily.

Esmè held out her hand, which he took ; and thus the friendly *entente* was sealed !

" You may be sure," she continued, " that I shall not breathe a hint of what has occurred to any one."

" Thanks ; how good of you ! "

" And I am sure no one in the house could suspect such a thing—you seem to have such a wonderful power of concealing your feelings— so that you need feel no embarrassment before the party."

" Oh, but, Miss Douglas, I must go away at once."

" Go away ? "

" Yes, to-day, or to-morrow at latest."

" Why, Mr Wyedale ? "

Tom was only too glad to find that there was any question about it.   He had understood that his departure would be considered a matter of etiquette.   " Why ? " he repeated, rather at a loss for a reply ; " oh ! you know my—ahem !— my feelings would scarcely permit——"

" Now, Mr Wyedale, we are friends, are we not ? "

" Certainly."

" Then I beg you, as a friend, not to go away."

"I would do much to please you, but this is really——"

"No, I will take no refusal; you *must* stay."

She had now quite decided that Tom's declaration was the result of a sudden fancy which had sprung up in his spasmodic mind the day before yesterday, destined to evaporate the day after to-morrow, and which, though utterly undeserving of the honours of a *grande passion*, yet demanded, from her compassion, the healing balm of kindness and consolation, during its brief existence.

"And you know," she added, "there is the great deer-hunt on Saturday. How could you go before that? It would look strange, so sudden a departure—it might cause remark."

"True," said Tom, as if this reflection had weight with him; "there is, certainly, a good deal of truth in that. I fear it might cause remark; but——"

"No, no, Mr Wyedale, I will have no 'buts.' You will stay?"

"Well," said Tom, after some reflection, "I will try to discipline myself. I *will* remain till after the deer-drive, at whatever cost of personal suffering. Your wish shall always be my law."

"And this, I am sure, is for your good. I

wish it because I wish you not to suffer, but to enjoy yourself, which I hope and think you will."

Tom shook his head despondingly, but repeated, in the resigned tone of a martyr, that he would remain till after the drive. And now, having reached the house, they separated.

Tom felt that he was entirely master of the situation. His financial strain was relaxed; he had honestly fulfilled his pledge to his sister; he was done with her long importunities; his autumn plans were in the *status quo ante;* and not a soul but Esmè and his sister, neither of whom seemed to him to matter, was a bit the wiser. Peace and contentment steeped the spirit of the rejected suitor; and his only anxiety was for the ordering of his countenance, which, he felt, might be apt to betray the unseemly joy raging within his breast. In this halcyon frame he sought his sister, who, seeing the brightness of his face, clapped her hands, and cried "Victory!" Tom had the decency to sadden his face a little, as he replied, "No, Lucy, alas! not victory,—a cropper."

"What is that? You don't mean that she has refused you?"

"Yes, I do; to her shame be it said."

"Why did she refuse you?"

"Why? I didn't press her on that point; but I presume it was due to some defect in her intellectual arrangements."

"And you joke about it!"

"I don't. I've had an awful time of it, I can tell you."

"You must have mismanaged matters somehow. This comes of your conceit and neglecting my hints."

"No, I managed it beautifully, and came off with flying colours."

"But without the lady, it would seem."

"Yes, but with all the moral results of a victory."

"Stuff! Well, there is ruin before you now."

"I hope not."

"Oh, but there is. You can never hope to have such chances again."

"Well, I couldn't abduct her forcibly, could I?"

"But you might have played your cards like a reasonable being."

"I have told you that I had my own scheme, which was to make a waiting race of it. If you chose to come and force my running, you have only yourself to blame for the catastrophe."

"I am utterly disgusted with you."

"I am sorry for that; but it is not an argument."

"Tell me *exactly* what took place. Remember, I shall get it all out of her."

"I'll tell you exactly; but you'll get nothing out of her—she is far too loyal and good."

Tom then told his story briefly; and when he had finished, she said—

"And when do you leave?"

"Leave? I'm not going to leave, that I know of."

"How?"

"Because I am going to stay where I am."

"You mean this—gravely?"

"And most distinctly."

"You can't be so utterly callous and abominable!"

"Well, I have sufficient fortitude and manly dignity to enable me to protract my residence amidst what Lord Germistoune calls 'our unrivalled scenery.' That, perhaps, is a more graceful way of putting it."

"Wretch! you have no shame!"

"Shame implies a gallery,—and there is none in this case."

"There is Miss Douglas."

"I stay at her special request."

"Oh, that would be a mere form, dictated by good-nature and a desire to let you down easily."

"Not a bit of it. In any case, I have yielded to her importunities. I really can refuse nothing to a woman, even to the woman who is 'red-hand' from refusing me, so I have pledged myself."

"And how, pray, do you expect me to look?"

"Well, I confess I had formed no theory on that subject. But I think, Lucy, you are quite old enough a soldier to look after yourself. Seriously, no one knows anything about the matter except Miss Douglas, and she need never know that you know anything about it; so how can you be compromised? See how unflinchingly I sacrifice my just susceptibilities to Miss Douglas's wish. Take an example from me, and sacrifice your own morbid *mauvaise honte* to your own convenience."

This so far silenced Mrs Ravenhall, to whom a move at the moment would have been gravely inconvenient; but she wound up the session by assuring Tom that he was heartless, selfish, false, and maddeningly self-sufficient; also that she now formally washed her hands of him for ever.

"But you mustn't forget our compact, dear Lucy," said Tom, sweetly.

"What compact?"

"Touching that tiresome further sum of a thousand pounds, which will require to be forthcoming, almost at once, I fear."

"I'm sorry I promised; but I'm not like you, I keep my engagements."

"I see you are embittered by my disaster. In a limited sense, that is perhaps to your credit; it shows heart, strong family feeling. and so on. But to turn and rend the poor sufferer himself, argues a kind of feminine logic which a woman like you ought to despise."

"Go away, you hypocritical horse-leech!"

And this was the lame and impotent conclusion of all poor Mrs Ravenhall's Machiavellian plots, sacrifices, and endurances.

CHAPTER XXXVI.

FOR several days succeeding the events just related, Cosmo had to endure a total cessation of intercourse with the lady of his love. Once he had the courage to contrive a pretext and call at the castle; once, in a forlorn hope, and sailing under the tourist's flag, he had revisited the ruins. But on the former occasion, his sole reward was the sight of Lady Bugles engaged in some mysterious process of imitative decoration at an upper window; and on the latter, when he had recrossed the river, half-deafened and crazed by old Maggie's "entertainment," he had the gloomy satisfaction of beholding Esmè, escorted by her father and Lord Ribston, arrive on the scene he had just abandoned. At church on Sunday, where he had hoped to see her, he found himself so placed in relation to the Duncrlacht pew, as to command a perfect

view of the heads of Lord Germistoune, Lady
Bugles, and Lord Ribston, all placidly swaying
in a harmonious trio of slumber, but nothing
else ; and although at the conclusion of the diet
he was rewarded by a little fluttering bow,
smile, and blush—this last, by the by, was not
quite a certainty—all these things constituted
but meagre fare to appease the hunger of the
heart withal. Cosmo was very feverish and
restless, and but sorry company for Phil Denwick, who, though he consoled himself pretty
well by unwearied devotion to the moor, mar-
velled greatly at the new indifference to sport
displayed by his host, whose otherwise spasmodic ways of life also excited his attention,
and eventually his suspicion. And so it came
about, that, before long, Phil was intrusted with
his friend's secret, and had to endure those terrible outpourings, and those circular maunder-
ings, which Love, the leveller, extracts with
equal hand from all his victims. It was hard
upon Phil, but a great relief to Cosmo, when
the latter had once unbent,—for Phil was both
sympathetic and sanguine, and regarding his
benefactor with a sort of hero - worship, invariably laughed to scorn the notion that his
superlative merit could fail of recognition in

any quarter whatsoever, including even Lord Germistoune.

"He may be prejudiced, you know, and that sort of thing, but, hang it! he isn't blind. Men like you don't grow on every hedge. Take a common-sense view of the matter. Remember that we live in the nineteenth century."

Thus Phil: and though Cosmo felt that, in reference to Lord Germistoune, the latter consideration had little virtue, still his friend's confidence assured him, and confirmed him—if, indeed, he required confirmation—in his policy of—

"Let the great river bear me to the sea."

This policy did not, as yet, go the length of leading him to direct and aggressive action. Hesitating and perplexed, he waited upon circumstances and the inspirations of impulse. With all his friend's sympathy and encouragement, these few days were days of torture and unrest; and it was in a tumult of delight that he received, on the Thursday evening, the following note—

"DUNERLACHT CASTLE, *Thursday.*

"DEAR SIR,—A good many of our deer are stated to be obstinately harbouring in the woods, and, for our stalking operations, it is expedient to dislodge them and send them to the forest. Moved by this consideration, and at the urgent request of my friend the Marquis de Saut du Loup, I am induced to decide upon having a deer-drive on Saturday. It is a form of sport which (viewed as sport) I distinctly disapprove of, but the above considerations prevail with me. Should it tally with your arrangements to join our party, we shall be glad to have your assistance, and that of any of your men whom you can spare for beating purposes. Ten o'clock is the hour decided upon, and the rendezvous will be at the cairn on the western shoulder of Dunerlacht, where the ladies propose to give us luncheon in the afternoon.—Yours truly,   GERMISTOUNE."

A similar missive arrived for Phil from the laboriously formal old gentleman; and it is needless to say that the invitation was joyfully accepted by both recipients.

END OF THE SECOND VOLUME.